THE KILLER'S DAUGHTER

KATE WILEY

Storm

Ebook ISBN: 978-1-80508-439-6
Paperback ISBN: 978-1-80508-441-9

Cover design: Lisa Brewster
Cover images: Trevillion

Published by Storm Publishing.
For further information, visit:
www.stormpublishing.co

ALSO BY KATE WILEY

As Sierra Dean

The Secret McQueen Series

Something Secret This Way Comes

A Bloody Good Secret

Deep Dark Secret

Keeping Secret

Grave Secret

Secret Unleashed

Cold Hard Secret

A Secret to Die For

Secret Lives

A Wicked Secret

Deadly Little Secret

One Last Secret

The Genie McQueen Series

Bayou Blues

Black Magic Bayou

Black-Hearted Devil

Blood in the Bayou

The Rain Chaser Series

Thunder Road

Driving Rain

Highway to Hail

The Boys of Summer Series

Pitch Perfect

Perfect Catch

High Heat

As Gretchen Rue

The Witches' Brew Mysteries

Steeped to Death

Death by a Thousand Sips

The Grim Steeper

The Lucky Pie Mysteries

A Pie to Die For

For all the girls who took out big books on serial killers from the library way too young, this one is for you.

ONE

The house was already haunted when Margot Phalen arrived.

Even with the bright California sun shining down on the gabled roof, the place looked empty, all the life evaporated from it. The thing that made it a home was gone. Now it was just shingles and drywall.

Inside, it was a crime scene.

Margot sat in her white Honda Civic, the window cracked slightly to allow a breeze in. Barely eight o'clock and already the heat was stifling, and of course her air conditioning was on the fritz again. The car had a sense of humor that mostly revolved around making Margot miserable.

Whatever happened to the promise of brisk, cool air from all that San Francisco fog? In her six years living by the Bay, she had never been able to get a grasp on the weather.

She slipped on a pair of mirrored aviators and sipped the already lukewarm Starbucks in her hand. There were two SFPD black-and-white cruisers in the house's driveway, and yellow police tape blocking off the arched entry that separated the drive from the main house.

No one was moving outside, which meant the real draw was inside the house.

A woman in black yoga pants and bright pink shoes jogged slowly past, trying to pretend she wasn't keenly interested in what was happening behind that tape. A few other neighbors had come to the ends of their driveway, not bothering to fake their curiosity. Another man had been watering the same bush since Margot had parked ten minutes earlier. She had meant to get out when she arrived but had spent longer than anticipated observing the neighborhood.

Forest Hill was one of the nicer neighborhoods in San Francisco. The houses all had wide front lawns and trees out front, spaced out like a proper suburb, unlike the rest of the city where the Victorian houses were all wedged so tightly together they looked like brightly colored library books.

Here, Margot was reminded of the big lawns in Missouri where she'd lived as a teenager.

She set the coffee back in the cup holder and sacrificed herself to the hot weather gods outside the car. A quick flash of her badge got her through the front door, and once she was inside, she was in complete business mode.

Pushing her sunglasses up and looping her long, light red hair into a bun at the top of her head, she took a deep breath just inside the foyer.

The air conditioning was going full blast, and the thin film of sweat turned cold on her skin. Just under the Freon scent in the air was something else, faintly sinister: a fetid copper smell.

"Detective Phalen?" Evelyn Yao, clad head-to-toe in white, appeared in front of her.

Margot was tall, almost five feet nine, so most women seemed petite by comparison, but the chief medical examiner was especially compact, coming in at five feet on the button. Under the white hood she had short, black hair shaved low at the sides, with purple tips. She might have been the coolest sixty-something woman Margot had ever known.

Evelyn handed her a pair of white paper shoe-covers, which Margot slipped on over her heeled ankle boots. It was an awkward look, but one she'd grown accustomed to over time.

Margot noted the bloodstains on Evelyn's own booties.

"How bad is it?"

"It's sure as shit not pretty," Evelyn huffed, scratching her nose. "Fox is already upstairs."

Margot stiffened, and let out a sigh. She was going to owe Wes Fox five bucks because he'd beaten her to the crime scene yet again. "Show me what we've got down here first. I need the caffeine to kick in before I see Wes this morning."

"He told me to tell you you'd better have cash in hand," Evelyn teased.

"I bet he did."

They walked into a formal sitting room, where the morning light turned all the white walls and furniture a soft cream color. Dead in the center of the room, a perfect bullseye in the middle of the white and gray rug, a large pool of blood had formed.

"This the scene?" Margot edged around the red circle, looking for signs of a body. Or, in this case, bodies. Nothing.

Evelyn pointed up, and Margot's gaze trailed in the direction of the ME's finger. On the ceiling, the drywall was bloated and bubbling, a wide red stain still glistening at the center, *drip drip dripping* in a steady rhythm to the carpet below.

"Ah."

A trip upstairs would need to happen sooner rather than later. Still, Margot took her time looking around on this level first. There were no bloody prints around the area, with the exception of a few spots that were likely from Evelyn's boots since they'd been marked.

The main floor was spacious and open, all painted in clean shades of white or gray, with minimal furniture and only a few professional black-and-white photos showing the smiling Ramirez family as they had been.

Margot grimaced at the largest family portrait, feeling a faint, uncomfortable itch at the back of her neck.

She took a pair of latex gloves from Evelyn, and wandered into the kitchen, checking the drawers and knife block to see if anything was out of place, but everything looked neat as a pin. Whatever the killer had used probably hadn't been a convenient grab from the kitchen. If it had been, then the murders would have been spontaneous. No, chances were good this had been planned.

There was a door in the kitchen that led to the backyard, and the casing around the latch had been damaged. Margot pulled the door in toward her and crouched down. Someone had kicked the door, and hard. The wood was splintered, and there were faint traces of a bootprint.

"Hey, did someone photograph this?" she shouted to the uniformed officer combing through the backyard.

"Yes, ma'am."

The uniform was maybe twenty-three, so Margot would give him a pass on the whole *ma'am* thing. "Make sure no one messes this up, OK? And see if there's any drying mud around here where the debris might have come from. Could be a better print there."

He nodded.

Returning inside, Margot steeled herself and headed upstairs, where the sound of muted voices made it feel like she was entering a funeral home. Everyone was whispering, and the coppery smell from the main floor was more pronounced.

There were a few more people dressed all in white here—Evelyn's team—and two more uniformed officers milling around. In another room a flashing light and shutter sound told her the crime scene photographer was hard at work. She followed the sound, and had barely arrived at the door when someone stepped out, blocking her path.

Standing at six foot three, Wes Fox was a rare figure who could make Margot feel small.

"Nice of you to join us, Phalen." He was chewing gum, the minty smell a welcome reprieve from the overpowering copper stench. She knew what lay beyond him without having to see it.

"I haven't had enough coffee to deal with you yet, Wesley," she told her partner.

"You should have gotten here sooner. I brought you one and had to give it to Evelyn."

He was handsome, but the kind of handsome where he knew it. At forty-two, he still had the boyish charm to make him irresistible to younger women, something he used to his benefit frequently. His dark blond hair was perfectly styled, and he had deep creases next to his brown eyes, giving the impression he smiled a lot.

Margot glanced down, checking out the freshly dry-cleaned mint-green shirt, and the wrinkle-free slacks and stopped when she spotted the little white booties over his feet. There, they were on even footing in the looking-cool department.

For some petty reason it made her feel better about losing their bet.

"Welcome to the party." He winked before stepping out of her way.

Margot rolled her eyes as she edged past him. Wes was so impossibly at ease in his own skin that, no matter what he did, he came across to most people as a pompous dick. She knew him well enough to know he really *was* a pompous dick a lot of the time, but he was also a damn fine detective, and a genuinely nice guy to those he cared about.

The room she walked into was darker than the rest of the house. The blinds were drawn, motes of dust suspended mid-air in the hot space. The walls were painted a rich chocolate brown, built-in bookshelves adorned every wall, neatly sorted spines filling each one. A large television was mounted on one wall, letting her know this was likely a living room or family den. The TV was muted, but still tuned to a nature documentary channel. The shifting images on the screen cast a flickering blue light into the room, giving the false impression that the bodies still had some life left in them.

One victim was slumped in a chair that looked out of place under the television. Not an obvious place to put a heavy leather recliner. Before she approached the body she scanned the area nearby, and sure enough there were deep divots in the rug, indicating the recliner had been moved.

The body belonged to a middle-aged man. Latino, probably about forty-five. He was a little overweight, a small belly protruding over his khakis. As far as Margot could tell, he was the kind of guy who took his appearance seriously. His brown loafers were still shiny where she could see them beneath the blood.

So much blood.

His head was slumped to the side, mouth hanging agape, and his eyes rolled back. Margot leaned in to take a closer look. Where the irises were visible, they'd already gone milky white. His tongue looked swollen. A fly buzzed near Margot's face, and she waved it away. Of course they'd have found their way inside already. She didn't think the bodies had been up here long enough for the flies to have come from them. But it was hot, and flies always managed to find their way in to where they were most unwelcomed.

There was a revolver lying on the ground next to the man's feet, as if it had dropped from his hand. His brains were splattered over a bookshelf nearby.

Looked like a textbook suicide.

Looked like.

Margot skirted round the impossibly large pool of blood

until she was standing behind the recliner and facing the door she'd entered. Wes was watching her, waiting to hear what she had to say. He had the upper hand, since he'd gotten here before her.

The air was stiflingly warm and reeked of blood. Margot swiped her arm across her brow to keep the sweat down. Three other recliners faced her, and each contained a body. Three women—two of them too young to properly be considered women—each lay slumped; their bodies having long given up anything that animated them, they were like discarded mannequins. Empty.

Each of them had a clear bag over their head, the plastic coated thickly with a film of condensation. The last breaths these women had taken were trapped inside with them.

The bags seemed unnecessary, since Margot could tell they hadn't died from asphyxiation. All three had their throats slit. Their fronts were soaked with blood, which pooled at their feet, mingling with that of the man in the other chair.

On average a human body held about five liters of blood. The amount changed based on the size of the person, but there was easily twenty liters of spilled blood on the floor.

No wonder it had soaked through to the floor below.

Jesus, what a goddamn mess.

"What do you think?" Wes asked, watching her intently.

This was the version of Wes she'd learned to appreciate early in their partnership, before she learned to like the real man under the asshole shell. When the investigator in him took over he was focused and all business. He was a great counterpart to bounce ideas off of. They worked well together.

"I know what it *looks* like," she replied, turning back toward the dead man. "It looks like Mr...."

"We assume this is the homeowner, Hector Ramirez, but that hasn't been confirmed yet. We're not sure about the others, but it's a safe bet they're his wife and kids."

"It appears Mr. Ramirez killed the women and then himself."

Wes nodded. "Yes, that would be how things look."

They stared at each other, and she wasn't sure which of them would break. Was he testing her? This was hardly her first day on the job. She'd been working homicide for SFPD for almost seven years.

Finally, she acknowledged that Wes would never blink first, and she sighed. "Of course, if it *was* a murder-suicide, Mr. Ramirez wouldn't have blood spatter on his shirt that was consistent with the spray from the ladies." Margot indicated a spray of blood across Hector's yellow polo shirt. If he'd slit their throats, the way the crime scene suggested at a glance, he wouldn't have gotten blood on him like that. Even if he'd stood in front of them to cut their throats—which seemed like a stupid move—the blood would be much thicker from the initial gush.

He'd been sitting where he was when the women were killed.

Women.

Something nagged at her, beyond the way the crime scene was staged.

"You said you thought the vics were his wife and kids?"

Wes nodded. "Yeah, but we obviously haven't removed the bags yet. Can't be a hundred percent sure."

Margot was shaking her head before he even finished speaking. Her pulse was pounding and her breath came out short.

The portraits downstairs, the ones showing the Ramirez family, hadn't shown Hector with a wife and two daughters.

The kids had been a girl... and a boy.

Margot looked at Wes. "Where is their son?"

TWO
OCTOBER 3, 1980

Just outside Petaluma, California

She looked skinny.

It was hard to tell underneath the hulking coat she wore, but skinny legs pale as the face of the moon stuck out the bottom of the coat's hem. They looked pearl white in his headlights.

She'd had her thumb up, but when he pulled the station wagon up beside her, she let her arm drop, and seemed to be considering changing her mind. He leaned across the front seat and cranked the window down, smiling at her as he did.

"Evening, miss."

The air outside was cold, and the girl shivered in spite of her coat. Her breath fogged as she let out a sigh.

Pretty little thing.

Her hair was blond, but the kind that he'd heard referred to as "dishwater blond" where it bordered on light brown. Not his usual favorite, but she had round cheeks and a small, pursed mouth. Her big eyes were watching him carefully.

"Hey," she replied. Her voice was high, babyish.

"Where are you headed?"

She chewed the inside of her cheek, glancing up and down the road hesitantly. "Novato?"

"Are you asking me?" His smile stayed steady, unwavering. The girl finally cracked. Her shoulders unhunched and she laughed.

"No. I'm going to Novato. You headed that way?" She chewed on a bit of skin by her thumbnail, awaiting his response. Ugly habit for a pretty girl.

"Sure, come on in." He popped the passenger door's lock with a satisfying *thunk*.

She brought the smell of sandalwood into the car with her, and as she rolled up the window and nestled in, she fluffed her coat around her like a downy shell. "It was so cold out there, I'm glad you came by."

"You mind me asking what you're doing out here all by yourself?"

She was still chewing on her thumbnail, and it took a moment for his question to register. "Oh, me? A friend of mine is throwing a little party, and normally I get the car on Friday, but my brother decided at the last minute to go to this stupid football thing in Sonoma, so he got to take it, leaving me stranded. So stupid."

"How old are you?" He kept his eyes on the road, his tone as smooth and neutral as his driving. Nothing to worry about here.

"Nineteen."

It had the taste of a lie to it, but he wasn't sure if she was aging herself up, or down. If she wanted to seem more innocent, she'd play younger; if she wanted him to think she was used to this sort of thing, she'd act older. One way or another he didn't believe she was nineteen.

His pulse quickened and in the warm interior of the car he felt sweat begin to pool along his spine and under his arms.

"What's your name?" she asked.

His answer stuck in his throat, and he thought about it, probably a second too long. "Ed."

"Ed." She giggled, a sweet, girlish sound that made him suspect she was probably closer to sixteen or seventeen. "Just Ed?"

What was the harm? "Ed Finch."

"I'm Laura."

He gave her a teasing smirk. "Just Laura?"

She stopped chewing on her thumb and grinned. "Guess I deserved that. Laura Welsh."

"That's a nice name, Laura Welsh."

She shrugged. "Sure."

His headlights skimmed a sign for Olompali State Historic Park and Ed felt his stomach tighten with excitement.

"You want to put on some music?" he asked.

"Oh, sure." Laura gave him a cautious look, then leaned over to fiddle with the radio dial. The radio buzzed in and out of stations until a syncopated drumbeat caught her attention. "I *love* this song."

The opening chords of Fleetwood Mac's "Tusk" filled the car as they passed a second sign for the state park. Laura, busily drumming along to the beat, slapping her palms on her knees with her eyes closed, seemed blissfully unaware of their surroundings.

Ed pulled off the highway and down a gravel road leading into the park.

It was only when the highway was well out of view and the only lights around them were his twin beams cutting through the night, that Laura stopped to look around.

"W-where are we going?"

"Shortcut. We'll get there a few minutes faster."

Laura looked at him, her face ghostly white. "There aren't any shortcuts to Novato."

Ed pulled over to the shoulder of the road and put the car

into park, then slid his finger over the power lock mechanism next to his arm. Once again, the *thunk* sounded. "No. I don't suppose there are."

She tried the door handle, futilely groping at it, and fighting with the lock, but each time she thought she had it up, he'd snap it back into place. Her breath came in short, desperate pants, fogging up the glass.

"Let me go," she begged. "I won't say anything. I swear. Please, just let me get out."

"Well, I can't do that, Laura."

"Why?" She hiccuped, and when she looked at him there was black mascara streaking down her cheeks and her pale white skin had gone red.

"Because I told you my real name."

Before she could reply, he grabbed a fistful of her hair and smashed her face against the dashboard. Bone crunched and she went limp almost instantly.

He stuck his hand between the seats and pulled out a long knife, its blade gleaming coldly.

In the back seat, the baby started to cry.

Ed turned the radio down, the Fleetwood Mac song fading out. He lifted the knife to his lips as he turned toward the wailing child.

"Shh, shh, baby. Daddy will be right back."

He left the car running as he pulled Laura out and dragged her into the trees.

Inside, the baby stopped crying.

THREE

Margot pushed past Wes and was halfway down the stairs before he managed to catch up with her.

"A son?" He jogged down the carpeted stairs behind her, and she guided him into the formal sitting room and pointed to the black-and-white portrait on the wall, the same one she had noticed on her way in.

Hector Ramirez—whose brains were now splattered all over his lovely custom bookshelves—his beautiful wife, their teenage daughter, and—

"Oh, Christ, Margot."

"Yeah."

The fourth member of the family was undoubtedly a little boy. Maybe nine or ten years old. The three victims upstairs sitting across from Ramirez were all women, and while Margot couldn't be positive without the medical assessments, she was betting the two younger ones were teenagers.

No ten-year-old boy in sight.

Down here, away from all the hubbub on the upper level, the house was eerily silent again. Wes stood next to her, staring at the portrait, like if he looked at it long enough something would change.

But no, there was still a boy in the photo whose body wasn't upstairs.

Margot's mind raced, immediately going to the darkest place possible. She couldn't help herself, it was how she was programmed. She thought of Dennis Rader, the BTK Killer. She'd thought a lot about Rader over the years, so it wasn't surprising how quickly he came to mind.

Rader had been obsessed with a little eleven-year-old girl named Josephine Otero. So obsessed, in fact, that he had murdered her entire family in order to have access to her. Mother, father, little brother, all dead.

What if someone had done that here?

It was certainly possible that the Ramirez family were victims of a homicide where none of them had been the target, just like the Oteros.

Margot snapped her fingers at Wes, getting his attention back from the picture. "He might still be in the house."

As much as she teased Wes sometimes for being slow on the uptake, she saw the flicker of immediate understanding on his face. He was a homicide cop after all, and he'd spent enough time working alongside her that his train of thought would head down the same depressing path hers had.

On her way to the kitchen she waved over a uniformed officer. "The Ramirezes had a son, probably eight to ten years old, he isn't upstairs. Let's get an APB out on him immediately, and get everyone you have looking through the house and yard, OK?"

"Does this place have a basement?" Wes asked. "I didn't see one on the way in."

Basements, at least proper full-sized ones, were few and far between in California, but not totally unheard of in more modern builds like this one. A lot of homes also came equipped with a so-called "California basement" which was a glorified crawl space that could house a furnace below ground and maybe a few boxes, but little else.

They'd had a basement like that where Margot grew up.

There was a reason her own apartment was on the top floor of the building she lived in.

She made her way into the kitchen. In spite of all the alarms going off in her head, telling her there was a fifth body some- where in the house, she still moved with slow, methodical steps, ensuring she didn't overlook anything because she was in a state of panic.

She'd learned a long time ago that bad things happened, and losing your shit over them didn't undo anything. It was part of the reason she'd become a cop in the first place; she could at least put that awareness to good use and help people when they needed it most.

The Ramirez family couldn't be saved, but someone had done this to them, and she could turn her laser focus toward getting that person off the streets.

A narrow door that looked like it might lead to a broom closet or a pantry was next to the fridge in the kitchen. It was so small, and so blandly painted, she hadn't even noticed it when she walked through the first time. She turned the glass knob and pulled it open, half expecting to find a Swiffer or neatly stacked boxes of Cheerios, but instead the open mouth of a stairwell greeted her, black and wide, ready to swallow her up.

A white string dangled a few feet down, and Margot took one step toward it, then froze.

She reached beneath her blazer, removed her service pistol from the holster clipped at her hip, and disengaged the safety. It seemed impossible that anyone would still be in the house after all this time, but she wasn't going to take any chances.

"San Francisco Police Department. If there's anyone down there, identify yourself." Right, because a mass murderer lying in wait in a dingy basement would just give himself up because she asked nicely.

Worth a shot.

She took a few steps down, then pulled the white string in front of her. A single bare bulb flared to life, swinging gently back and forth from the pressure of her pulling on it. Dim yellow light bathed the small basement, but shadows played tricks on her eyes, growing and shrinking as the bulb swayed.

"Wes, can you back me up down here?" She knew he couldn't be far behind her, and sure enough he came to the top of the stairs, his body blotting out any of the warm sunlight coming in from the kitchen. Though she was glad of the backup Margot immediately felt trapped, and it made sweat bead at the base of her neck.

The basement was small, just a narrow room with a concrete floor and exposed two-by-four beams for walls. The furnace was tucked in a corner, and as she had prophesied, there were a few stacks of cardboard boxes marked with Sharpie. "Christmas" a few proclaimed. "Mateo's baby clothes." "Evangeline's crafts." A sick feeling tugged in Margot's belly; these boxes represented a full lifetime of events, milestones, and hobbies that the Ramirez family would never again get to experience.

Sometimes this job really fucking sucked.

"Do you have a flashlight?" she called up to Wes. The darkness stuck to the corners of the room much the same as spiderwebs did.

Wes turned away and she heard his muffled voice. A moment later he took a few steps down into the basement and handed her a flashlight. It was a small but heavy black Maglite, something a beat cop might have on his belt. She pushed the button on, and a beam of light cut through the darkness.

Wes, she noticed, hadn't bothered to unholster his weapon,

which was either very stupid, or his way of telling her she was being overly cautious.

Either way, it was an amateur move and he was being cocky instead of smart.

She wedged the small light between the fingers of her left hand, then adjusted her pistol grip so she could still maintain a two-handed hold on her weapon, controlling the light and the gun at the same time.

She cleared the basement quickly, checking behind the furnace, and ensuring there were no sections of insulation pulled up to hide a person, or perhaps a murder weapon. The only thing remaining was the stack of boxes in the corner. She realized she was holding her breath.

Margot approached slowly, knowing if someone was hiding, they'd use the element of surprise and knock the boxes at her.

"See anything?" Wes asked. He hadn't sat down or retreated. His hand was resting on his hip, just behind his own holster. She recognized the actions of a man coiled to draw.

Maybe he wasn't so flip after all.

"No."

She nudged one of the boxes with her toe, trying to spook anyone behind them out of hiding, but also testing the weight to see if they could be moved without her surrendering her grip on either her gun or her light.

No such luck, the stack had a surprising amount of heft to it.

She heard a muted sob, and immediately stepped back three feet.

"Mateo?" The sound had barely been audible, but she knew how to tell the difference between a child and an adult. That had not been a grown man's voice. "Mateo, my name is Detective Margot Phalen, I'm with the San Francisco Police Department. I'm here to help you."

She lowered her weapon but didn't immediately reholster it.

She was also taking a gamble on his name, but she'd be a pretty shitty detective if she couldn't make the leap based on the box labels.

Silence once again filled the basement, a quiet that was so loud she could hear the blood pounding behind her ears as she strained to make out even the slightest sound.

A slight scrape, like something brushing over concrete.

"Mateo. I'm here with my partner, Wes Fox. Can you put your hands out, so I know where you are?"

Another long, exhausting pause. Wes must have heard the noise too, though, because when she glanced at him he was staring at the exact same place she was watching. Finally, when it seemed as if they might both be hallucinating, a very meek voice asked, "Where's my mom?"

FOUR

Mateo sat in one of the interrogation rooms, his legs not quite reaching the floor, feet swinging idly as he pressed his fingers into the can of Coke someone had gotten for him.

He was so small for nine years old. All skinny limbs and scabbed elbows.

Margot tried to remember what she'd been like at his age, but all of her old memories carried a stain, and she usually tried not to think about herself back then.

She'd once been a skinny little thing like him though.

She and Wes were standing out in the hall, staring through the small window that looked into the interrogation room. They could have had a better view of the boy if they'd gone into the room on the opposite side of the two-way mirror, but that felt invasive and somehow wrong.

A gray blanket was draped around the boy's shoulders, covering up the X-Men pajamas he was wearing.

They'd only returned from the crime scene a few minutes earlier, and Mateo had been waiting for them for an hour. He'd been taken to the police station after being checked at a hospital to confirm there were no hidden injuries. Since an initial search on the Ramirezes turned up no immediate family, they had called Children and Family Services.

There was no law against them speaking to Mateo on his own, especially since he wasn't under arrest for anything, but Margot wanted to tread lightly. His whole family had been murdered, and while he seemed to be holding it together pretty well, the second the reality of his situation sank in, they would want to have an expert here to help him deal with that.

Margot wasn't great with kids to begin with. Hysterical ones who had just learned they were orphans were way outside her wheelhouse.

She eased the door open, and she and Wes entered together. While Wes went to the corner to turn on the video camera, Margot pulled out the chair across the table from Mateo and took a seat. The CFS agent should be here soon. In the meantime, the sooner they started asking the kid what he remembered, the sharper his recollection would be.

They couldn't risk waiting any longer and losing precious details that might help catch whoever had killed his family.

And if that person *had* been his father, Mateo would be able to tell them.

"Mateo, do you remember me?" she said gently. It had only been an hour, but he'd met a lot of new people in that time.

Mateo sipped his Coke and nodded. "Detective Phalen."

Margot gave him an approving smile. "And my partner, Detective Fox. But you can call me Margot if you want. And he's Wes." This would be a lot easier if she could establish good rapport with him right away. "I want to tell you right away that you're not in any trouble, OK? But I still want to let you know that you have some rights." Mirandizing minors, especially those not under arrest, wasn't exactly a requirement, but with a case like this she wasn't about to take any chances that Mateo's statement might later be rendered inadmissible.

She'd seen enough lawyers pull dirty tricks to get their shithead clients off in the past. And while she honestly believed the victims in every case she took on mattered and deserved justice, this case in particular would demand a lot of her. She was going to play this one by the book. After telling Mateo his rights and getting him to agree that he understood them, she began her questioning.

"Do you know what happened at your house today?"

He stared at his Coke.

Margot didn't push him, she waited patiently and tried to read what was happening on his face. He looked angry for the briefest of flashes, then his brows knit together, and his face fell. His lower lip quivered, but to Margot's surprise, he didn't break down.

What a tough kid.

"I think they're dead, aren't they?" He glanced up at her, big brown eyes shining from under black eyebrows. Those eyes had depths to them, making him seem so much older than his nine years. She felt a pang of kinship with him, and that recognition made her feel sick to her stomach.

"Yes, they're dead," she said plainly, not wanting to lie to him. "Do you have two sisters?"

He shook his head. "Val had a friend over."

Val was Valentina, the older of the Ramirez siblings. They'd been able to gather that much from the neighbors, but the ID of the second young woman had remained a mystery. In fact, until the bodies were back at Evelyn's office, they wouldn't even know which of the two was Valentina.

"Do you know her name?"

"Emily."

"Do you know her last name?" Wes asked from the corner.

Mateo seemed to have forgotten Wes was in the room because he jumped slightly at the masculine voice. "Potter, I think."

Margot didn't even need to give Wes the nod. He was

already on his way out of the room, to see if they could find any record of an Emily Potter and hopefully locate her family. This was going to be a very, very shitty day for her parents. Margot breathed in through her nostrils and chased away the thought. It was so easy to get lost in what the living would think and feel, but her job was to work on behalf of the dead.

Emily, Valentina, Hector, Evangeline. They were her focus now.

"Did you see what happened, Mateo?"

He was so quiet and still she thought perhaps he hadn't heard her, but when she opened her mouth to speak again, he squeezed his eyes shut tight like he was trying to chase back a memory. Margot waited.

"I heard," he whispered.

"You heard it?"

The can crinkled softly under the pressure of his fingertips. Margot folded her arms on the table. "You can tell me anything. I'll believe you, even if you think it sounds scary, or strange. You can tell me."

"I heard Mama yelling at someone."

"Do you know who she was yelling at?" She had to stop herself from asking if Evangeline had been yelling at Hector. She didn't want to put the idea in Mateo's head that his father was guilty of something. It would be up to the kid's memories as to whether or not she drew that conclusion. It would be all too easy to ask him leading questions, but then he would only be telling her what he thought she wanted to hear.

She needed the truth, not a convenient lie.

"I think it was a man. Not Papa, someone else. I don't know who." He'd managed to cover most of her follow-up questions.

"Did you see someone?"

Mateo shook his head. "No."

"Did you hear anything before your mother started yelling?

Something unusual?" She thought back to the boot mark on the back door of the house.

"No."

So much for the idea that the killer had busted open the door and charged into the house. Though, given how the bodies were arranged, the killing hadn't been sudden; it had taken time. There were a lot of things about this murder that didn't add up. The answers wouldn't be easy or obvious, it seemed.

"When did you hear your mother start yelling? Today?"

"Last night. I got scared, I hid." He traced the lip of his Coke can with a fingertip. His cuticles looked like he chewed them frequently. She used to do the same thing.

"Were you in bed?"

Mateo's cheeks flushed pink, the color climbing all the way to the tips of his ears. "No."

"Can you tell me what you were doing?"

Wes came back into the room and returned to his place by the camera. He'd probably shared Emily's name but hadn't hung around to help with the search. Margot had to hope the interruption wouldn't throw Mateo off track and keep him from telling them what he'd been doing.

The boy's gaze cut to Wes, then back to Margot. She didn't bother to look back to see what Wes was doing but kept her eyes on the boy, and said, "Don't worry about Wes, he can keep a secret."

Mateo's shoulders slumped and he let out a sigh. They had him.

"Sometimes when Mom and Dad go to bed, I sneak downstairs and take things out of their jackets." He quickly looked between them again. "Like money and stuff. I was doing that when I heard Mama upstairs yelling at someone. I thought it might be Papa at first, but then Papa was yelling too, and when Emily and Valentina started screaming..."

Ah, the plot thickened.

"You heard them screaming."

"Yes."

"Do you remember what time that was?" Wes asked.

"After midnight?" Mateo sounded unsure, and Margot wasn't willing to bet their whole timeline on his guess. Still, it was something.

"What happened then?"

"They kept screaming, and I got scared, so I went and hid in the basement. I thought if something bad happened Mama would come find me. Only, Mama never came." His chin flopped toward his chest and his thin shoulders trembled slightly.

Margot, not sure what else to do, put her hand on his arm and gave it a squeeze. "You were smart. You did the right thing." She believed that to her very core. Had Mateo gone upstairs to see what was happening, he'd be dead now, too.

She thought about his words, though, trying to decide what was merely a passing comment and what bore more consideration. He'd specifically said *Mama* would come find him if anything bad had happened. Did that mean Hector wouldn't have looked for his son? If so, was there something more going on behind closed doors with this family, perhaps something that might indicate Hector Ramirez really had been the killer?

She'd hoped the boy could help her figure out if the killer had been inside his family or not, but now she only had more questions and uncertainty. Mateo had said he thought Evangeline was yelling at a man who wasn't Hector, but the boy had also been on the main floor. There was a chance he *had* heard his parents arguing and possibly hadn't recognized the voice for some reason.

Or maybe there had been a second man.

Regardless, there were no easy or obvious answers to be had, which made the headache looming at the back of Margot's skull grow a little bit bigger. Before this day was over it would be a migraine, no doubt.

A knock on the door interrupted them before she could ask anything else. Wes opened it up, and after a moment's hushed discussion, let a portly man into the room. He wore a sweater vest over an Oxford shirt, and his pants were so smooth they looked as if they'd just come off the rack. He had a bushy black mustache, which was almost the only hair on his head, aside from a ring of black fuzz circling the back of his skull.

"Detective Phalen, my name is Richard Jimsen, I'm here from Children and Family Services. If you're done with Mateo, we've been able to locate a cousin of his mother's who will be taking him in for the time being."

Mateo gave Margot a questioning look, and she wondered if he'd ever met this mysterious cousin. She felt for the kid, but she also couldn't do anything to help him. It wasn't like she could make up the pull-out sofa in her living room and start looking after a nine-year-old.

"I think we're done here for the time being." They'd need to get a better handle on what the crime scene meant before she could ask Mateo more specific questions. "But Mateo, if you think of anything, please call me, no matter how small, how silly. If you think of *anything*, I want to know." She slid a card across the table to him, her cell phone number on it.

He looked at it as if he wasn't sure what he was supposed to do with it, and she realized this was probably the first time anyone had ever given him a business card.

Wes was speaking quietly with Jimsen, and writing a few things in a small notebook. The two men exchanged cards of their own before shaking hands. The whole interaction took less than three minutes, and before she knew it Mateo Ramirez was gone, leaving her and Wes alone in the room together.

He shut off the video camera, then sat down in the seat across from her.

"What do you think?" he asked.

"I think this case fucking sucks, and I wish I'd let Wallace take the call." Margot leaned back in the chair and stared up at the water-stained ceiling.

"What do you think of the kid?"

Margot looked at Wes, trying to read his expression. She wasn't entirely sure what he was getting at, but she knew the question wasn't an altogether innocent one.

She'd known Wes long enough to know that everything he said, he said for a reason. Whether it was a cutting jab managed with only a few words, or a question like this, loaded with a meaning she wasn't entirely sure she understood.

"What do *you* think of the kid?" Since he was obviously dying to get something off his chest, she might as well give him the opportunity to say what he wanted to say.

"Didn't you find him a little... strange?"

That was one of those relative things, the strangeness of children. Margot didn't really know what normal kids were supposed to be like, since in her experience they all tended to be a little bit bizarre. She'd never been a normal kid herself, so her frame of reference was missing a control group.

"He seemed OK to me."

"Jesus, Phalen, I swear someone would need to be painting the walls of the room with shit before you thought they were acting weird."

"My threshold for *weird* is pretty high."

"I'll say." And there it was: for a fraction of a second his expression changed, and had she not been looking right at him when it happened, she'd have missed it. For a brief instant, instead of his usual smug superiority, Wes Fox looked at her with pity.

Pity.

"Don't do that," she sighed.

"Do what?"

"The thing your face just did, don't do that."

He sat back in the chair. "Hey, babe, my face is permanently handsome like this, I can't do anything about that." He was pretending not to know what she was talking about, and it was infuriating, but at the same time it saved them from having to discuss it. Maybe she should be grateful.

She should definitely let it go.

But it nagged at her all the same, because she didn't *want* his pity. She didn't want anyone's pity. What she wanted was to be treated like Margot Phalen, detective, shitty cook, normal-ish thirty-seven-year-old single woman.

OK, so maybe that garnered its own kind of pity in some circles, but that wasn't the reason Wes had been looking at her like she was a puppy who had been kicked, and she knew it.

She had created a very specific life for herself in San Francisco. Sometimes she wondered if she should have gone further away, if staying so close to where it happened was a mistake. Distance was meaningless, though, she knew that. She could have moved to New York, or Tampa, or New Zealand for that matter, and it would have followed her.

Wes usually did a good job of pretending she was normal, she had to give him credit for that.

"You're not that pretty," she said finally, a gesture she was letting it go.

"You're a terrible liar."

Margot snorted. "What's your issue with the kid?"

"For starters, I think it's weird he stayed in the basement all night if the murders really did happen at midnight. Patrol got the call something was hinky around nine in the morning. We showed up, what, shortly after ten?"

"Yeah."

"That's a *long* time to hide in the basement. That's hiding not only through a murder, but through some obvious sounds of people going through the house."

"He was scared."

Wes shrugged, a half lift of both shoulders. "Maybe. Maybe not. Another thing, why wasn't he more torn up about his whole family being dead? He just sat here like he was in the principal's office, drinking his Coke and answering your questions like it was no big deal. Weird."

"You wanted him to be shrieking and flailing and crying so much there was snot all over our table?"

"Maybe."

She gave a long exhale, a dull throb building behind her eyes. "People grieve in different ways, Wes. Kid's probably in shock. I'm not sure anyone gave him the manual on how to act when you're the only survivor of a mass murder."

Wes drummed his fingers on the metal tabletop and watched her carefully. "You've got a lot of good excuses for him, but I still think you felt it."

She was quiet for a while, still trying to read his face so she might better understand what it was he wanted from her. Margot had no intention of telling Wes what he wanted to hear if it wasn't what she wanted to say, but at the same time she felt like it gave her the upper hand if she understood his motivation.

He was a tough nut to crack.

"I grant you, Mateo didn't behave how I anticipated a kid in his situation would. That said, there could be an element of denial to the whole thing. He never saw the bodies, so maybe part of him doesn't think they're really dead? It's hard to process a loss if you don't fully believe the people are gone."

"If that's the case, I feel really shitty for the rude awakening that kid is going to get in a couple days when he realizes his mom and dad aren't ever coming back."

A soft knock on the door preceded the entrance of Officer Libby Hart, a small-faced young woman who seemed chronically incapable of meeting anyone's gaze directly. "Detective Fox? I found the information you were looking for." She came into the room just far enough to leave a piece of paper on the table between Wes and Margot.

For a fraction of a second, Libby's gaze met Wes's, and as she left the room there was a distinct flush of red on her cheeks.

Margot looked at Wes. "Did you sleep with her?"

"Inappropriate work discussion."

"Did you?"

"No, do you think I ought to try?"

Margot snorted and picked up the paper. "You ready to go meet Emily Potter's family?"

FIVE

They took Wes's car.

The Potters lived in a Victorian house, the exterior painted shades of mint and sunshine yellow. Wes had to circle the block twice to find a parking space, and in that time, Margot had searched for Emily online, finding her Facebook and Instagram profiles. Everything Margot found depicted a cheerful teenage girl with dark hair and beach-tanned skin.

In photos with Valentina—who was a constant co-star in Emily's timeline—the two could have easily passed for sisters.

Not impossible to imagine that a killer who only knew the Ramirez family had two children might be confused and kill Emily instead of Mateo. Sloppy, but plausible.

Emily and Valentina were both beautiful girls, flashing bright, toothy smiles and blowing kisses to the camera, or posing for pouty selfies, or applying silly filters that made them look like puppy dogs. Seeing video clips of them laughing proved to be too much for Margot.

Technology was great sometimes, but it often had the unforeseen side effect of making the victims seem too alive.

She didn't need to empathize or bond with these girls. She just needed to know who killed them.

Right now, that meant she and Wes had the unpleasant task of informing Emily's parents that the girl was most likely dead.

Outside, the air was as hot as it had been in the morning, if not worse. Margot was regretting the blazer she had chosen to wear, as sweat made the satin lining stick to her skin like plastic wrap. She removed her sunglasses and draped them in the V-neck of her plain white T-shirt. As they walked to the house from the car Wes, ever the gentleman, let her take the lead, which also meant she'd be the one to break the news to the Potters.

Margot rang the doorbell and waited, her heart hammering.

This part never got easier.

The door opened, revealing a pretty, plump woman with a gray-streaked black bob and thick-framed black glasses. "Hello?"

"Mrs. Potter?"

"Yes?" The woman was rightly suspicious of them. Margot noticed the way she wiped her palms on her jeans and kept looking between Margot and Wes, not sure which of them she should be paying the most attention to.

Margot pulled back the front of her blazer and unclipped her badge from her belt to show it to the woman, who didn't simply glance at it, but rather pulled it close and gave Margot a few incredulous sideways glances.

"I'm Detective Margot Phalen, this is my partner, Detective Wes Fox." Margot took a deep breath, and that moment was enough for Mrs. Potter to put the pieces together.

"Where's Emily?" she asked, her hand going to her chest, clasping at the gold cross around her neck.

"Ma'am, was your daughter staying with the Ramirez family last night? We understand she was close friends with Valentina Ramirez."

Mrs. Potter nodded her head, but all the color had drained from her face. The gears had started to click. She must have asked herself why two police officers—two detectives, no less— would be at her front door on a Sunday afternoon. She had to be asking herself how long it had been since her daughter had texted, was probably wondering what the last words Emily had said to her were. She'd think about those words for a long time.

She might also be wondering why Margot was using the past tense.

"Emily went over last night. They had a project to work on, so they were going to spend the weekend together."

"Mrs. Potter," Wes said, "is your husband home?"

She blinked, slowly taking in his words, adding them to the witch's brew of bad news that was bubbling up inside her. She left them in the doorway, wandering back into the house. "Peter? *Peter*, there are two policemen here."

A moment later footsteps from above announced the arrival of the unfortunately named Peter Potter. He was at least a foot taller than his wife and had sandy blond hair that had begun thinning at the temples. He was a handsome man, and Margot recognized a lot of Emily's features on his face.

"Hello."

Margot introduced herself and Wes again, then said, "Do you mind if we come in, Mr. Potter?" They hadn't been waiting for the man of the house to ask permission, rather it was easier to talk to both Potters at once, instead of repeating their story a second time, with one parent already inconsolable.

"Oh, of course. Jean, did you offer them a drink? It's sweltering outside. Come in, come in." Peter ushered them in and led them into a sitting room off the front hallway. Their home was cluttered, but in a warm, inviting way. The walls were all painted in light shades, and hung with original art. There were some classic movie posters Margot recognized, but the rest were black-and-white prints or bright modern paintings that looked as if they'd been done by a very talented toddler. Bookshelves lined a second room, wedged full of so many volumes the shelves had begun to sag under the weight.

Margot and Wes sat side by side on a squishy love seat, the cushions so plump they ended up sliding toward each other in the middle until their thighs were pressed together.

Jean Potter, despite her husband's polite suggestion, made no move to get them beverages, for which Margot was infinitely grateful. Yes, she was sweating like mad, but she didn't think she could drink homemade iced tea and tell these lovely people their daughter was dead.

There were framed photos of Emily over the fireplace. Margot saw no evidence to suggest the Potters had any other children.

"Mr. Potter, your wife confirmed that your daughter Emily was with her friend Valentina Ramirez at the Ramirez house this weekend."

"Did the girls get into trouble?" He shook his head and plopped down in an armchair across from them. Where Jean had apparently already reached the conclusion, Peter was arriving there quite a bit slower. "Kids, you know?"

Wes shot her a quick look, but Margot didn't turn her head. She said, "I think you should sit down, Mrs. Potter."

Jean hesitated, then sat in a matching armchair to the one her husband was in. Her hand was still clutching the cross necklace, and Margot knew from the woman's expression she had already steeled herself for what was coming next.

"We were called to an event at the Ramirez house earlier this morning. When we arrived, we found four bodies, and I'm afraid we believe one of them is Emily. We'll need you to make a positive identification, but the Ramirezes' son indicated Emily was the other person in the house last night."

"An event," Peter said. "What does that mean?" He had managed to totally gloss over the major bomb Margot had dropped in his lap and was focusing on her word choices instead.

Jean, on the other hand, had started to sob, taking big soundless gulps of air as tears streamed down her red cheeks. Peter wasn't even looking at her.

"Mr. Potter, we're homicide detectives," Margot clarified. "We were called to the scene of a multiple homicide at the Ramirez residence. We believe one of the victims is Emily." She wasn't sure how much clearer she could get while still being kind. It wasn't standard practice to scream *Your daughter was murdered, come look at her body* to grieving family members.

An uncomfortable silence filled the room, punctuated only by Jean's periodic choking gasps for air.

"I'm very sorry," Margot concluded. "If you're able, we can take you now so you can identify her. And we'll have some questions." She tried to look penitent for mentioning this last part, as now was not an ideal time for questioning, but she wanted to make the expectations clear.

Peter seemed to realize then what Margot had said, and that his wife was crying. The color drained slowly from his cheeks as it dawned on him that his daughter hadn't been arrested for mischief. This wasn't a case of kids being naughty. He wasn't going to have to think about teaching Emily lessons on responsibility, or footing the bill for something she'd damaged.

Margot saw the precise moment he understood that his daughter was dead, and it crushed her. Everything that he'd been only a minute earlier vanished in the space of a second. His features slackened, the shine in his eyes dulled. All it took was a few words from her, and these two people would never be the same.

"Someone killed our baby?" His hands started to tremble, and he placed them on his knees to keep the shake to a minimum.

"D-d-did..." Jean struggled with her words, barely able to

get out the syllables, let alone the sentence. She took a deep breath and Margot waited quietly, patiently, giving Jean time to find her way. "Was it b-bad?"

As opposed to a gentle murder?

For the first time since they'd sat down, Margot glanced at Wes. She knew he was better at this than her, at the fake kindnesses. She had a bad habit of being too blunt, and it sometimes came across as cold. The last thing she wanted to do was make this worse for the Potters.

Wes leaned forward, inviting intimacy and a friendly rapport. As if drawn magnetically to him, Jean edged forward on her seat. Even Peter's gaze seemed glued to him.

"I don't want to give you folks false expectations. What happened in the Ramirez home last night was very unpleasant, and when you see Emily it's going to be upsetting. It won't be easy, and I'm very, very sorry for that. But I've been doing this job a long time, and from everything I saw this morning I don't think Emily knew what was happening. I don't think she suffered."

Margot bit the inside of her cheek.

He was helping them. This was what had to be done to keep them from falling apart. But she had been at the same crime scene as Wes, and she knew exactly what a crock of shit he was selling. She'd seen the thick fog of breath coating the inside of each clear plastic bag. She'd seen how much blood there was.

The victims had been awake.

And they'd been alive when their throats were slit.

No matter what kind of bow Wes put on it, Margot knew Emily had suffered a great deal before she died.

SIX

JANUARY 16, 1981

Petaluma, California

A small piece of paper, ripped from a steno pad, rested on the dash of the station wagon, the hastily scrawled address lit by a single streetlight.

The night was barren, too cold by California standards for anyone to be outside. The apartment building across the street was blazing bright, most of the suites well lit. Several occupants hadn't bothered to draw their curtains against the early arrival of night, and Ed could see into their private spaces.

On the main floor a family was sitting down to dinner, their hands linked in prayer around a cheap dining table. Two floors up a man was feeding a parrot whose cage rested near the window. Ed wondered about parrots. What kind of pets did they make, really? He didn't want to own anything that could talk back to him. Too creepy.

The upper floor was where he spotted her. She was too high up for him to see her as well as the others, but she was speaking on the phone, wrapping the coiled cord around her finger as she spoke. She stopped briefly in front of the window, pushing her long, dark hair back over her shoulder and laughing at something her conversation partner had said.

Ed shifted in his seat, watching her with rapt attention.

She drifted away from the window, but her shadow still teased him as she moved around the room on her phone. He waited. He waited an hour, then a second hour. Slowly the other lights in the building began to switch off. A few brave souls ventured out, others returned from work, all bundled up against the chill in the air.

Eventually, shortly after ten, her lights went out, replaced by the flickering blue glow of a television set. Ed turned off the car and waited, watching the street until he spotted someone moving with purpose toward the apartment. There wasn't much else on the block to draw a person down this way, just an empty lot, and a garage that was closed for the night.

Ed got out of the car, putting on a pair of wire-framed glasses and turning up the collar of his coat. He was wearing a wig he'd bought from a local costume shop, and the synthetic fibers were already making his scalp itch.

As he'd expected, the man coming up the street stopped in front of the building and hit one of the call buttons. A moment later someone buzzed him in, and Ed was there to catch the door as the man jogged up the stairs, blissfully unaware or not caring that he'd let someone in behind him.

Waiting until the thump of footfalls stopped and a door closed, Ed slowly made his way up the stairs. On the second floor he turned left, marking the number of the apartment first from the stairs. 2B.

She would be in 5B, then.

He smiled, pleased with his detective work. This was proving to be very easy, much easier than he'd anticipated. Surely something should have stopped him by now if he wasn't meant to do this. Perhaps the man at the door would have blocked his way. Or the woman would have had company.

There was a whole universe of signs that would have told him to turn back and go home.

Instead the universe seemed to smile on him.

He made his way up the stairs slowly, with practiced patience, careful to not make too much noise. Anything that would make his presence in the building memorable was something he had to avoid.

Be a ghost, he told himself.

By the time he got to the fifth floor, he was already hard. His erection pressed uncomfortably along the inseam of his jeans and he shifted from one leg to the next.

There was a bulb burned out toward the end of her hallway, creating shadows that made it look as if the hall simply ended in a black abyss, rather than extending to more apartments. Ed stared into that blackness, waiting for a sign, something to tell him whether or not he should proceed.

Again, there was nothing that told him this was wrong, and everything in his gut told him it was so very right.

He approached her door and listened. A comedy laugh track made a tinny echo, muffled voices indicated she was watching a show, but he couldn't make out which one, and it didn't matter. The TV was the only noise coming from inside the apartment.

She might be asleep.

That didn't matter either.

Ed knocked on the door, softly enough someone inside would hear it, but nosy neighbors would be likely to miss the sound.

After a few moments of silence, he heard footfalls from within, then the lock turning. When the door opened, she was standing next to it wearing a loose T-shirt and a pair of shorts. She rubbed her eyes, looking as if she'd just woken up.

"Hello?" Her voice was groggy.

"Hi, oh man, I woke you up, didn't I?" He feigned a

sheepish look, the kind of aw-shucks apologetics that he hoped she'd find endearing.

"What? Oh, no, it's fine. I was watching TV. Sorry, do I know you?"

"I live in 4D, I think I've seen you in the hall before."

"Sure." She lifted a shoulder in a half-shrug, too sleepy to question him. Thankfully she didn't appear to know whoever lived in 4D. "What's up?"

"My girlfriend is working late, and I forgot she had our keys. So stupid. Now I can't get into the apartment. Would you mind if I came in and borrowed your phone to call her?"

The woman paused, looking him over briefly. Whatever she saw didn't deter her from stepping out of the way to let him inside. He followed her into the kitchen where she indicated the cream-colored phone hanging from the wall.

"What'd you say your name was?" she asked.

"I didn't." He tried not to stare at her, even as he wondered how the wig looked under the light. Should he have spent more money? Was it obvious he was covering something up? His heartbeat pounded, pulse hammering in his ears. "My name is Frank."

"Frank from 4D."

Ed nodded happily. "Guess so. What's your name?"

She was quiet for a minute, playing with the sleeves on her shirt. Her dark hair was shiny and smooth under the kitchen lights. Ed wanted to touch it.

"Beth."

"Well, I thank you for this, Beth. You're a real lifesaver." He jerked his chin in the direction of the phone.

"Oh." She laughed softly, finally releasing the pent-up nerves that seemed to have followed her from the front door. "Yeah, no problem."

She wandered off, leaving him to the phone, but he could tell she wasn't far. In the background the sounds of studio laughter came from the TV. He still couldn't make out what she was watching, but in truth he didn't pay much attention to what was on. All the shows seemed the same.

He picked up the phone and held down the receiver button while dialing seven fake numbers. After enough time to make it seem like he'd waited for a ring, he started reciting the script he'd come up with on his way up the stairs.

"Is Kim there?" A beat. "Hey baby, I'm so sorry to call you at work, but you took the keys, and I can't get in." Another pause, this one longer, punctuated by a sigh. "No, I know, I know." Another short intake of breath. It wasn't hard for him to imagine this sniping argument. He could have called his real wife at home and she'd have started reading him the riot act immediately for being out so late. "Do you think you could bring it back... baby, you have the car."

Beth peeked around the corner, her expression somewhere between bemused sympathy and something resembling worry. She raised an eyebrow at him, and he gave her a comforting smile that implied a *what can you do* attitude.

He hoped.

At the base of his spine, the knife was a cool presence against his skin. Knowing it was there, feeling it so close, gave him all the comfort and courage he needed to keep going.

It would be in his hand soon.

This would be over soon.

Beth smiled at him softly, a pretty curve of the lips. She tucked her hair behind her ear, leaning up against the wall. The faint scent of vanilla hung in the air. A lotion, maybe, or her shampoo. Whatever it was, it was strikingly feminine.

"Kim, baby, I know. I know that. I already said I was sorry. Can you come on your break maybe?" He rested his head against the kitchen wall and took a deep breath in through his nose to really maximize the drama. "No, I'm upstairs. One of our neighbors on the fifth floor let me use her phone. Yes, her."

He gave Beth a quick look and she made an apologetic face, like she realized her presence was causing him trouble. "Baby. Baby. Come on now, what was I supposed to do, you had the keys." He scratched his stubbly cheeks, then nodded mostly to himself. "I'd appreciate that, thank you. Yes, thank you. I love you, too. Bye."

Once the phone was back in its cradle, Beth let out a little whoosh of breath. "She seems like a handful."

"Love is never as easy as they make it seem in the movies, right?"

"I wouldn't know." She was playing coyly with her hair. Was she... flirting with him? That took him aback. He'd expected rigid politeness, maybe a passive friendliness that would befit a neighbor helping someone she didn't know that well.

Her being smiley and batting her lashes at him didn't fit in his plan.

"I really appreciate you being so kind. You're a real life-saver," he told her again. For the first time that night he wondered if he should leave. The door was close, he could just beg off and tell her he would wait for his girlfriend downstairs.

It's not too late.

"Did you... I dunno, did you maybe want a drink while you wait for her to come? I'm only watching TV. Beats you having to sit in front of your door, bored."

Ed's palms started to perspire.

"I-I should probably head downstairs." His upper lip was damp with sweat, and he was itching to get out. Things had gone so well, everything had been perfect. What was happening?

"Don't be silly. It's no problem at all, seriously. I was only sitting around here, you know. By myself. You'll be doing me a favor by hanging out. I mean, what kind of girl falls asleep before ten on a Friday? That's sad. You'd be my hero, basically."

His throat was dry. "I suppose I c-could use a drink."

Get your shit together, Ed.

Beth's face broke into a wide smile. "Yeah? Oh, that's great." She moved into the kitchen, brushing against him as she passed. His erection, which had begun to wither, roared back to life, and a shudder racked his sweat-chilled body. The smell of her this close was intoxicating.

"Are you wearing perfume? Something vanilla?"

Beth laughed, not bothering to look at him as she spoke. "No, nothing like that. It's a lotion. Does your girlfriend like vanilla? I could tell you the brand."

"No, she's not really into the girl-stuff like that." He thought of his wife, seemingly allergic to makeup since giving birth to Megan. Her once-long hair cut into a short, boyish style. She was barely a woman at all anymore. Saggy tits, no lipstick. Ed sneered to himself. "Doesn't really take much pleasure in looking nice, I guess."

"Ugh," Beth groused. "Seems so unfair. Single girls bend over backwards to look good, and it's the girls with boyfriends and husbands who get to be lazy about it. Guess my mama would have said that once a fish is on the line, you don't need a lure anymore." She laughed, then handed him a glass of amber liquid.

"What's this?"

"Bourbon, with a little splash of water. Come on." She took her own drink into the living room and plopped down on the couch with practiced ease, then patted the cushion beside her.

Ed hovered a few feet away, pretending to be distracted by her bookshelves. The stacks were filled with Danielle Steele and other well-read romance novels. Framed photos adorned the shelves showing Beth at different stages of her life, from graduation to family vacations. She wore the same toothy, confident smile in all of them.

The confidence brought Ed back to his purpose.

She was a shiny, beautiful, untouchable creature.

He slid the knife out of the back of his pants and held it flush against his sleeve so she wouldn't see it if she happened to take a look back at him. Sipping the bourbon, he set the glass down on the nearest bookshelf, then moved to stand behind her, his gaze locked on the back of her head rather than on the television screen.

"Do you watch this one?" she asked, indicating the screen.

"No." He moved, then, with the speed of a natural-born predator. His hand clamped down on her mouth, his other lifting the knife to her throat, cool metal pressing against the delicate skin there. All it would take was a little too much pressure and he could end her then and there.

Mutely she breathed heavily into his hand, her legs kicking out, fingernails trying to find purchase on him, but to no avail. Her cheeks were suddenly wet with tears.

"Beth, if you're a very, very good girl tonight, I will let you live, do you understand?" His fingertips dug into her cheeks, pushing her lips open. "Say you understand."

"Y-yes," she said into his skin. Her hot breath sent a chill through him. He was in control again.

"Good. If you do anything I don't like, Beth, I'm going to use this knife on you, and I won't start with your throat. I'll start with your pussy. I'll cut you open from the inside so you can feel me in there while you're still alive. Do you understand?"

Beth sobbed, tears streaming down her face and chin, her nose slick with snot.

Not so confident now.

He took her into the bedroom.

An hour later, he washed her blood off in the sink, then wiped the phone down with bleach. He finished off the last of the bourbon in the glass he'd left on the bookshelf, and took the tumbler with him when he left.

SEVEN

It was Emily.

Of course, it was Emily. Margot didn't live in a world with surprise happy twists. She lived in a world where whole families could be murdered overnight, leaving parents without their children and little boys without their parents.

By the time she left the station about twelve hours after starting her day, she was physically and emotionally drained. Watching the Potters weep over their daughter's body had been the thing that finally cracked her. It had been a long, hellish day, and she was ready for it to be over.

She stopped her car in front of one of her favorite dim sum restaurants a block away from the station and waited at the counter while they made her order. Since she was there about once a week, she knew the staff. They'd long ago realized she wasn't one for idle chitchat, but they smiled politely and left her a Diet Coke while she waited.

At home, with her car parked in the locked garage under the apartment building, and her three deadbolts engaged, she put her dim sum on the secondhand coffee table and poured half a bottle of white wine into a glass.

She didn't bother getting changed.

Kicking her shoes off, she flopped onto the couch and turned the TV on, leaving the volume muted for the time being. Her head was throbbing and the last thing she really needed was a loud laugh track or explosions adding to the din in her brain.

Her phone chimed.

For a moment she considered ignoring it until morning. She didn't have a lot of friends, and her brother never messaged her. There was a limited pool of options as to who could be texting her at ten thirty on a Sunday night and none of them were people she wanted to talk to.

She picked it up and checked the message.

Wes.

Groaning, she took a big gulp of wine.

> Hell of a day.

Really? He wanted to chat about this?

> Yeah, I was there for it. I remember.

She watched the three dots as he texted back, then the message appeared.

> You think this could be something… more?

Margot clutched the phone tightly. She knew what he was asking, and more precisely she knew *why* he was asking, and there wasn't enough goddamn Riesling in the world to make her OK with that right now.

> I don't know. It's too soon and we don't know enough.

She wasn't lying. Wes wanted to know if she thought this might be the work of a potential serial killer. There were too many uncertainties, though. If the killer was, however improbably, Hector, then the case was tied up in a neat ribbon and no one else would die.

But if the man Mateo had heard was a stranger—or more likely someone the family knew somehow—and he'd been the one to leave the bootprint on the back door, then their killer was in the wind. Whether or not he killed again had everything to do with his motivations and nothing to do with Margot's hunches or personal history.

Not wanting to see what he wrote next, she put the phone face down on the table and picked up her dim sum. The TV was playing a re-run of *Bob's Burgers* and Margot couldn't think of a single thing better to distract her from the day's events.

That was, of course, until she remembered the show was about a family, with three kids, and that tenuous connection was enough to turn her stomach.

She flipped the channels a bit before landing on a nature documentary and figured that learning about the secret lives of wombats might be her safest bet for stress-free viewing.

The dim sum had gotten cold on her ride home, but a steamed pork dumpling is still a steamed pork dumpling, regardless of how cold it is.

Her phone buzzed again, then a second time, but she couldn't bring herself to flip it over. She didn't *want* to think about the case. As it was, she'd be up most of the night mulling it over. Why couldn't Wes leave her alone for five seconds and let her think of *anything* else?

Shouldn't he be off using his easy charm to lure some unsuspecting woman into his bed? Margot was fairly certain that was the only thing he did in his free time.

Another buzz.

"For fuck's sake."

Picking up the phone again as she munched on the pork bun, she scrolled through Wes's messages.

> I want to talk about this.
>
> Can we meet up?
>
> Something is bothering me.

She was about to respond to him when the phone buzzed in her hand, startling her. This time the message wasn't from Wes, but rather a number she wasn't familiar with.

> Ms. Phalen, your father would like to see you.

Margot dropped the phone on the carpet. The pork bun suddenly tasted like stale ashes in her mouth.

How the fuck had he found her?

EIGHT

Three file boxes were emptied out on Margot's floor by the time Wes arrived.

She sighed with annoyance when he knocked, because she realized the three deadbolts made it impossible for him to come in on his own. Sort of the point of a deadbolt, really, but a pain in the ass when she was on the hunt for something.

Leaving the mess laid out on her floor, she checked the peephole to ensure it was him and he was alone. It took a moment to undo all the locks and the chain, and when she did finally let him in, he picked up in the middle of a conversation they hadn't been having.

"You know, when I said I wanted to get a drink I wasn't trying to get an invite to your place. It wasn't a come-on."

"There's beer in the fridge. Don't worry, I have no intentions of trying to seduce you." She watched him walk into her kitchen like he lived there, comfortable wherever he went, not a care in the world. The fridge light illuminated his dark blond hair, and when she realized she'd been watching too long, she left him and returned to her bedroom, where envelopes were strewn all over her bed, and files were spread out over the rug.

Some of the tension she'd been carrying all evening felt lighter just knowing there was someone else in the house and she wasn't alone with all this anymore.

Margot had foregone a glass and opened a new bottle of white, this time drinking it straight. After a few moments Wes joined her in the bedroom, beer in hand, and let out a low whistle.

Unlike her, he had changed out of his work clothes and was wearing a pair of snug-fitting jeans and a black sweater that seemed tailored in order to say, "Hi, I go to the gym."

"What are you up to, Phalen?"

"I'm trying to find something."

"If it's the killer, I don't think he's in there."

"Ha ha." She flipped through one of the folders in the box closest to her, and a stack of neatly folded newspaper clippings fell out. As she was stuffing them back in, Wes crouched down next to her and picked a few up.

"God."

Margot snatched the story out of his fingers and put it back in the folder. "It's not what you think."

"Oh, good. Because it looks like you're collecting material for a fucking *insane* scrapbook." He moved to sit on the bed, but finding it too covered, he settled down on the floor a few feet from her and took a pull off his beer bottle. "What the hell are you doing?"

She handed him her phone without saying a word, the text message still on the screen.

It had been almost an hour since she'd received it, and she still hadn't been able to bring herself to call the sender, demand answers, tell him to leave her alone.

Now that it was after midnight, there were all sorts of people she wanted to call but couldn't. Her brother, for one. Their family lawyer, for another. The Clinton Correctional Facility in New York. She wanted answers, and someone at the other end of a phone had them.

But all those people were asleep.

Wes took some time, seeming to read and re-read it before he looked up at her, frowning. "Do you know who sent this?" he asked.

"No, but it's a local number, and that's bothering me more than anything."

"Why?"

She sighed, shoving the folder of clippings back into the box. "It bothers me because the last time I checked, his whole legal team was in New York. If someone is writing to me on his behalf, that person needs to have been in contact with him. So, either this is another one of those fucked-up groupies that seems to attach to him every few years, or it's a lawyer. And if it's a lawyer, I want to know why he has a lawyer with a local area code." She said all this without pausing for a breath, barely taking her eyes off the papers around her.

Classified Killer trial begins Monday a stray paper clipping called out from the floor. Margot picked it up and scanned the article.

Edgar Finch, the man better known as the Classified Killer, who terrorized inhabitants of the Bay Area for the better part of a decade, will begin his trial this coming Monday.

She couldn't read any more. The story was ingrained in her head, she knew how it all played out. She hadn't been present at the trial, but she'd been able to watch most of it on YouTube in the years since.

Ed, sitting at the front of the room, looking ghostly pale and without even a shadow of remorse on his face.

Pictures of him from his arrest and trial still popped up, used whenever a particularly violent crime struck, especially one against young women.

Edgar Finch.

The famed serial killer.

Her father.

"Margot, what are you looking for?" Wes asked softly.

God, when he wasn't intentionally being a jackass, he could be such a nice guy sometimes.

Why had she even asked him to come over?

Because since the minute she got that text, she'd felt like she was being watched. She'd felt as if Ed were in the room with her, standing over her like he'd done sometimes at night when she was young. The memory made her skin crawl.

She hadn't wanted to be alone, and she'd known Wes wouldn't say no.

Margot took a deep slug off the wine bottle next to her.

"I'm trying to find letters from his last doe-eyed idiot fangirl. Connie, I think her name was. That might have been the one before. Misty? They all sound like wannabe Patsy Clines fresh from a trailer park." She sneered, not feeling particularly generous toward the women who threw themselves at a convicted serial killer who was on death row.

What kind of woman professes love for a man who had killed people?

Margot had never been able to figure it out. They'd started coming out of the woodwork during his trial, and in the years that followed he had developed a steady following of female fans. He'd briefly married one—Abigail—but she had come to her senses, and to Jesus, not long after. The divorce had been quick, and Abigail hadn't stuck around for the media attention.

It had been impossible for Margot to avoid Ed, even after he was in prison. Stories about him resurfaced every few years. There were dozens of websites devoted to him, either simply exploring his crimes, or some establishing online fan clubs. Items from Margot's childhood home periodically popped up on eBay, though the house itself had long since been purchased by a different family.

She had done everything in her power to disconnect herself from the constantly building legend surrounding Ed Finch, but his fingers always seemed to reach just far enough to graze the back of her neck when she let her guard down for a fraction of a second.

Her family had left California, they'd moved to Missouri, they'd changed their names—first and last—they'd put a wall of red tape between themselves and Ed, but someone always managed to find them.

As Margot got older, the interest in her had died down slightly. Now that she was in her thirties she didn't get letters— usually sent through her lawyer—as often. They used to be a weekly ordeal, and he only forwarded them to her so she could maintain a record of people who might want to do her harm. If some whack job was out there planning to kidnap her or some-thing, she wanted to know.

Those letters had varied from marriage proposals to reli-gious messages of hope. People sent her dozens of copies of the book written by Special Agent Andrew Rhodes, the FBI profiler who had tracked Ed down, as if she hadn't known it existed.

There were other letters that suggested because her father was a killer, that evil was in her blood too. She had been born from a monster, so she was a monster.

Those had been the ones her mother couldn't handle. After a decade of being told she was complicit in Ed's crimes simply because she'd been oblivious to them, Kim Finch had killed herself.

All of this was rushing to the forefront of Margot's mind right now, because of one stupid fucking text message. While

she might have instructed her lawyer to pass along fan mail, she
had made it abundantly clear she wanted zero contact from Ed
himself. He was not to have her mailing address, her phone
number, or her new name. Anything sent by him to her lawyer
was to be destroyed.

He might be a ghost that would haunt her life forever, but
she didn't need to give him more power over her.

Power was the one thing he could still get pleasure from,
and she wouldn't give him that.

So how, then, had someone connected to him figured out
her name and number?

Margot was aggressively rifling through the box of papers,
tossing things on the floor that weren't what she was looking for.
She was so focused on finding the *one* thing she thought she
needed that she was barely processing her actions.

"Margot, can you stop doing that for a second?" Wes placed
a hand on her arm, and she immediately jerked away from his
touch. "Sorry."

"I need to find the letters from his last groupie. I think she
said something I might have overlooked at the time. About Ed
wanting to see me, or about the weather, or *something*. I need to
know how he knows where I am. *Who* I am."

"So what if he knows who you are?"

Margot shot him a look she hoped was withering, but Wes
didn't shrink back in the least. "How can you say that?"

"Because it *doesn't matter*. Ed Finch is locked up in a maxi-
mum-security prison. He's never getting out. Even if he does
know where you are, or what your name is now, it's not the
same as being able to get to you, Margot. He can't hurt you."

She froze, because despite generally being about as deep as
a bird bath, Wes had managed to cut right to the core of what
had her spooked. Logically, she knew he was right. Ed would
never leave prison, he would be behind bars for the rest of his

days, however many they may be. And yet the mere thought of him having her name made it feel as if he could knock on her door at any moment, like he'd done with all those girls so long ago.

"I thought..." She let out a heavy sigh and dropped the folders back into the nearest box. "I thought it was safe to come back here. He's in New York, and there was nothing for me in Missouri, and I missed it here. The closest thing I remember to being happy was being here, before everything went fucking south, you know?"

Whether he understood or not, he said, "Yeah."

"I didn't want to go back to Petaluma, but I thought I could come *here*, start fresh. It had been long enough, and I had a new name. No one needed to know. But people know."

Whether it was conscious on his part or a tick to keep him busy, Wes started to pick up the scattered piles of paper, creating some sense of order to her disaster. He glanced down at an old issue of *Newsweek* with Ed's famous trial photo on the cover. "People would know no matter where you ended up."

She picked up the bottle of wine and gulped some back. It wasn't cold anymore, but she didn't care.

Wes knew about her history because she'd told her captain, and when she and Wes had started working together more frequently, the captain had told him. At the time she'd been furious about it, but now it felt nice to have someone around she didn't have to pretend with. Wes knew she wasn't normal, and it was a relief.

At this point, it was about the only thing that was a relief.

"You know what might make you feel better?" he said, putting the stack of papers he'd finished organizing back in a box.

"If you say *sex*, I swear to you, Wesley, I will break both your legs before the last letter is even out of your mouth."

"I was going to say a trip to the range. But your suggestion is good too." He smirked and finished his beer.

God help her, she smiled. "Not a chance in hell. Goodnight, Wes."

NINE

Photos of the Ramirez crime scene were tacked up over several corkboards in Margot and Wes's cramped office, each victim given their own space. Hector bothered Margot most of all. His polo shirt was stained with blood—much of it consistent with the gunshot wound to his head—but also the dotted modern art spray that would have indicated he was sitting in the chair while the women had their throats slit.

Not really something that he could have managed if he'd been the killer.

Margot was, for the time being, alone with the boards. She hadn't been able to sleep after Wes left, so she'd continued to sort through the boxes, but hadn't been able to find any letters that implied one of Ed's girlfriends knew where Margot was.

When the sun came up, she decided she might as well head to work early, because sitting around her North Beach apartment was only succeeding in making her feel crazier.

She'd left a message for her lawyer, but it was still early on the East Coast, so she wasn't anticipating a call back for several more hours. Wes would arrive at normal human hours, so Margot had the board to herself. Her first hour in the office had been spent arranging things to her liking, and now she was poring over every sordid detail.

It didn't take long for her to stop seeing the victims as people and start seeing them as puzzles to solve. She didn't think the way she disassociated from victims had anything to do with her parentage, she knew it was a necessary evil of her job. If she saw a mother, and children, and a father, she would get too emotionally involved. She needed to be unfeeling if she was going to get justice for these people.

Still, it sometimes unnerved her just how easy it could be to turn off her emotions.

There were days she worried she might not be able to turn them back on again.

For now, though, she looked at the board, wanting it to distract her from the unanswered text message on her phone.

The deaths of the women seemed to be the most straightforward. The medical examiner still hadn't had time to perform a complete work-up on the cause of death, but based on the blood, the women had been tied up, had their heads covered with plastic, then had their throats slit while they were still alive.

Not a pleasant way to go.

"Ugh, what a mess." Detective Leon Telly had snuck up behind her and leaned against the nearest desk, sipping his coffee as if it didn't taste like hot dirt.

Leon was in his early sixties, one of the few established lifers in the homicide unit. Most cops only lasted five or ten years tops working homicide cases before moving on to something different. Leon arrived when he was twenty-eight and hadn't left. Margot admired that. He was a man who saw the worst of the worst and didn't flinch away from it. He also hadn't let it make him hard.

She hoped she could live up to the expectations men like Leon Telly had unknowingly set for her.

"Don't you wish you'd picked this one up?" she asked.

"Wasn't Wallace supposed to get this one? Guess you shouldn't have taken that call then, should you? Me, I got a nice basic robbery shooting. Guy didn't wear a mask while knocking over a convenience store, has a record. We'll have him locked up in a few hours once we confirm location."

"Boring."

"Wallace ended up with a mugging gone wrong. Maybe he'll trade you."

Margot's lips puckered, as if his words were something sour she'd been forced to swallow. Sure, this case was going to be a hideous pain in her ass, but she wasn't going to pawn it off on someone else because she thought it might be a bit difficult.

Easy cases weren't quite as satisfying. Sure, finding a solution felt good at the end of the day, but really digging her teeth into something and finding the answers that were buried beneath the surface, that was what kept this job interesting year after year.

Wes arrived then, and handed her a steaming cup of Blue Bottle coffee. He had forgone a tie and his white button-down shirt was open one button too many to be wholly work-appropriate. He looked freshly showered but like he might not have shaved. "Good morning. I see you went a little bit *Beautiful Mind* before I got here." His eyes narrowed as he looked at the boards. "Was the copy room out of red strings for you to start constructing a nice little insanity map out of?"

Leon chuckled.

"Don't encourage him," Margot scolded, smacking Leon in his round belly, a level of jovial play it had taken her several years to earn in an old boys' club like this one.

Leon gave her a wink as he headed out of the room. "Wouldn't dream of it. Now, if you'll excuse me, I'm off to close a case, like a real detective."

As Leon left, Wes plopped down in his desk chair and wheeled it up beside her.

"You normally get Peet's." Margot looked at the cup in her hand. "Not that I'm complaining."

"Sure. When I'm coming from my own place."

Margot raised an eyebrow at him, then lowered her voice to avoid being overheard by anyone wandering past. "You left my place at one in the morning, where the hell else could you go that late?"

Wes smirked and shrugged. "Somewhere near a Blue Bottle, I guess."

"Gross."

"Don't hate the player."

"Wes, you are forty-two years old. Please never say that again."

So, he'd managed to find a booty call after one in the morning on a school night. Margot had to wonder what type of woman eagerly agreed to such a charming proposition. She was almost more impressed that he'd brought such a nice change of clothes with him for the event.

"You're welcome for bringing you coffee," he reminded her coolly.

"Thank you, Wesley."

"Did you actually come up with anything while doing arts and crafts this morning?" With his long legs stretched out in front of him, he was the very picture of casual ease. He was a mystifying creature, someone who could make a homicide department look like the VIP lounge at a football game.

"I am pretty convinced Hector's suicide was staged. We'll still need to wait a couple hours before Evelyn will let us talk to her about the bodies, and even then, we'll only get a preliminary report, but I'm willing to bet she'll back me up with the physical evidence." Margot waved her hand in front of the board, drawing Wes's attention to one of the pictures of Hector. "There's way too much blood on him."

"I agree."

"Good." She sat on the edge of her desk, staring at the photos, hoping if she looked long enough, the big picture would unlock itself in a sudden *whoosh* of realization.

The office had begun to fill up slowly, the morning shift moving in to replace the evening crew. The noise level escalated, but aside from some grunted hellos, no one stopped to talk to them.

"Let's go back to the house," Wes declared, pushing himself up and tossing his empty cup in the nearest trashcan. "I want to take a look through now that it's empty."

The house was still, and felt especially quiet and eerie as they walked through the doors for a second time. With all the police and forensics teams gone, the silence was almost overwhelming. Margot hadn't realized how much of a buzz had permeated the place the day before, but now that they were the only ones present, the difference was shocking.

Wes shut the door behind them, and they walked slowly through the main floor together. The pressure of the first day on the scene was finding the obvious, the things that would tell them the most about their victims and the crime.

This time around the goal was to find what they'd missed, because there was certain to be something. The bonus of having a closed scene like the house was that nothing was going to wash away in the rain, or in the pockets of curious passersby. They had more time than usual to pick things apart.

Margot circled back toward the kitchen, opening the back door to where the boot had left its distinctive dent. She crouched low to get a better look at it, though a dent was a dent, it couldn't tell her much beyond the obvious.

"This bothers me. If someone broke in, wouldn't Mateo have heard it? He said he was downstairs at the time. If this *was* a burglar, then why would the yelling be the first thing he heard?"

Wes stood above her, touching the door jamb. "And if someone had kicked the door in, why isn't this damaged at all?"

She'd missed that the day before, and scolded herself for not seeing something so obvious. "We should see if the family called in a previous break-in. Maybe someone had tried to get access before. It's a long shot, but it's something."

"Yeah, family in an area like this, they strike me as people who would call it in."

"Unless it was someone they knew." Ever the optimist, Margot had to wonder. In cases of murder like this, it was highly unlikely the perpetrator was a stranger to the Ramirez family. There would always be outliers, convenience or serial killers who targeted their victims for reasons beyond simple comprehension, but in ninety percent of the cases she saw, the victim knew their killer.

Someone willing to kill a whole family likely had a bone to pick with one of them.

"Didn't know them well enough to not kill the wrong kid," Wes reminded her.

Margot grunted. The Emily and Mateo mix-up was a strange element to the story. If someone had wanted to kill the family—and punishing Hector seemed the most likely motive, based on how he had been displayed in the room, observing the dead women—then how had that person not known Hector had a son?

Margot frowned and thought of the little boy. Mateo himself seemed unusual in the wake of his family's murder. While there was no right way to grieve—and Margot knew better than to judge someone for crying too much or too little—

she'd kept going over the interview with Mateo in her head ever since Wes had commented on the kid seeming weird.

Was he weird because his reactions hadn't felt right at the time, or was there a deeper strangeness to him that might indicate a reason he was withdrawn from his family? There were plenty of social and mental disorders that could start to show themselves in a kid his age. If Mateo had some kind of anxiety or perhaps early symptoms of an avoidant personality, he might not have exhibited normal childhood behaviors and could have been absent frequently from family activities.

A killer who was observing the Ramirez family from a distance might never know they had a son if the only thing they ever saw was the Ramirez parents on outings with Emily.

Curiouser and curiouser, and unfortunately none of it was bringing her any closer to an obvious answer. Like any good puzzle, she knew all the pieces were there, she just wasn't sure she *had* them all yet. Maybe she had missed something in the way the crime scene was set up, or in the victimology. Going through everything at the site might give her the right nudge. As it was, she was starting to wonder if taking over Wallace's mugging gone wrong was still an option, because this was turning into quite the tangled web.

They went upstairs, where the cloying smell of aged blood hit them with its oppressive coppery fist. Amazing how death's presence clung to a place.

No wonder people didn't want to live in murder houses. The stain of the crime remained even after the blood had been wiped clean.

Instead of going back to the den to poke around the part of the house she was most familiar with, Margot was drawn away from Wes and down the hall to where the home's three bedrooms were arranged.

The bed in Hector and Evangeline's room was half-unmade, sheets in a tangle and pillows on the floor. Someone had either gotten up in a big hurry, or had been dragged out against their will. Margot circled to that side of the bed, where a dog-eared copy of *The Kite Runner* rested next to an empty water glass. A pair of reading glasses with slightly smudged lenses waited for their owner on top of the book. The purple plastic frames of the glasses suggested they had likely belonged to Evangeline.

Hector, Margot recalled, had still been wearing a polo shirt, and maybe hadn't gotten into bed yet.

On his nightstand, a newspaper was folded to show a half-completed crossword puzzle from the Saturday *New York Times*. The pen was missing.

Margot got onto her knees and peeked under the bed, not sure if she cared about the pen, but curious about what might have happened to it. She found a single woman's slipper, and a few stray pieces of Lego.

"What are you doing?"

She peered up at Wes, who was standing in the doorway. "I'm looking for a pen."

"Why?"

"There's a half-finished crossword on the nightstand."

He scratched his jaw, waiting for her to offer him more insight, and when she didn't he gave a little shrug. "And you wanted to finish it?"

"No, the pen is missing."

"While I'm sure Chekov's pen is going to be instrumental in breaking the case, I want you to have a look at something."

He led her back into the hall, past the den, where the bloody carpet and spatters on the walls were all that remained of the grisly scene from the previous day. They stopped in front of a bathroom, where Margot saw a floral-print cardboard box on the counter. "Take a peek."

Margot pulled a pair of latex gloves out of her pocket, slipping each one on with a snap. She peered into the box and found it was filled with two or three dozen prescription bottles. The yellow plastic canisters were so deep into the box she couldn't get a good read on how many there were.

Almost every single one had Mateo Ramirez's name on it, with a few mixed in for Valentina. Nothing in the box was labeled for the parents.

"My God, what the hell are all these?" She investigated the labels, wondering if she could make sense of them based on the names and directions for use, but it was almost impossible. They'd need to consult a doctor or pharmacist to know what each one was for. But the sheer number of different prescriptions struck Margot as being especially unusual.

If Mateo had a condition that required him to take regular medication, then wouldn't that medication be at least somewhat consistent? Ten or more different prescriptions seemed like an impossibly high amount for a boy his age, especially when the hospital hadn't mentioned any serious medical concerns during his checkup.

"Do you know what any of these are for?" she asked Wes.

"No idea. We can take them with us and have a full list made up. If he needs medication, CFS has to know about it ASAP."

That hadn't even occurred to her. Mateo might have medications in the house he needed. Would a nine-year-old think to mention something like that?

She left the bathroom, taking the box with her and leaving it at the top of the stairs to bring along with them when they left. Moving back down the hall, she looked into one bedroom—clearly Valentina's—its walls painted soft pink, and a sleeping bag in a heap on the floor. As in Hector and Evangeline's room, the blankets on Valentina's bed looked violently unsettled, as if she had been pulled out by force.

This wasn't what Margot was looking for though.

Crossing the hall, she found herself in Mateo's room. The

walls were papered in a green-and-blue plaid, and the curtains were so thick the room was completely dark even in the morning light. She pulled open the curtains, a bright spear of light plunging into the gloom, immediately making the space more inviting and alive.

The room was surprisingly neat for such a young child. His bed was also unmade, but there was a slim dent where his body had been, and none of the same rough distress. He'd gotten out on his own, just like he'd told them.

Margot stood in the doorway, not sure what it was she was after. The pill bottles in the bathroom suggested Mateo must have been incredibly ill, or struggling with a chronic issue of some kind, but this room was that of a completely normal little boy. There were posters on the wall for the Giants and 49ers, he had little red and gold trophies above his desk for soccer, medals dangling from the side for track and field events, and various shades of participation ribbons stuck to the wall.

A huge Lego model of the Millennium Falcon from *Star Wars* was displayed on a bookshelf, alongside various tattered paperback books, and clear plastic bins filled with more Lego. On the surface it all looked normal, like Mateo was no different from any other child his age. Yet an uneasy feeling lingered in her stomach as she glanced around the room. It was so clean, so tidy. She thought back to the way her brother's room had looked when he'd been Mateo's age, and the word *wasteland* came to mind. This space was *so* well organized that the toys barely looked like they'd been used.

She sat down on his bed, and a metallic rattle caught her attention.

Shitty bed frame?

Bouncing once, she heard the sound again, from the opposite side of the bed. Circling around to the side nearest the wall, she traced her fingers along the edge of the mattress until she came to the headboard. Her hand brushed against something cold and metallic.

She pulled, but the item yielded only a little before snagging in place with a loud *clack*.

Margot tugged at the blanket and sheets, exposing the corner of the mattress, which she lifted to expose whatever it was she was holding.

Her blood went cold.

"*Wes.*"

He appeared a moment later, looking at her quizzically. "Find something?"

Instead of answering, she got to her feet and grabbed hold of the mattress, yanking it out of the frame, and pulling it back so it tumbled to the floor, landing quietly in a heap of dirty clothes. Wes seemed like he was about to protest, but fell silent when he looked down at the bed frame.

On either side of the headboard, a pair of handcuffs with long center chains were clasped to the bed; the loose ends had been tucked under the mattress and now lay exposed. At the end of the bed, a pair of padded ankle cuffs were clamped to the footboard.

Suddenly, the prescription bottles were the least of Margot's concerns.

TEN

"Holy Christ on a bicycle," Wes said.

Margot, who was still wearing her latex gloves from the bathroom, stooped down and lifted one of the handcuff bracelets with one finger. They weren't toys, they were the real deal. She let it drop back to the back seat.

The Ramirez house of horrors had just gone to a whole new level of disturbing.

Wes met her gaze and they both simultaneously glanced across the hall to Valentina's room. Moving in silent unison, they went in and had her mattress lifted in no time, resting up against the wall.

Valentina's bed had no shackles, but when Margot looked at the wooden frame, it was obvious from the distinctive spots of wear on both the headboard and footboard that cuffs had been there previously.

"We need to get a unit in here and search the house again. We need pictures of all this." They'd touched too much as it was, but this was never what they'd expected to find. Instead of answers, Margot only had more questions, and with the Ramirez family dead, she wasn't sure if anyone would be able to tell her what she wanted to know. The gnawing, uneasy feeling she'd gotten standing in Mateo's room resurfaced.

Even here in the kids' bathroom, a space that should have been cluttered with Mateo's bath toys and Valentina's first forays into makeup, everything was Spartan and almost too clean. Each child had a toothbrush holder, with the toothpaste precisely rolled up at the base; and as Margot opened drawers, she found them lined with plastic organizers. Everything had its place.

The hairbrushes didn't even have hair in them.

It looked more like a set than a space anyone actually lived in.

"I think we need to talk to Mateo again," Wes said.

"No shit." She traced her fingers over the deep grooves in the wood at the foot of Valentina's bed. What had happened to these children?

Wes left the room, pulling out his cell phone as he went. She could hear him calling the station to get backup sent over. The preliminary work done by the team the day before had been largely focused on the crime scene and getting as much physical evidence related to the murders of the family as possible. Since the house was a secure scene, the team knew they would have ample opportunity to come back and continue their investigation later.

Margot wasn't surprised they'd missed all this, but at the same time she was furious, both with the crime scene unit and with herself, for not having uncovered something this substantial sooner.

She sat down at Valentina's desk, facing the girl's bed with her feet resting next to Emily's twisted sleeping bag on the floor. A headache had begun to squeeze at her temples, threatening to build into a doozy if she left it unattended. There was some aspirin in her bag, which she'd left in Wes's car.

Her phone rang, and without thinking to check the caller ID, she answered it. "Phalen."

"Miss Phalen?" The voice on the other end of the line seemed surprised to hear her voice. Perhaps they hadn't been expecting her to answer.

"Detective Phalen," she corrected.

"Megan Finch?"

Margot went stone cold, frozen in place on the bed, too shocked to hear the name to say anything in response. The headache doubled its efforts and suddenly her throat was bone-dry.

"Who the fuck is this?"

No one had used the name Megan Finch in twenty-two years. As far as Margot was concerned, Megan was just another one of Ed's victims.

"Miss Phalen—"

"*Detective* Phalen," she said again, acid boiling on her tongue.

"My apologies." He didn't sound particularly sorry. "Detective Phalen, my name is Ford Rosenthal, and I represent your father, Edgar Finch."

Margot gritted her teeth. "How did you get this number?"

This question, apparently, took him by surprise. "From your brother."

Margot wasn't entirely certain she believed that Justin would just give her number to a lawyer without asking her first, but she also knew he sometimes acted without thinking. If he wasn't on the other side of the country, she would have kicked his ass.

She loved her brother, but he'd learned to deal with his demons in more destructive ways than she had, and sometimes in the haze of whatever binge he was coming out of, he would do or say things thoughtlessly. They tended to have their worst fights when he was in the ugly sober valleys between bottles.

Justin was a good guy, but he was also one more thing Margot had long ago realized she couldn't fix.

"Were you the one who texted me last night?"

"Yes, I'm glad you got that. You see, now that your father is so close to you, he is really very interested in seeing you in person, and he's—"

"What did you say?" Now she was on her feet, moving out of Valentina's room. It seemed wrong to be having a conversation about Ed Finch in a dead girl's bedroom. He would have enjoyed that too much.

"As I mentioned in my text, your father would like to see you."

"No, before that."

"I don't understand the question."

Fucking lawyers. "You said, *now that your father is so close to you.*"

"Well yes. With him being at San Quentin now, he's practically in your backyard."

An electric jolt of panic sizzled through her, and she had to count to ten before she was able to speak again. Setting aside the fact that this proclamation gave Margot the impression Ford Rosenthal had never spoken to a real human person before—because who would talk about having a serial killer in your backyard as if it was a good thing—Margot kept circling back to the meat of his revelation.

"Ed is at Clinton Correctional."

"No, your father was moved a month ago. He's at San Quentin."

She wasn't sure when she had left the Ramirez house, but she was standing on the front lawn now, the blinding morning light completely unable to warm her skin. Her hands were shaking and the dryness in her throat had become a suffocatingly thick pressure. Margot sat down on the front steps, all the air sucked from her lungs.

"That's not possible."

"It's quite possible. I visited him a few days ago. He said he was delighted to be back home."

Home.

Some idiot had let Ed come back to his old stomping ground, less than thirty miles from the scene of his first murder in Petaluma, and now he was living less than a fifteen-minute drive from where they'd found several of his victims.

He'd come right back to where it all began.

For Margot, who had thought two decades was enough time, and enough distance, she was suddenly fifteen again, sitting in the back seat of a police cruiser, watching her mother scream at the police as they tackled Ed on a neighbor's lawn.

She felt so stupid for believing there was ever going to be an end to this, that it was ever something she could have escaped.

"Detective Phalen, are you still there?"

"Yes," she croaked.

"Would you be willing to set up a meeting with your father?"

She wiped her clammy hands on her knees, momentarily distracted as a van pulled up and parked behind Wes's car. The first crew had arrived. They must have already been on their way to pick up on the previous day's work.

Kismet.

"Will you tell him something for me?" she said quietly.

"You could tell him yourself."

"No, tell him something next time you see him."

"What's that?"

"Tell him Megan Finch is dead."

ELEVEN
JULY 4, 1981

Petaluma, California

"Ed, hon, can you hold Megan for a second?" Without waiting for a response, Kim thrust the baby into his arms.

Megan, at just over a year old, was at that strange stage of her babyhood where she was starting to develop a personality but was also still a squalling bundle of highly breakable parts. Her ginger hair was downy, sticking up in all directions despite Kim's best efforts, and she had Ed's brown eyes.

His daughter stared at him, bemused, or temporarily stupefied, her tiny mouth parted in something that could have been a smile or a burp.

"Hey there, Meggy-May." He tickled her belly and she let out a bright peal of laughter, her whole face erupting into an expression of unadulterated joy.

She was such a curious little being, all need, no giving, and yet when he was near her his own demanding id was at peace. With Megan, the impulses that drove him shifted into a different gear, and he thought about things like building her dollhouses, teaching her how to ride a bike. The things that commanded his attention weren't nearly so dark as they were often inclined to be.

Megan held on to his thumb, pulling it into her mouth and gnawing on it with the little stubs of her first teeth. Sharp needles of pain kept him focused on her, but it didn't hurt so badly he would make her stop.

"What an adorable baby," a woman's voice gushed.

Ed glanced around, noticing that Kim had vanished, likely back to the car for some forgotten item. They were forever forgetting something essential to Megan's survival, either in the house or the car, and while Ed was of the opinion that three hours without a soother wouldn't be the end of days, Kim agreed to disagree.

The woman speaking to him was a slender girl in her early twenties, her dark hair worn in a high ponytail, bright blue eyes shining even as the sun dipped below the horizon.

"Her name is Megan."

Megan turned her gaze toward the girl and gave her one of those glorious full-faced smiles that were like a reward to whoever she happened to be looking at in that given moment. The charm trap worked, and the young woman made a soft cooing noise, like her insides were melted fudge and Megan was the sundae.

Ed glanced around and saw no sign of his wife anywhere nearby. "Do you want to hold her?" In his experience women rarely turned down the opportunity to hold a baby, regardless of whether or not they knew the parents.

"Can I?" she asked, practically gasping.

"Sure." Megan wasn't exactly floppy and delicate anymore. She could hold her head up just fine on her own, was starting to speak, and had already learned to take some halting steps. She wasn't going to get damaged. He handed the baby to the woman, who hugged Megan to her chest, bouncing her softly in place. Megan giggled and grabbed a fistful of the girl's hair.

"Oh, ow." The girl laughed good-naturedly, but Ed knew how strong his daughter could be when she put her whole focus into something.

"Let me help, she doesn't know her own strength." He smiled and moved closer to the girl, helping disengage Megan's tiny hand.

The woman's hair smelled of lavender, and this close Ed could still feel the heat of the summer sun radiating off her bare arms. Her skin was smooth and tan, and he had to stop himself from trailing his fingers down the long line of her neck.

The sound of a clearing throat brought him back to reality faster than a swift dunk in ice-cold water. Kim had returned, a bottle and baby blanket in hand. The items they had evidently forgotten in that car. Somehow that would be his fault, though he wasn't sure how.

Kim, on the other hand, had had the whole walk to and from the car to figure out just what he'd done wrong, and she wouldn't hesitate to let him know.

"I was making friends with your beautiful daughter," the woman said, seemingly oblivious to the tension radiating off of Kim in waves so thick they tasted like rotten meat on Ed's tongue.

"She's very good at that." Kim held out her hands for Megan and the girl obliged, handing the giggling baby back to her mother. "Enjoy the fireworks."

And with that, the pretty girl had been dismissed.

It took about three seconds until she was out of earshot for Kim to fix Ed with a withering look somewhere between anger and pity. "Seriously, Ed?" she hissed.

"What?"

"I go away for five minutes and you're using our daughter to pick up women?" She bounced Megan in her arms and the baby closed her eyes, the rhythm of the movement and the familiarity of an argument lulling her to sleep.

"I wasn't picking anyone up. She stopped and saw Megan— what did you want me to do, tell her to fuck off?"

Kim wrinkled her nose. "You're so predictable."

His palms itched with the desire to slap that holier-than-thou expression off her face, but he wouldn't touch her, especially not when she was holding the baby. Besides, he needed to placate her. Angry Kim would haunt his every footstep, question every evening out. He had to make sure she went back to barely noticing his presence or lack thereof, and that would never happen if she was trying to memorize everything he did in order to use it against him later.

He moved toward her and Megan, wrapping them both in his arms and placing a kiss on the top of Kim's head. She smelled of milk and ever so faintly of baby powder. Megan's scents. It wasn't an unpleasant smell, but it did nothing to help him find her appealing.

"I'm sorry, Kim. I wasn't thinking."

She sniffed and let out a little exhale of breath like she might say more, but instead he felt her go loose in his arms, sinking into the hug. "Ugh, I'm sorry I'm such a bear, Ed. You shouldn't apologize for showing off the baby. I guess I just... I worry, you know?"

"Worry about what?" He pulled back and looked at her, trying to use the expression on her face like the clues in a puzzle. Except Ed wasn't particularly gifted at solving human puzzles.

"You know, I worry... since having Megan I sometimes think maybe you're not as attracted to me anymore." A sheen of tears clung to her lower lashes. Between their bodies, Megan squirmed and started saying, "No, no, Mom, no."

Megan hated it when Kim cried.

"Baby." Ed didn't tell her she was wrong, because he knew the lie would give him away immediately. But telling her she was right wasn't going to help him either. He tilted her chin up and kissed her, ignoring Megan's little kicks against his belly. For the moment, that seemed to be enough to appease Kim, as she let go of her anger about the young woman, and they were able to enjoy the fireworks without further incident.

Later, after they'd soothed Megan back to sleep from her exhaustive wailing over the fireworks, they walked together as a family back to the car. They passed the dark-haired girl again, and she smiled at them, offering a small wave.

Every bone in Ed's body said, *Follow her.*

But Kim waved back, and Ed knew he would never see the girl again.

Kim rarely forgot a face, and he was already imagining the way she'd look up from the newspaper and say, "Isn't that the girl who was holding Megan in the park?" when they found the body.

Best to let this one go.

TWELVE

Margot was quiet as the field team continued to pick through the house, this time looking for more evidence *against* the Ramirez parents, rather than to hunt down their killer.

The crimes still needed to be solved, but for Margot, the notion that she was seeking justice felt dampened, as if perhaps the act of killing these people might not have been an entirely bad thing. Her heart still ached for those girls, and for Mateo, who would have to go through the rest of his life as the sole survivor of a massacre, but she was having a hard time dredging up empathy for Hector or Evangeline anymore.

There was a myth, perpetuated by the greeting card industry and the ideal of the nuclear family, that parents were always good, and always loving. But Margot knew that love—even parental love—could be an ugly, toxic thing when it came from the wrong person.

It still wasn't clear what had happened to the Ramirez children, but the signposts of serious abuse were littered everywhere, and suddenly Margot understood why Mateo's reactions to the death of his family may not have been typical.

Maybe their death had been the first time he'd been able to breathe freely in his life.

What she knew with absolute certainty, though, was this house of horrors had entirely new depths to its endless basin of secrets. And she aimed to find them all.

She focused on the case, blotting out her conversation with Rosenthal as best she could. Still, his words haunted her as she moved from room to room. Ed was here. Ed was back in San Francisco, so close she could probably see the faintest hue of San Quentin's walls from the roof of her apartment, if she really wanted to try.

Coming here, she'd thought it was the last place he'd ever be. Margot had done everything possible to sever the ties between herself and her father. She'd changed her name, she'd ignored all his letters, she'd refused to go on a woe-is-me press tour or write a tell-all book. Other people had written those books, almost a dozen of them at her last count.

People were still fascinated by him in a way that was hard for her to fathom.

Perhaps she could have turned the tragedy of her past into a meal ticket. Maybe then the burden of student loan debt wouldn't have trailed after her well into her thirties. A lifetime of being a figure of pity and scorn, though; that wasn't how she wanted to live her life.

She didn't want to be another one of her father's victims.

At least, she'd told herself that right up until now. Now she felt small and helpless, and angry in a way that defied categorization. She wanted very badly to lash out at someone, and the only target available to her right then was the memory of Hector Ramirez.

Standing in the den, Margot stared at the chair where they'd found his body. The books behind his head were still splattered in the congealed goop of his brain matter. When they finally let a cleaning crew come in to scrub the house down, those once-beautiful leather-bound volumes would be headed right into an incinerator.

As far as Margot was concerned, they'd need to burn this whole house to the ground to get rid of all the bad juju left behind.

She paced around the periphery of the room, imagining it as it had been yesterday, with Hector slumped in his chair, gun on the floor beneath his outstretched fingertips.

After all the things they had discovered this morning, perhaps the idea of a suicide wasn't out of the question. Crouching in front of the chair, she looked at the blood soaked into the upholstery. Where Hector had been, the light blue fabric was untouched, only a few lines of what had dripped down from his head and shoulders marred the otherwise clean microfiber.

Still, there was a possibility Hector could have orchestrated it all somehow. She pivoted on her heel so she was facing the other chairs at about Hector's sitting height. Maybe he had instructed the women to cut their own throats as he watched.

No, their hands had been bound. Also, while fear of being shot might make people do a lot of crazy things, Margot would have taken the bullet to the head before willingly slicing her own neck open. So much for that theory.

This new inkling of how the Ramirez parents were treating their children did make her more willing to believe Hector might have killed himself out of guilt. The handcuffs could have meant a lot of things, whether it was a way to keep the children in bed at night, or something a lot more sinister. The evidence on Hector's body, however, wasn't changed by their discovery. The evidence still told her someone else was involved in this, and she wasn't sure how that fit together. Was this still a random event?

Wes came to the door, the box of prescription bottles tucked under his arm.

"See anything new?"

"No."

"Then stop staring at that chair like it's a crystal ball and come with me. Evelyn called—she's ready with the preliminary autopsy results. She also said she could tell us what most of the pills in this box are for, so we might as well kill two birds with one stone."

Margot stared at the stains on the carpet where the blood of Evangeline, Emily, and Valentina had pooled so thickly it had leaked through the floorboards to the level below. Now it was just a blackened mark in the fibers.

If the secrets she was looking for were written there, she didn't yet have the vocabulary to read them.

She got up, her body protesting at all the stooping and squatting she'd been doing. Considering the shitty sleep she'd had, curled up on her couch rather than sleeping in her bed because she had folders all over her duvet, it was a miracle she wasn't even sorer.

As it was she felt like someone had stuffed her body inside a tractor tire and rolled it down a bumpy hill.

Could be worse, right?

Wes drove them to the city morgue and found parking nearby. Before she was able to open her car door, however, he engaged the locks, trapping Margot inside.

While she knew deep down there was no danger to being alone in a car with Wes, her pulse started to stutter erratically, and she broke out into a cold sweat in an instant.

Ironically, it had been Ed who taught her the danger signs when she was alone with a boy. She'd gone on her first date at fourteen and Ed had been there, standing in the window, when the boy's father dropped her off that night.

Ed, who taught her to always ask for photo ID before letting someone into the house.

Ed, who taught her locks were only useful when they were engaged.

He knew how she could keep herself safe because of all the ways other girls had failed to protect themselves against him.

And she had to wonder how many of those women had trusted Ed the way she trusted Wes.

Calm the fuck down.

She was just on edge because of the phone call. It was making her crazy. But all the same, she wasn't able to use logic to tell her anxiety to take a hike. Panic attacks had very little interest in logic or reason, she'd found.

Her breath started coming up short, and her hand gripped the door handle with so much force her knuckles turned white.

Wes, who might have been insensitive but who wasn't blind, recognized what was happening right away.

"Hey, whoa, I just wanted to talk to you alone before we go in there."

"C-can you, unl-lock the door, please?" She wasn't prone to stammering, a stutter hadn't been one of the side effects of her trauma, but all the same she sometimes had trouble vocalizing her needs when she panicked. Fear could do incredible and terrible things to the human body.

Wes unlocked the door, and before he could say anything else, Margot was out on the sidewalk sucking in deep lungfuls of air as she wiped her sweaty hands on her jeans. This, she realized, was why the captain had wanted Wes to know about her past. There were things she could hide from others, but working in close quarters with another person created an unintentional intimacy. Had Wes not known the truth about her, they never would have been able to work as partners.

She could deal with the pitying looks he gave her from time to time if it meant he didn't think she was totally batshit crazy.

Though, the way she was acting right now, she wouldn't have blamed him if he did.

He got out after her and locked the car again, then took her gently by the elbow and guided her toward a nearby set of concrete stairs, where he eased her down into a sitting position.

"Take a deep breath."

She wanted to tell him that she was perfectly aware of how to deal with a panic attack, but it would have taken too many words, so instead she did what he suggested and took a deep breath.

"Another."

She complied.

It took about five minutes, but eventually Margot's breathing and pulse returned to a normal rhythm, and she groaned, settling her face into her hands. "I'm sorry."

"No, I wasn't thinking. Locking you in was so stupid. I didn't want you to get out before we had a chance to talk, but I should have realized."

"How could you realize? I don't come with special care and handling instructions. Hell, even I don't know what's going to do it sometimes. I heard a man call his daughter 'Buddy' in the grocery store the other day and I just left. Like, I dropped my basket right in the middle of the aisle and left."

"You haven't really been yourself since last night, and I'm not exactly worried, because you're obviously still fine at your job, but... what the fuck is going on with you? Is this still about that text?"

"They called me. While we were at the house."

"And?" Wes had straightened up, looming over her with his full six-plus feet. For some reason it wasn't as menacing out here as it had felt inside a locked car. She was once again able to remind herself that he was—if not her friend—someone she could trust not to hurt her.

It was hard for her, though, for obvious reasons, to believe that anyone in the world was a hundred percent trustworthy.

Wes would have to do.

Such a depressing option.

"Ed is in San Quentin," she admitted, cutting right to the chase. "They apparently moved him about a month ago. So... yeah."

"They moved him here? Fuck, I'd have thought that would have been much bigger news, considering..." He let the sentence drift off when he realized what he would have to end it with.

Considering Ed had killed seventy-six women, primarily in the Bay Area, over fifteen years?

Considering the cloud of terror he had cast over the city that had rivaled even that of the infamous Zodiac?

Yeah, Margot was a bit surprised it hadn't hit the papers, too.

Maybe it had, as a little blurb on an inset column. Margot wasn't exactly known for keeping up on local news. But she had to believe her sometimes-friend Sebastian at the *Sentinel* would have called her if that was the case. He was one of the very, *very* few people in town who knew who she really was, and she doubted he would stay quiet if he had heard something about Ed coming back.

"You're sure he's really here, it's not someone playing a prank on you?" Wes asked.

"What a weirdly specific prank that would be."

"You know those serial killer fanboys, they like to get themselves involved in the story, find their way into the thick of it. Can you imagine the raging boner on a guy who managed to figure out who you were and convince you your dad was in the same city? He'd be all over the message boards bragging about that."

Margot felt sick to her stomach imagining such a person, though she didn't have to stretch her imagination much to get there. The message board types, those who were still trying to "solve" the case even decades later, were a constant thorn in her side.

Why couldn't people leave the dead in their graves and let the living go on living?

"I think he was legit. I'll look him up when we're back at the office, and get some independent confirmation from the prison."

"What does he want?" Wes asked.

"The lawyer?"

"Your dad."

The words sounded almost tender in Wes's mouth, and for a minute Margot imagined Ed as he had been. Weekend barbecues, football games on TV, teaching her how to ride her bike. *Dad* memories.

But that man was nothing more than a fancy illusion. That had been an act Ed had put on for years, while the real monster inside him did its dirty business.

"Apparently Ed would like to see me."

This was enough for Wes to take a seat beside her, no longer in a rush to hustle her off to Evelyn's office. A million things played across his face over the span of a second. Shock, confusion, repulsion. He let out his breath in a little *whoosh* of surprise. "No shit?"

"No shit."

"Does he need a kidney or something?"

Margot barked out a laugh, taken aback by this question. Of all the reasons she could imagine Ed beckoning her to a prison visit, she hadn't even considered that he might want something from her. Obviously, he wanted *something*, but could it be as base and simple as an organ?

That would be so Ed.

"I think it's far more likely that now that he knows where I am, he wants to fuck with me."

Wes rested his arms on his thighs, leaning forward. A

woman passed by them, and he watched her go. Margot found his predictability soothing, like the ticking of an old clock.

When Wes looked back at her, she could tell it was taking him a bit longer to pick up the threads of what she'd been saying. "Fuck with you?"

"Yeah. When he got locked up, I was fifteen. He was still a parent, still in charge of my life. For twenty-two years he hasn't been able to lord that power over me, and I think he'd like to have it back." Wow, way to bust out the pop psych 101. "I think he's probably very, very bored in there, and I probably seem like a fun challenge."

He winced like he'd been physically injured by her sentence. "That's fucked up."

She smiled, her breath finally back to normal, everything feeling right, or whatever her version of right was. "Yes. It *is* fucked up, isn't it?"

"You want to go look at some dead bodies? Think that'll make you feel better?"

Ah, there it was, classic, callous Wes. But, in truth, looking at some dead bodies actually *might* take her mind off things.

At the same time, considering what they now knew about the Ramirez parents, she wasn't feeling very charitable about their status as victims. For once, she wouldn't scold Wes for being so cavalier about the once-living.

When they got to the morgue, Evelyn was waiting for them. Instead of the head-to-toe white ensemble she'd been sporting at the crime scene, she was now in basic green scrubs, a white lab coat, and comfortable-looking white running shoes. Her black and purple hair was slicked back, most likely owing to the paper cap sticking out of her lab coat pocket, which had likely just been on her head.

"You know, if you guys decided to open a bar, I bet the

hipster kids would love it. Phalen and Fox. Sounds like a hipster bar name, you know."

Evelyn had a habit of picking up conversations right in the middle, and usually on a topic that had never once been discussed. It was easiest to simply roll with it.

"Maybe I should open a bar with him," Margot replied. "Having all that free booze on hand would make my work day a hell of a lot more enjoyable."

Wes snorted.

"You kids want to play a little game of Guess that Cause of Death with me?" Evelyn asked.

Lordy, now even the coroner was being inappropriate. Must have been one of those days. Or maybe Margot was too sensitive. That was always a possibility.

Also a possibility: all of them spent way, way too much time around death and it was starting to make them a little bit squirrelly.

"Which vic?" Wes asked, obviously willing to play along.

"Walk with me." Evelyn headed down a long, tiled corridor. Where her footfalls were so silent she might as well have been floating, Margot's boots clacked with every step. There was no way to come into this building with an ounce of subtlety.

Evelyn led them down a flight of stairs, and as they descended the temperature got progressively colder with every step. The lights were brighter down here, but all fluorescent, making the space look as cold as it felt. The medical examiner unlocked a pair of large double doors with her swipe card, and ushered them into another room, this one even colder still.

It spanned the length of the basement hall and had ten side-by-side metallic tables lined up. The back wall was a series of metal lockers. The floor was cement, and dark gray rather than white. The slightest tilt angled the floor toward a series of drains, meaning the whole space could be hosed down at the end of the night if need be.

Margot wondered how often the place needed that kind of scouring.

As it was, the floor beneath the four closest tables was shining and damp, with the faintest pink streaks creating an almost pretty marbling against the dark floor.

On four of the tables, the Ramirez clan and Emily Potter were laid out beside each other, their skin grayish blue under the blinking fluorescent bulbs. Each was covered up to the chest with a clean, white sheet, though there was evidence of blood and viscera on the tools next to each table, which Evelyn had evidently not had a chance to clean up yet.

Beside the bloodied tools, each table had a clipboard with a thick bunch of papers attached, starting with an anatomical drawing on the top sheet of each. Margot wasn't close enough to read the notes, but she could make out annotated marks indicating the throat slits and other wounds.

"Who do you want first?" Evelyn asked, slipping on a new pair of latex gloves.

"Doesn't matter." Margot glanced over each of the bodies. She marveled at how utterly non-threatening Hector Ramirez looked. His skin was slack and waxy, scrubbed clean of blood. There was no menace in him, nor any sign of what might have been likable. It was difficult to see him as the same man from the family portrait in the living room, or even the man she had found when she entered the den for the first time.

This version could have been an anatomical doll, he was so unassuming.

"Our friend Hector has drawn the good detective's eye, so let's start there, shall we?"

Wes breathed out through his nose, and Margot briefly caught his eye. His expression said, *Are we paying extra for the sweet talk?*

Margot smiled to herself. Evelyn, who spent most of her day cooped up with only the dead to keep her company, sometimes overcompensated when there were actual people around. Margot actually liked the plucky cheer and constant chatter. If Evelyn was talking, Margot didn't have to say anything.

Wes set the box of pill bottles on a nearby countertop and followed them over to where Hector's body was laid out. The hole in the side of his head was so neat and clean it hardly looked real. His forearms and face were marked with bruises, like he had taken a hell of a beating before taking the shot to the head.

"He looks like shit," Wes said.

"You wouldn't look great if you were in his position either, buddy," Evelyn retorted. "As you can see, he has defensive wounds on his arms, and the bruising on his knuckles indicates he probably got in a few blows of his own before he died. All four victims show signs of defending themselves from attack, but since the women were all bound, they have fewer. Hector landed a blow or two of his own."

"Any chance the women's wounds correspond to the damage to his knuckles?" Margot asked. "Just covering my bases."

"I can assure you whoever they were defending themselves against, it wasn't Mr. Ramirez." She made a note in the margin of her clipboard. "Or if it was, it wasn't *just* Mr. Ramirez. But let's not get ahead of ourselves here, OK?"

Wes had sidled up next to Margot, and every time Evelyn said something that Wes wanted to reply to, he leaned against Margot's side. She had to keep her expression completely stony every time he did it, despite how badly it made her want to laugh.

Being around death all day made people weirdos. Wes, Margot, and Evelyn were evidence of that.

"More important than the defensive wounds, is this." Evelyn drew their attention to the now-clean bullet wound at Hector's temple. The skin was ragged and the dark hole was edged with white bone. It seemed so peculiar that a wound could be that nasty-looking and not bleed, as if perhaps it wasn't real at all.

Evelyn prodded the skin next to the hole with the end of her pen, and Margot hoped to hell Evelyn wasn't the type of woman who nervously chewed on things. She also made a mental note to never borrow a pen from the medical examiner.

"So, you guys weren't sure if this was the real deal or staged, right?"

"We're leaning toward the latter," Wes confided.

"Well, lean back, my friend. Based on gunpowder residue tests, and the angle of entry, I can say with almost absolute certainty that Hector Ramirez shot himself."

Margot tried to keep her jaw from falling slack, but Wes wore his incredulity bare and open. "That doesn't really fit with what we saw at the scene."

"Eyes lie, Wesley. Evidence doesn't."

"You're sure?" Margot asked.

"There's a narrow possibility the killer could have crouched down next to him, held the gun to his temple and pulled the trigger, sure. But who holds still for that? Maybe if he was unconscious? I don't know, that's your department. What I'm telling you is that from everything I see here, this man killed himself. Ten out of ten times, if not found in the setting he was, I'd rule this a suicide."

"The killer." Margot circled back to the beginning to Evelyn's explanation. "You said he killed himself, but also said *the killer*."

"Yeah, that's the best part." Evelyn beamed. "There's no way Hector killed his family."

"How can you be sure?"

"Because he was dead at least an hour before the rest of them."

THIRTEEN

Wes didn't speak the entire way back to the station, and Margot was in no mood to be the first to break the silence. They had listened to everything Evelyn had to say—no surprises about the cause of death for the women—but nothing had topped her bombshell reveal about Hector.

That his death had been a genuine suicide was interesting.

That he had died at least an *hour* before the rest of his family was something Margot still couldn't quite process. All the ways she had imagined the crime unfolding, in each instance they required him being alive for the murder of the women.

Possibly even responsible for it.

Now, in spite of how the crime scene looked, it appeared that Hector was not the audience for the show, but rather the star of it.

Had the real killer made him do it? Had the women been forced to watch, knowing their turn would come? Another question nagged at Margot, continually swirling around to the front of her mind: why hadn't Mateo mentioned the gunshot happening first? Perhaps he hadn't heard it down in the basement? But she was bothered by it nonetheless, because if three women had to watch Hector blow his brains out, they probably would have screamed. Mateo had heard the initial argument between his mother and the supposed attacker, but not the ensuing mayhem and terror?

They'd left the box of prescriptions with Evelyn as well, but her initial assessment told them the medications were primarily for treating asthma and heart disease. Unusual things for a seemingly healthy child to be taking.

Margot bit a hangnail next to her thumb, letting the sharp red-hot pinprick of pain distract her momentarily from her thoughts.

Wes parked in front of the precinct but didn't turn off the car. Instead, he stared straight ahead, his grip on the wheel tight and his face unreadable.

"Aren't you coming in?" Margot asked, already aware of the answer before she'd even asked the question.

"No." He glanced at the clock, the time well after six. Shift change had taken place, so he was within his rights to call it a day. For Margot, she couldn't imagine leaving without at least taking another look at the crime scene photos, knowing now what she hadn't known this morning. "You going to be OK?" he asked, finally turning to look at her.

She'd all but forgotten the near-meltdown she had outside the morgue.

"OK is sort of a relative term, and it's been a long time since it applied to me. But I'm not going to go inside and start crying or anything, if you're worried about that."

He sighed and stopped looking at her. "That's not what I meant."

"Look... this thing you know about me, the reason I don't tell people is because I don't want them to treat me like I'm a victim. Which they inevitably do. And I'm many things, but I'm not a victim. Ed had seventy-six of those, and I don't deserve to be counted alongside them. And you might want to pretend like you're not treating me differently, but you are. Please don't. Just be your normal, jackass self. I don't think the real Wes Fox would handle his partner with kid gloves."

"The real Wes Fox," he repeated. "Christ, Margot."

"Forget it."

She got out of the car without another word, letting the click of the door end the conversation for her. She wasn't even sure why she was so mad at him. Because he wasn't being an asshole? Because he genuinely seemed to give a shit how she was doing?

How dare he? What a prick.

Margot sighed and considered knocking on the window to apologize, but Wes pulled away, leaving her with nothing but an empty parking spot to look at.

Not yet ready to go home to an empty apartment where a treasure trove of her father's crap was waiting to be put away, she jogged across the street and into the police station, making her way up to the second floor where her board of photos was waiting, tucked into the small office she and Wes shared. Since the shift change also meant shared space had changed, the board had been turned backwards, and Leon Telly was sitting at Wes's desk. Leon hadn't had a partner since his previous one, Diane Domingo, had retired the previous year.

He glanced up as Margot entered the room. "Hey, wasn't expecting to see you. Your sidekick along for the ride? I can make room." He moved to grab his laptop, but Margot waved him off.

"No need, Wes is gone for the day."

"What does he think this is, a nine-to-five?" Leon smiled softly. That was the thing about Leon. When Margot had first worked with him, she'd thought he seemed aloof, because he rarely talked and didn't invite close friendships with those he worked with. But she soon realized that once he opened up, he was the kindest, sweetest man. He didn't keep photos up at the shared desk, but she knew he had two daughters and had been married to his wife, Lori, since they graduated high school.

Leon kept his work life in a tunnel. He didn't want to see outside it. He wanted to do the job, then go out into the light of the real world and enjoy his life.

For Margot, the real world often felt darker than her job.

"You mind?" She pointed to the board.

"Nah, go to town. I'm just finishing some paperwork on that drug case from Sunday."

Margot wheeled the board out, turning it around and positioning it in front of her desk so she could sit in the armchair near the door. She continued to chew on the hangnail on her thumb while processing the images of the crime scene through fresh eyes. What did Evelyn's news mean?

She'd barely been sitting for five minutes when someone knocked on the door. "Hey, Telly, we got a call for a stabbing in Golden Gate Rec Area, you're up."

Leon grunted. "All right."

The desk clerk left, and Leon gathered his jacket and car keys. "Hey, Phalen, you want to come along?"

Margot was about to decline, to point out that she had her own case to work on, but it was so damn rare for Leon to invite anyone to do anything with him that it seemed impossible to do anything but go with him.

"Yeah, sure."

It was not unusual for the detectives on either shift to juggle multiple cases at once. Some crimes were easier to solve than others, and since she didn't see an easy conclusion on the horizon for the Ramirez case, it might be nice to focus on something a little less complicated, more cut and dried. Right now her brain was so full of questions about Hector's death, the things they'd found in the Ramirez house that morning, and Ed reaching out to her, she would take any excuse to think about something else.

It felt morbid to welcome a stabbing victim as distraction, but there it was.

Leon was a books-on-tape guy. Or, since it was the twenty-first century, a books on his phone guy. As soon as they got in the car and his Bluetooth synced, the soothing voice of a woman started to describe a luxurious ballroom in elaborate detail. She lavished attention on the gowns of the women queuing up to dance.

Leon reached for the power button, but Margot said, "No, you can leave it."

She wouldn't have taken him for a romance fan, let alone a historical romance fan, but it delighted her to unearth this private detail about him.

"Now you know the truth about why I don't have a partner anymore."

"Is this the real reason Diane retired?"

"Probably."

"Maybe I should ask for some recommendations and start playing them in the car with Wes."

"He'd probably think you were flirting with him."

Margot snorted. "So, romance novels, hey?"

"I asked myself, what's the polar opposite genre of murder? Lori suggested I read one of her Johanna Lindsey books one summer vacation and I don't mind telling you I was hooked. So now this is what I listen to, and it's cheaper than therapy, let me tell you."

The sun was fat and orange in the sky, not ready to set but not at its most oppressive anymore. The interior of the car was warm, but Leon hadn't bothered to turn on the air conditioning, and Margot found it wasn't necessary. She felt comfortable for the first time all day.

He navigated the car across the Golden Gate Bridge. It was

a rare occasion where the fog wasn't clinging to the upper reaches of the red suspension bridge, giving Margot a clear view of the Bay, and the high spires rising above her. Instead of enjoying the uninterrupted vista, she was staring at the pedestrians, bike riders, and the people standing to the sides of the bridge snapping photos.

Golden Gate was the number one most common destination for suicide attempts, and after being called to more than one scene involving a body crushed by the impact of hitting the water below, Margot couldn't help but keep an eye out for those who might be thinking of taking the plunge.

When she'd been younger, she'd loved the bridge, found it beautiful even. Now it just represented another way for people to die.

She shook her head. *You are one cheerful motherfucker.*

The Golden Gate National Recreation Area was a sprawling park area on the opposite side of the Bay from San Francisco proper, and was so large it was actually twice the size of the city itself. It technically included the Presidio in San Francisco, as well as Alcatraz, but the area they were heading to was inside Muir Woods National Monument. Since Muir Woods was under the jurisdiction of the National Park Service, they were ill-equipped to handle a murder investigation, and the Marin County Sheriff's Department wasn't built for murder cases either. They were going to meet a lieutenant from the Sheriff's Investigation Division, along with the park ranger who had originally called in the body, but the case would be theirs.

When Leon parked in a visitor lot inside Muir Woods, the low-hanging sun could barely penetrate the dense canopy of tall redwoods, giving the place a creepy, green-tinged darkness, as if night were suddenly upon them in spite of it not even being seven o'clock yet.

A woman dressed in a Sheriff's Department uniform waved at them as they got out of the car. Behind her was a tall man wearing the crisp uniform of a park ranger, including a flat Stetson, which he took off as Margot and Leon approached. As soon as she was standing in front of him, his true height was much more apparent. He was at least six foot eight, making him seem as if he had grown alongside the trees.

"Detectives, thanks for joining us." From someone else it might have come out sarcastic, but the lieutenant sounded earnest. She offered a hand first to Leon, who was closer, then to Margot. "I'm Lieutenant Baker. You can call me Amanda if you want. This is Interpretive Ranger Abbott."

"Simon," said the tree-man, shaking their hands in the reverse order Amanda had.

"I'm Detective Telly, this is Detective Phalen."

Leon didn't offer their first names, but Margot gave hers, anyway. These people were welcoming them in, sharing their jurisdiction. If they wanted to be first-name people, she could be a first-name person. She got the feeling Leon would stick to titles, and that was fine, too.

"You found the body, Ranger Abbott?"

Abbott shifted uncomfortably, scratching the back of his neck, his tan cheeks turning ruddier as he flushed. "No, sir. A group of hikers on a self-guided walk found her, but I was the first person on the scene to get things under control, and I called the sheriff to come out."

It was probably pointless to have involved the sheriff, but the Marin County office did have a special unit in place to assist with investigations like these, even if they didn't handle them themselves, so both Baker and Abbott would have their uses here.

Abbott nodded toward the nearest trail. "We best head up there now if you want to see things before it gets dark. We have a couple guys there waiting to cover the scene when you give them the OK, just to keep things as dry as we can overnight. Even when it doesn't rain it sure can get wet. We didn't call the ambulance yet to remove her—figured you'd want to see everything as-is."

"I'll call the medical examiner direct," Margot offered. "No reason to bring an ambulance out here."

"Are the folks that found her still out there?"

"We sent them to the visitor center. They're with another ranger right now, but we still have them," Baker offered, and Margot could tell she wanted to prove they weren't fucking this up.

It wasn't a contest. Margot and Leon weren't here to judge them. Inevitably, though, it always ended up in a grandstanding display as each group attempted to show how good they were at their jobs.

Leon didn't speak or ask any additional questions while they hiked out. The path wasn't too difficult, but it was still a hike in the woods, and neither Margot nor Leon had dressed right for it. She found herself sweating profusely in her leather jacket by the time they reached the area Baker had sealed off with police tape. The sun might not be able to penetrate the woods, but the humidity had no problem wrapping its stifling arms around Margot and giving her a suffocating hug.

Abbott, with his long legs and intimate knowledge of the area, led the way, and the three law enforcement officers did their best to keep up with his confident strides. Margot liked to think she was in good shape, but by the time they were ducking under the tape she had to dismiss that notion outright.

Leon, who was a smoker, wheezed and coughed into his fist.

There were a group of men standing on the path ahead of them, but the body wasn't so obvious to locate. Abbott hesitated on the path, and Baker must have sensed it, because she led them from that point. "We've asked everyone to stay on the trail for now, until you guys have had a chance to see her. Figured the fewer people we have stomping around near her body the better."

"Appreciate it," Margot said.

They followed Baker over a low wooden fence meant to keep people from leaving the designated walking path. Leon and Margot tried to keep in Baker's footsteps as they traipsed through the poorly lit undergrowth, where roots and bushes threatened to knock them down every few feet. When they arrived at the scene, Margot glanced back and realized they'd come quite a distance from Abbott and the other men.

"How did the hikers see the body from that far away?" Dogs weren't permitted in Muir Woods, so the old *my dog found the body* excuse wouldn't fit here.

"They found her about four hours ago. It was quite a bit brighter then, and it's hard to tell now, but her sweater is a very bright pink. One of the hikers climbed over the partition to get a better look and as soon as they realized what they were looking at, they hightailed it out of here."

In the dim light of evening, the body looked like a surrealist painting exploring the concept of death, rather than an actual corpse. She was lying on her stomach, her blond hair caught in the twigs around her, making it fan out unnaturally around her head. As Baker had mentioned, she wore a pink hooded sweater, but her lower half was bare, her pants missing entirely and her underwear clinging to one ankle like a shackle.

Margot sighed. She'd been almost relieved at the Ramirez crime scene to find no signs of sexual violence against the women—something Evelyn had confirmed after the autopsies—but out here in the woods she was dragged back to reality. Usually, crimes against women had a sexual aspect to them, and it certainly appeared that this poor girl had been assaulted either before or after she was murdered.

Leon was writing something down in a notebook, so Margot carefully circled the body, trying to get an angle from above. It was impossible to gauge how old the woman at her feet was. She might have been a teenager, or in her fifties. Her skin was smooth and unwrinkled, but that didn't mean anything.

Stooping down, Margot lifted the hood of the sweater and found the sweater stained dark red, a color so deep it nearly looked black. Without having gloves on yet, Margot couldn't inspect the material to see how many holes there were, but judging by the spread of the blood there were at least two or three different stab wounds.

She stayed in a crouch, and from where she was, she could no longer see anyone on the path, even the railing was out of sight.

"Perfect area to do it. Not sure how long she's been dead, but I'm willing to bet the killer attacked her when it was still dark. Night, or possibly the twilight or dawn hours. We'll need to come back when there's better light, but if it was this dark for him, then he would have had no trouble keeping hidden from anyone on the path."

"What about the girl though?" Leon asked, his voice calm and even-keeled. "He assaults her, stabs her, and she doesn't make a single noise? With the path only a hundred feet away? I don't buy it."

"And it's pretty unlikely he would drag a body out here that he killed somewhere else. It's a terrible place to try to haul in a corpse. Too many risks. So, night then, he would have killed her at night when there weren't any tourists or hikers around."

So much for Margot's dreams of tagging along for an easy case.

Margot put on her gloves to better investigate the body, and pushed back some of the victim's hair, noting the dark roots indicated she wasn't a natural blonde. Her skin had started to change from the waxy white of the early dead to the unpleasant blue of decomposition. It was nearing the point where she was barely recognizable as having once been human. Bugs were crawling out of her nose and mouth. Based on what was left of

her, however, Margot suspected she was older than they'd originally believed, closer to forty than twenty.

Dropping the curtain of hair back into place, Margot
steadied herself and turned away, taking a few deep, steadying
breaths. She'd been doing the job for a long, long time, and
while very few things surprised her anymore, some of them
weren't that easy to adapt to.

The fresh dead were a lot easier to stomach than those who
had been gone a few days. Hell, the ones who had been dead for
weeks were easier still, since they seemed like something an
archaeologist might find at a dig.

This woman was at the stage where death was at its most
unforgiving.

"She's been out here a couple of days," Margot said when
she turned around. "Advanced decomposition."

Leon scratched his chin, then followed in Margot's footsteps. While he didn't take time to steady himself, she could still
see the change in his complexion, his dark skin dampening with
sweat and a vaguely haunted look casting over his eyes briefly.

"Doesn't make sense. That level of decomp, surely some
animals out here would have been taking some liberal bites out
of her." He moved in a circle around the body, each step careful
and hesitant, lest he step on something important. The light
continued to peter out, and everywhere Margot looked the
image of the woman's rotting face seemed to float in front of her.

Finally, Leon returned, jamming his notebook into his
pocket and shrugging.

"Get that tarp set up, if you don't mind." He nodded toward
the park rangers lingering on the periphery, who seemed to have
been awaiting this very command.

Without another word, Leon started marching back to the
main trail, following the same rough line in the undergrowth
they'd come in by.

Margot took a last look at the woman's body, another

mystery to be solved, then followed Leon back to the main path. Along with the growing darkness, the damp evening fog had started to roll in, giving the air a chill, and an eerie, hazy quality.

"Let's head back to the parking lot, wait for the team to meet us," Leon suggested. "This is turning into a hell of a day for you, Phalen. You sure you don't want to go home?"

Margot thought about what was waiting back at her apartment and shook her head. The corpse and a mist-soaked crime scene seemed preferable to being alone with her thoughts. "I'm fine."

"Attagirl."

Never mind that she was almost forty; to a guy like Leon she would always be a "girl." It didn't bother her, in fact it made her feel ever so slightly young again. Leon got on the phone, calling the coroner and the crime scene team, coordinating generators, spotlights—everything they would need to work well into the night. It was going to be a shit show, but better to do as much of it as they could before morning came.

The longer she was exposed to the elements, the more evidence they would lose. Given how decomposed the body was, Margot had a feeling most of the trace evidence on her skin would be long gone, but they'd have to do their best. If they worked through the night, they'd be able to move her body before morning. The parks folks would certainly be happy to have the cadaver gone, but Margot couldn't guarantee how soon they'd be able to open the trail up again.

What a logistical nightmare.

Leon hung up, having coordinated the last of the relief efforts, and they returned to his car for a few minutes to warm up, blasting the heat on their fog-chilled fingers. Margot had dressed for daytime weather, and in spite of it being summer, she found that the light leather jacket and T-shirt wasn't quite substantial enough to keep her warm now that evening had settled in.

Leon reached across her and popped open the glove box, pulling out a box of animal crackers. He opened it up, then offered her the first choice. Margot took a few of the little cookies out, only now becoming aware how hungry she was.

"How very Dave Toschi of you," Margot commented, referring to the famous San Francisco detective who had worked the Zodiac killer case. Based on Leon's age, the two wouldn't have been contemporaries but might have crossed paths at some point when Toschi was in the latter stages of his career.

"Can't give Toschi credit for this, I'm afraid. My granddaughter left a box in the car one weekend and I found they were a damn fine snack. Kept 'em around ever since. But don't you fucking tell anyone." He winked at her, biting the head off an elephant.

"I like that you're more worried about me snitching on the animal crackers than the romance audiobooks," she laughed.

In the dark of the woods, it was easy to spot the flashing lights approaching.

Leon put the cookies back in the glove box and sighed.

Their reprieve was over.

FOURTEEN
AUGUST 15, 1981

Petaluma, California

Ed had made a mistake.

He wasn't the type who did stupid things. He was a planner, a big believer in knowing what was going to happen when and having contingencies. The whole process of doing what he did meant he needed to be smart about things, needed a way out, needed to be clean.

His car hit a bump and the loud *whump* sound from the trunk made his whole body clench.

Why had she run?

Every detail had been laid out perfectly. He knew where she lived, and had watched her for almost a week, making sure he had a good idea of her schedule, when she arrived home, when she was most likely to be alone. She walked to the corner store every night to get a newspaper—who read the newspaper at night?—and an ice cream. It was after this trip, on the fifth night of watching, that Ed made his move.

He was going to follow her into the building and get her as

she re-entered her apartment, a basement suite in a small building where most of her neighbors were elderly couples.

Only as he went through the door after her, she turned around.

She'd forgotten something.

Ed had already had a mask on.

They came face to face in the dimly lit hallway outside her apartment door, and she stopped dead in her tracks, her mouth agape in slight surprise.

"What?" she managed to say.

Fuck, thought Ed.

Then she seemed to register what she was seeing. She dropped the ice cream on the floor, and he could see her scream before he heard it. It appeared first as a twist in her features. Her eyes squinted, and her mouth widened as if to swallow him whole.

He lunged at her before she could make the sound, the shriek turning into a *gulp* as she saw what he was doing.

She ran.

Ed, while strong, was not an athlete. He wasn't a runner. In fact, his cardio skills left a lot to be desired on the whole. He cursed this aspect of his physique as his intended victim bolted for the stairs that would take her out the back door of the apartment building and into the evening street, where he'd never be able to catch her.

He should have let her go. It wasn't as if she had seen his face, or any identifying marks. He had started wearing a nondescript navy-blue coat when he went out, and a pair of work boots that were a different brand from those he wore every day.

They were also a size and a half too large.

When he was simply walking or climbing stairs, the extra size didn't matter so much. But now that he was trying to best a lean, fast young woman in a foot race, he could see the error in his foresight.

He tore down the hallway behind her, and by some miracle caught her at the base of the stairs.

Ed grabbed her by her feet and yanked her back toward him with incredible force. The woman fell forward, her arms shooting out to break her fall, but there wasn't enough time. Her face smashed hard against the concrete steps, making a satisfying wet sound when she landed.

She wheezed, not about to start screaming again now. Blood spilled from her mouth, but she was still trying to find her way back to her feet. Ed wasn't accustomed to this kind of fight. Typically, the women he encountered knew better. They'd seen the knife, they'd heard his threats. This one had no idea what he was planning, but all she had needed was a glimpse of his mask to know he wasn't there for a friendly visit.

The woman clawed for the top of the stairs, as if she might still have a chance of getting out the door, even in her current condition. Her nail broke off, a tiny red crescent spinning into the dimly lit corridor.

It didn't matter.

The blood didn't matter.

Ed didn't care if the police knew the woman had died here —and she *would* die—as long as they didn't know he was the one who had done it.

He could paint the goddamn halls with the inside of her skull and it wouldn't matter.

Breathing hard, he hauled her to her feet. Her eyes were heavily lidded, like those of a drunk, and she stared up at him, barely able to show fear anymore.

"P-please," she whispered.

"You shouldn't have run," he snarled in return.

He had no patience for begging. People should keep their prayers for God, because He was just as likely to listen as Ed was.

There was no salvation. There was no last-minute reprieve.

Getting the woman's keys would take too much effort, and increase the chances of someone coming out into the hall to see what was happening. His only option was to take her outside and get it done in the alley. It meant he wouldn't have the time he wanted. He wouldn't get to savor it.

It meant he'd need to find another girl that much sooner.

He dragged her up the stairs, her feet limp and ineffectual. Ed was careful to sidestep the pool of her blood. One mistake tonight was more than enough.

The alley behind the apartment building was quiet. Scattered puddles pooled the light from the one yellow-tinged overhead bulb. The air around them was damp and ever so slightly cold.

The woman's head bobbed, her whole body getting heavy and her breathing more labored. He hadn't realized she had hit her head so hard when she went down, but now that he had her outside, she seemed as though she was half-dead already.

His desire for the kill dried up. This wasn't exciting for him, there was no thrill in it. She wasn't going to squirm and struggle, nor would he get the rush from her fear. She could barely keep her eyes open long enough to look at him, let alone show him those delicious flashes of terror he craved so much.

The knife felt like such a useless tool here.

Ed propped her against the wall, and she nearly sagged to the ground. When he grabbed her by the throat to keep her standing straight, she gurgled out a pleasant noise of protest that sparked his desire. He held her with both hands, the leather gloves he wore creaking with the exertion of his grip. He wished he could feel her skin against his, feel the clench of the tendons in her neck against his palms. But no. He had made enough stupid mistakes for one night.

When the survival center of her brain recognized it was no longer getting oxygen, her eyes snapped open wide and she began to kick her legs at him, her shoes scraping against the damp concrete of the alley. She let out a little mewling noise and Ed sighed, growing hard against her.

There was a little fight left after all.

She held his wrists, trying without any hope of success to pry his hands away from her throat.

He leaned in close, pressing his cheek against hers so his lips were against her ear. "I wish I'd had more time. I could have done this right." Ed licked her earlobe and the woman let out a sob.

When he was finished, she was limp, and heavy, too much weight for him to keep holding up. He dropped her to the pavement and she sank into a heap, nothing left to animate her or make her appear human.

It was then he realized the apartment complex didn't have any dumpsters. Only a row of regular household garbage cans, all of them much too full for him to use to hide a body.

Cursing his stupidity, he skirted around the building to claim his car, then returned to where her body lay. He didn't have anything in the back he could use to wrap her in, but one of Megan's baby blankets was in the back seat.

Without a pause to think it over, he wrapped the woman's upper half in the blanket, careful to cover her hair and bloody face. He couldn't have any obvious traces of her in the trunk. He had just finished tucking her away, and removing his gloves and mask, when a young man opened the back door of the apartment complex, a bag of garbage in his hand.

He barely even acknowledged Ed's presence except to say, "Can't park back here, man."

"Yeah. Sorry."

Ed got into the car and drove away, his shirt glued to his back with sweat.

Close. Too close.

He hit another bump, the body rocking in the trunk. There

was a span of open road between here and home, a length of backroad highway he'd driven dozens of times.

If he hid her far enough back, the bugs and animals would get to her before the cops ever did.

He'd need to get Megan a new blanket.

FIFTEEN

Margot woke to someone kicking her in the leg.

She sat bolt upright, sending a swath of papers falling to the floor next to her. A sharp pain in her neck was the first evidence she had of having slept somewhere other than her bed. Bleary-eyed, she glanced around and discovered she had fallen asleep on the ratty love seat in the precinct's break room. It was an ugly 1980s monstrosity someone had "donated" to the office when they cleaned out an aging parent's home.

It smelled of spilled coffee and other things Margot didn't want to think too long about.

She had one leg off the couch, her other bent at the knee in an attempt to fit her long frame onto the small surface. She was still wearing her boots, and someone had draped her jacket over her at some point while she was asleep.

Wes was standing over her with a coffee in each hand, one of which was currently on offer to her. Philz. He'd slept at home last night.

"You look like shit," he greeted.

She grunted.

"Were you here all night?" He set his own coffee on the

ground and helped collect the papers she had dropped. She doubted it was chivalry. He wanted to see what she was working on. "What's this?"

"Went out with Telly to a scene in Muir Woods last night." She was careful not to tell him too much, since it wasn't his case, after all. He might not want to know. He might be pissed she'd latched herself on to another case when they were working a quadruple homicide as it was.

Instead of saying anything, he handed it back to her. "Did you get any sleep, Margot?"

Margot yawned and rubbed her eyes with the heel of her palms, succeeding only in smearing what remained of her mascara.

"I guess."

In truth, whatever sleep she had had was short and dismal, but thankfully dreamless. She couldn't remember when she sat on the love seat to "rest," but it had been well after midnight. Now the morning shift had arrived, and she had to be ready to go for her day.

Taking a sip of the deliciously bitter coffee Wes had given her, she got to her feet, her whole body protesting with creaks and groans. In her twenties she'd been able to sleep almost anywhere—and had attempted to prove it—but now she didn't have that same flexibility and it showed.

Returning to the office they shared, she found a note from Leon written in his flawless handwriting, telling her the crime scene crew would be out at Muir Woods for the better part of the day if she wanted to go, but he didn't seem to expect it.

Good thing, too, because the Ramirez case needed to take top priority. That didn't mean the woman in the woods was nagging at her any less. She never should have agreed to go with Leon. Not because she regretted being there to help him, but rather she now felt as beholden to the Jane Doe in the forest as she did to poor living Mateo. She wanted to see that case to conclusion just as badly as she did the Ramirez family's murders.

Margot was no stranger to burning the candle at both ends. It wasn't a healthy way to live, but she wouldn't mind the distraction.

In her desk she found a spare T-shirt and deodorant, as well as a pack of Wet-Wipes and her emergency makeup kit and hairbrush. This wasn't her first time falling asleep at work, or pulling an all-nighter right into the next shift change. She'd learned to be prepared, because it was a lot easier to keep shit in a drawer than it was to spend the whole day in a wrinkled shirt stinking like you'd never met a shower.

She made quick work of her morning routine, then joined Wes back in their office.

"Look at that, like a brand-new woman," he said.

"Ever so slightly used." With the coffee in her hand once more she was starting to feel a bit more like herself. "Any strong feelings about what you'd like to do today?"

"I would like to solve a murder."

She rolled her eyes. "Yeah, cool."

Wes rolled up his shirtsleeves, exposing toned forearms and a watch that was a little too expensive for a detective's income. "I'd like to take another look at the house, then I want to talk to Mateo again."

"You think he's going to have anything different to say?" Her stomach rumbled, and she knew they'd need to stop somewhere to grab a greasy bite before she would be fit to carry on a patient conversation with a child.

Outside their conclave, phones were ringing and other detectives in the homicide division were being called out to their own wretched new mysteries. But in the office she and Wes shared, their focus was all on the Ramirez clan. The scent of coffee filled the room, and if anything made her anxiety worse.

She drank it anyway.

"I think something about his story doesn't line up, and I want to know why he didn't mention the gunshot that killed his father coming an hour before the death of his mother and sister." Margot wasn't sure why Wes was so hung up on finding things wrong with Mateo's story. He wasn't behaving like the perfect victim, certainly, but she knew a thing or two about how varied human responses could be to trauma. And they had no idea, really, what those kids had been put through by their parents in the months and years leading up to the murders.

"Time of death isn't exactly a perfect science," she reminded him. "I know Evelyn is good, but there's a chance she messed up. Maybe Hector *did* die at the same time as the girls."

"Maybe." Wes was obviously not convinced.

Neither was Margot, honestly. Evelyn would be the first to admit that timing the death of a victim was mostly guesswork, which meant if she was willing to make a point of calling out Hector's death as being earlier, she had to be pretty damned sure about it.

Margot's phone buzzed in her back pocket. Must be Leon calling her with an update on the Muir Woods case.

"Phalen," she answered quickly, not bothering to check the screen.

"Please don't hang up, Ms. Phalen."

At first, she didn't recognize the voice, only because she was expecting Leon's deep, gravelly one, and this man was soft-spoken and had more of a lilt to his consonants.

Then it clicked. The lawyer.

"Jesus, I thought we went through this yesterday. You know, I'm a cop, I know a thing or two about what constitutes harassment, Mr. Rosenthal."

"I understand that you probably don't want to speak to me—"

Margot barked out a laugh, cutting him off. "Probably? Pal,

look, you did your job, you asked if I wanted to see him and I said no. That's it. I know Ed might be hard to disappoint, but he's just going to have to deal with it this time."

"Miss Phalen. Megan."

"Margot."

He sighed, but Margot wasn't going to yield. She'd been Margot Phalen longer than she'd been Megan Finch at this point, and she wasn't going to let him call her by a name she barely recognized anymore.

"Margot," he continued. "I told your father what you said yesterday, and he wanted me to pass along a message."

"I don't want his message."

"I suspect you do."

"No, Mr. Rosenthal, I can assure you I don't want any fucking messages from Ed Finch."

At this, Wes's attention perked up. He'd been pretending to ignore her call out of politeness, but now that she'd said the magic words, he was all ears.

Ford Rosenthal plowed ahead, totally undeterred by her rebuffs. "Your father said, and I am reading directly from his message, 'Tell her if she says hello, I'll tell her about Seventy-Seven.'"

Margot's palms broke out in a sudden cold sweat and her balance wobbled. She braced herself against the edge of a nearby desk and took a deep, steadying breath through her nostrils. No matter how hard she tried to focus, she could feel the panic creeping in, wrapping its long fingers around her neck.

It had been months since she needed a Xanax, but damn if she wasn't desperate for one now.

Seventy-Seven.

Rosenthal was being clever, reading from the statement. The number could mean anything, it could have been a year, could have been an address, could have been so many things.

But it wasn't. It was something else.

Ed Finch had gone down as one of the most prolific serial killers in US history. He'd killed seventy-six women.

Seventy-six.

If she says hello, I'll tell her about Seventy-Seven.

Her father had more victims.

SIXTEEN

Margot hung up on the lawyer.

Had she been in a better headspace she might have come up with a response, might have even known what to do. But she was groggy, she'd slept poorly, and now someone had told her that her father might have killed more women than any of them had ever expected.

Seventy-seven.

If there was one more, who was to say there wasn't a seventy-eight? An eighty. Ninety? How many women were there out there still?

He left most of the victims in their homes, waiting to be found. But he'd moved Annie Wray. He'd dumped her body in the woods. Likewise, Laura Welsh, his first victim, had been found in a forested outdoor area. She flashed back to the woman they'd found in Muir Woods last night. Obviously, the fresh kill hadn't been Ed's handiwork, but what if there was another girl like her? Another body long vanished?

What if there was a cold case Margot could put to rest simply by sitting across from him in a room? It was quite literally her job to bring closure to the families of victims, to bring justice where there was only agony. More than that, it was something she believed deeply in, and was passionate about.

Yet with her father involved, she immediately got cold feet.

Fuck. Fucking fuck fuck.

"What was that all about?" Wes asked, as if he didn't already know.

She wanted to cut him with words, to jab back that his playing dumb wasn't helping people, and especially wasn't helping her, but instead she stared at her phone like an idiot.

"It was the lawyer," she managed.

"I thought you made it pretty clear you don't want to see him."

"He had a message from Ed."

"Yeah, I gathered. What did he say?"

Margot couldn't make the words come out. She wanted to tell him, wanted to share part of this burden with someone. If she could only manage to tell him, maybe he would have the right answers. Instead, she slipped the phone into her pocket, silencing the ringer in case the lawyer called back. She couldn't speak to him, or Wes, or anyone. Not yet.

"Can you drive?"

"Margot, what did he say?" Wes followed her out of the office, car keys jangling in his hands. "It's obviously got you rattled, just tell me."

"We'll head to the Ramirez house first. I'll call CFS to arrange a meeting with Mateo." She made a beeline out of the building in the direction of his car. He was hot on her heels, not too difficult with his long strides. She should have kept her shit together better in the office, now it was obvious something was wrong, and Wes was like a dog with a bone about it.

Sometimes it was nice knowing someone was in on her secret. She had the freedom to say Ed's name around Wes without him being shocked. But it also meant he wanted to *know* things. She wasn't used to people expecting to be let in.

One of the things that kept her safe, if only in her own mind, was that so few people in her current world knew who she really was. If she let Wes in about this, there would be more questions, more digging, more things in her past she didn't want to unearth. They would always end up circling back to *Why didn't you know?*

It was the question that plagued her the most. She had been a teenager, and in her own world, absolutely. But how had she not known? How had her mother not known? That, ultimately, was the question that took her mother's life, the one unanswered thing that had lingered over her life after Ed's arrest like a dark cloud.

How had we not known?

Of course, in the years that followed, Margot had learned plenty of answers to that question. Ed was a psychopath. He didn't feel guilt or empathy. It's easy to pretend nothing is wrong in your life if you genuinely believe there's nothing wrong. Because that was the truth, in Ed's mind. He did what the voice inside him told him to do, and as a result, seventy-six young women died.

Seventy-seven.

The number swam around in her mind, nipping at her, biting. There had been times after Ed's arrest that Margot had feared she might be like him. Any time she had a negative thought toward someone, or a violent urge, she wondered if the darkness that had piloted him was in her too.

But Margot felt guilt. She felt all the guilt Ed hadn't. She had begun meticulously researching all the women he'd killed, learning what she could about them, about their lives before. And whenever she found something she shared in common with one of them, it ripped her heart apart a little bit. These women, some of them weren't much older than she'd been at the time of his arrest when they died.

How could Ed have seen them the same way a lion sees a

lame gazelle, but still look at her and warn her to be careful around boys? How was it that Ed had seemed every ounce the doting, protective father until he was *the* Edgar Finch?

These were the spiraling questions she tried to avoid within herself, and the questions that she felt Wes might want to have answers to. Answers she simply couldn't provide him, because after more than twenty years she barely had answers for herself.

Which was why she didn't let anyone in. And why it was so dangerous that Wes knew even as much as he did.

"Margot." They were in the car now, and she hadn't said a word to him since they'd left the station. The silence was lessened by the radio on low, some new pop song filled the car with bass, but she could barely make out the words. Nothing was getting through.

Seventy-seven.

"Margot," Wes nudged again.

"I don't want to talk about it, Wes."

"I think you should."

"I'm sure you do."

"You've gotten this far by yourself, I get it, but at some point, you're going to have to let someone in."

"I don't think that's true."

He gave a heavy sigh and returned his gaze to the road. She hadn't actually seen him looking at her, but she could feel it. The weight of his stare was a tangible thing.

"I can't pretend to know what your life has been like. Not many people can. But I think if you're willing to share this with me it might help. Whatever that call was about, wouldn't it be easier to tell someone else about it?"

"Easier for who?" Her question was meant to be earnest, but it came out barbed with sarcasm, something she had difficulty keeping from her tone even at the best of times.

If she shared this burden with Wes, he would try to make it seem like it was her choice, and she didn't have to go see Ed.

Wes might even suggest she shouldn't. But deep down she would know what he was thinking, what he was expecting from her. He would want her to go, because it was the right thing to do. Putting her own comfort and years' worth of hard-fought mental stability on the line to get answers for some poor family.

She understood that was what she should do, but the struggle remained.

She didn't want to go. She didn't want to see Ed.

And telling Wes wouldn't do anything to make that decision any easier.

They arrived at the Ramirez house about twenty minutes later, and the entire time Margot had managed to avoid saying a word to Wes, and he hadn't pushed her. She'd also felt her phone vibrating, but couldn't determine if it was *actually* vibrating or if she was feeling phantom dread vibrations, waiting for Rosenthal to call back and continue to prod her to meet with Ed.

Everything in her body and brain told her not to give in, not to see him, but the detective part of her, the side that knew every victim deserved justice and every family deserved closure, wanted to find out if there was any truth to what he was suggesting.

She wondered, too, if Rosenthal had tried to contact Justin, or if this was Ed's sick treat for her and her alone.

Regardless, she should call her brother and let him know, just in case. He didn't deserve to be blindsided by it the way she had.

It also vaguely nagged at her that she should be calling Andrew.

The only person outside her immediate family who really understood what it meant to be a part of the Ed cycle of drama was Special Agent Andrew Rhodes. He was the profiler who had helped figure out who Ed was, how his victims were connected, and managed to catch him. He'd also treated the Finch family with more kindness than the police or public at large had. He seemed to realize that they were not responsible for Ed's actions and didn't deserve the fallout of his crimes.

Andrew had been the one to help them get settled in Missouri, and used connections to help get their names changed. It wasn't Witness Protection, but his assistance had been incredibly helpful in starting their new lives. Not that it had been enough for Kim... Cathy in the end. Her mother couldn't leave the past in the past.

And as it turned out, neither could Margot.

She hadn't spoken to Andrew in at least a year, but he lived and worked in the area, and had been a true friend to her when she moved back to the Bay Area. At thirty-seven Margot could admit that she had absolutely looked to Andrew as a surrogate father figure after she'd lost Ed and scrubbed him from her mind as having any attachment to them. They were Phalens now, he was a Finch.

Andrew had been a touchstone. He'd checked in with her and her brother—and her mother when she'd been alive—frequently, and he let Margot lean on him when she got genuinely frightening fan mail or threats from those who wanted to defend Ed. She'd never understood why they were so fixated on her, on Megan. She hadn't testified against Ed, she hadn't spoken up at his sentencing hearing, or condemned him to the media. She had simply melted into the periphery, wanting nothing to do with the three-ring circus of horrors that followed wherever his name was in the air.

Andrew was a comfort and consoler, and even though he'd been relatively young when he solved Ed's case, only thirty-five, younger than Margot was now, she had still put a lot of parental expectation on him, and that hadn't really changed over the course of twenty-two years.

The only thing keeping her from picking up the phone

immediately was the heavy guilt she felt for how long it had been since they'd spoken. Andrew had never forgotten Margot and her family, but in her efforts to escape her past, he had been one of the many things she'd withdrawn from. It wasn't intentional, per se. They'd never had a blowout, she'd never attempted to destroy their relationship, but she'd left it unattended to die all the same, like a houseplant forgotten in a bedroom window.

Could she just revive that connection now that it suited her?

Did he know Ed was back in the Bay Area? If he knew, why hadn't he reached out to her, issued a warning? The simple courtesy of giving her a heads-up would have kept the revelation from being such a punch to the solar plexus. There was no easy way to learn your serial killer father was living in your backyard, but better the news came from a friend than a stranger.

Wes parked in front of the Ramirez house, turning the engine off and letting true silence and sticky morning heat fill the car. This heat wave would need to break soon, because Margot missed foggy, cool days that generally matched her mood. This heat was bullshit.

He looked over at her, his blond hair mussed and an expression somewhere between annoyance and concern etched on his face. "You going to sulk your way through the crime scene, or can I have my partner back for a minute or twelve?"

Margot had a barb on the tip of her tongue but swallowed it. Wes, for all his faults, was trying to help her, trying to be a good friend to her, and it wasn't his problem that she was a closed-off, broken nightmare of a person. She couldn't let people in, but he didn't deserve to get her attitude on top of her cold shoulder.

Was this personal growth?

She sighed. "I know you're being kind, in your special Wes kind of way, and I'm sorry. I really wish I was one of those people who can take an offered shoulder, or be willing to share the burden, or whatever. My therapist will have a heyday with this later, and tell me I should let you in, but I think you can appreciate why I have a hard time trusting people, you know?"

"My special Wes kind of way?" He smirked, resting his arm on the back of his seat and half turning toward her. "What is that?"

"You know, giant shithead but a little nice."

He snorted. "You know how to keep a man's ego in check, Phalen, I'll give you that much."

"Controlling your ego is beyond even my exceptional powers."

"I'm glad you understand your limitations." He opened his door, letting his long limbs enter the outside world, and Margot followed through the passenger side.

The crime scene crew was still there; two white vans with SFPD logos on the side were parked out front. As with the day Margot had first arrived at the Ramirez house, there was no activity happening outside the home. The perfectly placed tall grasses swayed in their rock beds, and the planters filled with bright red geraniums that lined the front step were looking worse for wear having not been watered in the last several days. Their green leaves were curling in, protecting themselves against the aggressive sunshine, and their red heads had begun to droop.

Inside, she and Wes flashed their badges to a uniformed officer who was waiting near the front door, and he stepped back without a word, letting them enter. There was a box of white boot covers sitting just inside the front door, and Margot and Wes both slipped the booties over their street shoes. Even though the house was teeming with crime scene techs, the place continued to be burdened with a haunting silence. The air was still and hot; no one had bothered to turn on the air conditioning, in spite of how warm it was and how uncomfortable the technicians must have been.

Sweat beaded on Margot's forehead and back almost immediately. She hated this heat. Shucking off her leather jacket, she hung it over the banister leading to the upper floor, leaving her in only an emerald green V-neck. Her entire wardrobe consisted of tailored jeans and nineteen different colors of the same GAP V-neck. She didn't have the patience for shopping, so when she found something she liked, she bought it in multiples, either more than one of the same, or one in every color she thought she might wear. That meant drawers filled with soft cotton shirts that washed well, all in neutral tones that didn't clash with her hair.

She needed to be comfortable, and wearing pressed suits and high heels didn't help her solve crime. Heels would have also been incredibly awkward to wear with crime scene booties over them. She'd seen others try, and it was almost always a disaster. Her preferred boots had a low, chunky heel that suited her just fine.

Margot and Wes headed upstairs, assuming the bulk of the work was being done at the crime scene location as well as in the kids' rooms. The techs would have been scouring the whole house over the last two days, but those rooms would most likely be their primary focus even now.

Wes wandered toward Mateo's bedroom, where the forms of two white-clad technicians were moving around. Margot slipped on a pair of latex gloves in case she wanted to touch anything, but instead of going into Mateo's room, she drifted toward Valentina's. The mattress she and Wes had pulled from the bed the previous day was gone, probably taken to a lab somewhere for additional testing, though she wasn't sure what they might expect to find on it.

The box spring sat naked and empty, and the four wooden posts of Valentina's twin-sized bed were easy to see now that the mattress was out of the way. Margot grabbed a white chair from the desk in the corner of the room. The aging paint was decorated with cute butterfly and rainbow stickers, though it was obvious some had been peeled off, leaving sticky scabs behind, as if Valentina had wanted to remove any hints of childishness from the space.

It was a room caught in between being a little girl and a young woman, with pink paint and stuffed animals still adorning the space, but posters of bands and teen heartthrobs on the wall. Now Valentina would never get to make that full transition into adulthood, and the knowledge of that fact sat heavily on Margot's chest.

"What happened here?" she whispered, not sure if it was to the empty room, the ghost of Valentina, or a god she didn't believe in.

The scrape marks on each of the four bed posts stuck out like a sore thumb now, rubbed raw and exposing light wood underneath. The pits where the wood stain had been whittled away weren't violent or bloody, like someone trying to escape a one-time prison, but rather worn smooth, the way water carves canyons into mountains. The shackles weren't there now, but they had been, and it looked like they had been for a long time.

Margot put the chair next to the bed, sat down and stared at the place Valentina had been lying when someone dragged her violently out of the room.

They wouldn't have been able to take her if she'd been shackled.

And if Mateo still had the cuffs attached to his bed, how was it he had had the freedom to make his way downstairs that night? He told them he liked to sneak out when his parents slept, to steal change from their pockets and have free rein over the house. Was that why they'd chained him? It seemed like a massive overstep. They could have simply put a lock on his door, or emptied out their pockets ahead of time if they knew what he was up to.

And keeping Mateo abed wouldn't explain why they'd done the same thing to Valentina.

Margot's mind reeled, she couldn't make any sense of what she was looking at.

A crime scene tech appeared in the doorway, a pretty woman with soft gray eyes and blond hair so light it was almost white. Margot recognized her from other jobs, but didn't know her name.

"Detective Phalen?"

"Yeah?"

"Roxie." The woman pointed to herself, and now Margot was certain they'd been properly introduced at one point, and she had forgotten about it. Which made Margot feel a bit ashamed of herself since Roxie was obviously someone you made a point of remembering.

"Sorry," she said, abashed. "I know we've met before, I recognize you, but I'm terrible with names."

Roxie waved a hand, dismissing Margot's apology. "Don't worry about it, but I thought you might like to see something we found in the family room."

Margot followed the other woman into the den, marveling at how she seemed to step weightlessly down the hallway, as if she had been designed to leave no part of herself behind. The family room looked much the same as it had when Margot and Wes had been there the day before, only now the books covered in blood and brain matter were all neatly lined on a white plastic sheet on the floor, spines facing up. Roxie stood in front of the sheet and put her hands on her hips.

"Notice anything?"

Standing beside Roxie, Margot was aware of her own height, and of the sweat making her shirt stick to her skin. She felt incredibly self-conscious all of a sudden, which wasn't like her. Normally she was completely unaware of herself at crime scenes, unless it was related to where she stepped or what she touched.

"They're the books from the shelf." Margot jutted her chin toward the obvious empty space over the chair Hector had been sitting in.

"What else?"

Margot was being tested and she wasn't sure if she liked it. Was Roxie sure she would notice, or was she anticipating that Margot would miss it, and waiting for her opportunity to gloat over what she'd found? A competitive instinct kicked in and Margot crouched down in front of the books, resting her forearms on her thighs and tilting her head sideways, hoping a different angle might help her unlock what it was Roxie was trying to show her.

And there it was, clear as day. It was so obvious Margot wondered how they could have possibly missed it earlier, but like with the children's bedrooms, it hadn't been what they were looking for.

"One of the spines is completely clean." She tapped her finger on a black leather-bound volume that had no title or author name on the spine. It, and the others from the same shelf, appeared to be photo albums. "Is this the order they were in on the shelf?"

"Mmhmm." Roxie nudged her with her knee and an unexpected warmth flared in Margot's belly. "Now look over here." Leading her over to the now-empty shelf, Margot immediately saw what Roxie was sharing this time. The top of the shelf had a clear line where the books had been, and a smattering of blood and body matter above it. But there was a line about three inches wide where one of the albums had clearly been missing when Hector shot himself, the whole space filled with the same pink and gray flecks.

Returning to the album, Margot picked it up carefully and turned it over in her hands.

The title *Family Memories* was embossed on the front in gold letters, but it was covered over in a thick, smeared layer of blood.

Someone had had this book out before the murders and put it away after Hector was dead.

Which naturally begged the question, *why?*

SEVENTEEN
FEBRUARY 4, 1982

Penngrove, California

Ed blew into the cupped palms of his hands and pulled the zipper of his jacket up around his face. It was chilly, the nighttime temperature bordering on freezing, but he knew he couldn't risk turning the car on. It was one thing to run it if he were driving around the block a few times, but he had settled in, watching the trailer's bedroom window carefully. Sitting in front of the home for hours, idling with his engine on, it would bring attention at some point.

He'd worried just sitting there might raise a few eyebrows, but what he'd learned in all his time doing this was that people only saw what they wanted to see, what they were looking to find. A man sitting in a dark car didn't draw attention because no one was looking at his car. They assumed it was empty. It also helped that he'd learned over the past few nights of driving through that the owners of the trailer across the way weren't home, and he had been able to park in their driveway without anyone being bothered.

It was a lot easier to hide in plain sight than most people realized, Ed had learned.

Still, it was getting fucking cold, and his ass had grown numb. If she didn't go to bed soon, he might call it a night, come back when it was a bit warmer. The temperature might prove to be a problem anyway. She normally slept with her window open to let in fresh air, but with such a chill, she might think twice.

If the window was closed, he told himself, he would go home.

If it was open, well. A sign was a sign.

After what felt like a decade of waiting, she finally turned off the lights, and the bedroom sank into darkness. No lamplight, no flickering TV glow. Ed checked his watch, and it was a few minutes after eleven, a bit late for her, but not by much.

He picked up the slip of paper on his dashboard, one he had already folded and unfolded so many times the paper was soft to the touch and almost see-through in places. *Sadie Beckett, 6070 Old Redwood Highway, Penngrove.* Her phone number was there as well, along with the billing information she had given, and finally her chosen message.

Attractive female, 30, seeks outdoorsy man for companionship. Must love hiking and trips to the beach! Looking for long conversations, and love. Must be over 30. Non-smoker.

Ed had the passage memorized by now, knew every word of it, just like he'd known all the others. Each syllable stalked him in his sleep. *Outdoorsy man for companionship.* Did she want a husband or a dog? Nothing about the ad gave him much of a sense of who Sadie was, but watching her these past few days told him there wasn't much outdoorsy about her. Hiking and walks on the beach? More like nights in front of the television set, and not so much as a walk around the block.

He wondered, often, why women felt the need to lie so blatantly in their personal ads. Did they think they could fake their way into a relationship with the perfect man, and once he figured out what was happening it would be too late because he was just so in love?

Women. They were so manipulative. Duplicitous. He thought about Kim and the way she had looked when they first met. She put so much effort into her hair, her makeup had always been precise, and her wardrobe carefully cultivated from trends in the latest fashion magazines.

Now he wasn't sure if she even looked in a mirror anymore. She looked rumpled and exhausted all the time, and while he understood that being with Megan all day was a tiring task, it didn't mean she had an excuse to completely give up on being a good wife.

Ed sighed.

He needed to keep Kim out of his mind right now, lest he get too distracted. There was work to be done, and his wife had no part in what came next. If anything, thinking about Kim would only diminish the thrill of what waited for him across the street.

He checked his watch. Fifteen minutes had passed since Sadie Beckett had turned out her lights. He would wait another thirty. He had been watching her over the past week and gathered from his observations that it didn't take Sadie too long to fall asleep. She never got up in the middle of the night to pace, or watch TV, or even go to the bathroom. She was one of those people who was out when she was out, and that's what he needed.

Thirty minutes later and not a flicker of light or movement from Sadie's trailer. He reached over into the back seat to where his small duffel bag was sitting in Megan's car seat. He dropped it into his lap and looked inside, making sure everything was where it needed to be. His balaclava sat on top of the bag.

Ever since the girl had gotten away from him six months earlier, he had wanted a way to protect himself. Just in case. He didn't anticipate letting another one get away, but between the girl and the man who had seen him in the alley, it was much too close. He'd really expected the man to identify him after it was obvious the girl was missing, but it had been months and nothing had happened.

Ed had gone from looking over his shoulder every time he saw a cop car or an officer on the street, to feeling more confident. Bolder.

He was hungry again, and the fear had faded enough he didn't want to wait. Sadie's ad had been all the urging he needed. She'd sounded so sweet, so happy on the phone. She'd laughed at his jokes when he teased her about the ad.

She was definitely the right one to break him out of his funk. He could tell from the way she made him feel on the phone that day, and even now, waiting for her, waiting to be with her, he was sure this was the perfect thing to feed his soul.

He touched every item in the bag. The gloves, the ropes, the tape. Every piece was a lesson learned from one of his previous girls. Sadie would be perfect, he wouldn't make any mistakes with her, he'd take his time, savor it all.

There were three different knives in the bag. The one he had used for the last two girls, and two new ones. One he had picked up at an estate sale from a hunter who had died; his family was clearing out a lot of real gems at a low price, and Ed had picked up some gear, and the beautifully kept gut-knife. He'd also grabbed some older toys and baby items to show Kim he hadn't wasted his time at the sale. Megan loved her gently used Jolly Jumper, and he had a new toy of his own to play with.

The third knife he'd gotten at Whole Earth Access on a day trip into the city, telling Kim he needed to go see a specialist for a rattle in the car. The rattle had miraculously been fixed for about the same cost as a new hunting knife.

He liked having the options now, and was eager to see what the new blades could offer him. Tonight would be a good night to play with them, let them taste blood for the first time, show him what they could do.

Zipping the bag shut, he pulled on the balaclava and scanned the street one way and then the other, making sure he was alone and wouldn't be interrupted. No one stirred, not a soul was out walking their dog. The chill of the night air was working in his favor here, hopefully his luck would hold.

Stealing out into the darkness, he moved through the deepest shadows where porchlights didn't reach, and soon he was standing under Sadie's window. The cold evening hadn't deterred her from her routine. Her window was slightly ajar, only the screen blocking him from entering. Her window was big and, as if by invitation, was right above her large generator. He climbed up onto the generator with ease, and peered inside.

Sadie was in her bed, wrapped tightly in her floral comforter, with one creamy white leg kicked out.

It was as if she couldn't decide if she was too hot or too cold.

Ed zipped open the bag and pulled out one of the new knives, using it to silently slice open the mesh screen. The blade went through the screen like it was hot butter, he couldn't believe how easy it was to get access.

He crawled in, lowering himself onto a dresser below the window, his foot tipping over a small ceramic jewelry dish, which clattered its contents onto the floor. He froze, expecting this to be the mistake, the thing that would ruin all his perfect planning. Sadie didn't stir, her even breathing remained consistent.

Ed let out a little breath and pulled himself the rest of the way into the room, lowering his bulky weight and the duffel bag to the floor. He rifled through it once again, this time with-drawing a length of black nylon rope. Then, with one last steadying breath, he walked to the foot of the bed and yanked the blanket off Sadie's sleeping figure.

Maybe it would have been easier to climb on top of her first, to avoid the risk of struggle, but Ed loved that one perfect moment of fear when he saw them recognize him for what he was.

Sadie, rattled out of her slumber, blinked up at him. He saw it, the moment realization dawned on her, and she saw what waited for her in the shadowed recesses of her bedroom.

Ed held the knife up and pressed a finger to his knit-covered lips, signaling silence. Then he told her his favorite lie.

"Sadie, if you're a good girl, a quiet girl, I won't hurt you, OK?"

Her eyes, slick with tears, widened in horror, but she nodded mutely.

Then Ed went to work.

EIGHTEEN

Margot and Wes stood over the open pages of the Ramirez *Family Memories* photo album, slowly scanning each photo as if one might stick out, with someone who was so obviously the killer they could call off the investigation then and there.

Of course, this wasn't a weekly crime drama, and the villain of the piece was not leering up at them from the glossy photos. Or he might have been, but nothing they were seeing gave any indication that was the case.

Instead, the book was an unremarkable collection of family moments, afforded unusual gravitas because almost everyone in them was dead now. There were vacation photos from a camping trip that looked to be near Tahoe. A birthday party for Mateo, where he seemed to be about six and had evidently been going through a big *Iron Man* phase, given the decorations. Christmas, with both children opening gifts and wearing pajamas along with their gleeful expressions.

It was all so painfully normal, these expressions of familial happiness. Nothing in the pages indicated a dark family secret, or gave any hint that the Ramirezes were the kind of monsters who chained their children to their beds.

Most importantly, nothing explained why four people were now dead in a grisly mass homicide that defied all logical reasoning.

The books on either side of this volume were much the same. Family photos through the years, sorted in neat chronological order, with tidy handwriting next to each one that described the scene with a brief sentence. *Mateo's birthday, June 25. Valentina junior prom! Mateo's first soccer game.* In those photos Margot saw Mateo with big white teeth, the front two too large for his mouth as if they'd just grown in, wearing a uniform so fresh and crisp it looked like it was right off the rack. He was surrounded by a handful of other little boys and girls, and a man who appeared to be about thirty-five, wearing a T-shirt that bore the team's name, *Scorpions*, in bright red font. The coach maybe? Probably another dad.

Margot pinched the bridge of her nose, trying to chase away the headache that threatened to catch up with her at any moment. The house was stifling hot and smelled of aged blood. She turned to Wes. "Let's bag all of these and take them to the station. I'm not seeing much right now, but there has to be a reason this volume was out and then replaced before we got to the scene."

"And here I thought we were looking at these photos as a nice bit of brain bleach," Wes retorted with a wry grin.

She couldn't decide if she adored him or wanted to murder him, and the answer changed every day, several times a day.

"We'll get them all sent back to you by the end of the day," Roxie offered.

"Thank you." Margot tried to smile but it came out as a grimace, which was the best she was able to do these days. She turned to Wes, who was handing the photo album over to Roxie. "Let's go talk to Mateo again." In truth she wanted any excuse to get out of the house, whose walls felt like they were closing in on her with every passing moment.

The memory of Hector, Evangeline, Valentina, and Emily lingered, chasing Margot's footsteps even though their bodies were long since gone. They needed her to solve this, to find the missing pieces and put it all together, to give them the justice they deserved.

But everything she was discovering about this case made her wonder just what kind of answers she was going to find as she continued to dig.

She called Mateo's social worker from the car to coordinate a meet-up with the Ramirez cousin who had taken custody of Mateo for the duration of their investigation. She wasn't sure if that would be the long-term solution for him, or if perhaps there were plans built into the Ramirez parents' wills that would dictate a different home for him, but for now they at least knew he was being taken care of.

The social worker called her back a few minutes later, letting her know that Mateo wasn't at the cousin's house, but was actually at a community center not far from where the Ramirez family lived. Margot exchanged an uneasy glance with Wes after hanging up and directing him to their next stop.

"I know we talk a lot about how grief looks different for everyone, and no two people grieve the same, but don't you think it's a bit weird this kid is playing at a community center two days after his entire family gets murdered?"

Wes shrugged. "I think a nine-year-old isn't going to have the capacity necessary to process something this big, and is probably going to look toward the familiar during a really difficult time." He turned to look at her, then looked back to the road. "This kid bothers you, doesn't he?"

It was funny to hear him asking her that, because on Sunday night he'd had much the same reaction to Mateo's first interview. The boy was hard to work out, but Wes had seemed to be more bothered than she was. Margot stared out the window, watching the perfectly manicured lawns glide by. What Mateo was, she thought, was as much a victim as he was a survivor, and there was no way to know how someone like that *should* behave.

"I think something happened to those kids, and I think it could make a lot of sense if he didn't feel particularly bad his parents were dead. I'm not saying he killed them," Wes qualified, "I'm just saying that he weirds me out a little. That's allowed, isn't it? I mean we both saw what was going on in that house before they were killed. The kid can't be perfectly normal and well-adjusted after that. I guess I don't know what point I'm trying to make here. You agree that he seemed *off*, and I think it's a bit weird he's out kicking a soccer ball around or whatever."

Margot nodded, still gazing out the window. They were almost on the same page. "I don't think it's easy to know what normal looks like for a kid after all the shit he's been through. But yes, I agree, he's a bit unsettling."

What she didn't add was how *unsettling* she and Justin must have seemed in the wake of what had happened to them. Wes seemed to register what her meaning was without the words, though.

Wes didn't say anything. He parked the car in the small lot in front of the community center. It was everything one might expect from a community center in an affluent neighborhood: clean, brightly painted, with a well-maintained lawn and plenty of space out back for kids to play on the perfectly tidy soccer fields and the pristine tennis and basketball courts.

Margot felt a slight pang of jealousy from her inner child, who hadn't gotten anything like this in her own upbringing. She'd played at the school playground, skinning her knees on uneven concrete, and spent most of her summers on a hand-me-down bike one of their neighbors had outgrown. Ed had been thrifty, finding her plenty of decent-quality toys and clothes from garage and estate sales. He had *loved* garage sales.

Only later had she learned the real reason he spent so much time hunting through other people's junk on weekends.

Her stomach churned uneasily as she remembered.

They exited the car, getting slapped in the face by the heat. It did nothing to brighten her already dismal mood, and the aggressively sunny day and cheerfully lit community center felt like a personal affront to all the grim thoughts circulating in her head.

Didn't the day know that she wanted to be miserable?

Once again, she was met by the shocking shift in temperature as they entered the building, and here the air conditioning was set much too cold for comfort, causing goosebumps to erupt instantly on Margot's skin.

She and Wes walked up to the front desk where a teenage girl was sitting, reading a book with her white wireless headphones tucked into both ears. The girl didn't even look up as they approached, hunched over the desk, her whole focus on the book. Margot was torn between annoyance and admiration over how absorbed the kid was. She almost hated to interrupt.

Wes set his badge on the open pages of the book and the girl jumped, knocking her headphones out of her ears. She had the enviable perfect skin of youth, her dark complexion accented by a smattering of freckles. Her afro was pulled back in one big puff at the back of her head. Her cheeks flushed. "Wow, sorry. I didn't hear you guys come in." Bass thumped from the headphones she had knocked onto the desktop.

Wes smiled, turning the charm up to twelve, more than a poor sixteen-year-old could be expected to handle. The girl's blush deepened. "My name is Detective Wes Fox, this is my partner, Detective Margot Phalen. We're looking for a boy who is supposed to be here right now, according to his guardian."

Margot held her phone up, showing the girl a picture of

Mateo. The girl nodded vigorously, pushing her desk chair back and coming around to their side of the desk. She was taller than Margot had expected, given her terrible reading posture earlier. Now that she was standing, she was almost as tall as Margot.

"You guys are looking for whoever killed Mateo's family?" she asked.

The story had hit the news the previous morning, so it wasn't exactly surprising that someone with a connection to the family would have already heard about it. Margot was more relieved that the media hadn't gotten all the details of the case. She would need to send Sebastian Klein a gift basket for not reporting the story as what it was: a massacre. He had been leaving messages for her and Wes all day, though, so she knew he wanted more.

Seb never used his knowledge of who she was as a bartering chip when it came to their investigations, which Margot appreciated, and made her more inclined to share information with him. He was too young to have been around for the heyday of Ed's murders, but Seb was a second-generation crime reporter for the *Sentinel*, and his father Percy had been the one to cover the murders and Ed's arrest.

In a way, she and Seb had both grown up with the murders hanging over their family life. Percy had destroyed his marriage in the name of following the story, and for Margot, well... She shook off all thoughts of Sebastian Klein and the reports on the Ramirez family murders and tried to focus on the girl.

"We're not really at liberty to discuss an ongoing investigation," Margot said.

The girl from the front desk nodded eagerly. "Totally understand. It's all so *sad* though."

"Did you know Valentina Ramirez?" Wes asked.

"Not really. She picked Mateo up sometimes, but we went to different schools." She gave a frown. "Mateo adored her, though. He's a tough cookie, but he's got to be crushed."

Margot bit the inside of her cheek. The girl led them to a door at the end of the hallway. She rapped twice on the glass, then opened the door, showing them into a small room that looked like it might be a library. The walls were lined with low shelves at a good height for children, and several circular tables were in the center of the room, with bright orange plastic chairs surrounding them. At one of the tables, Mateo was hunched over a paper, a spread of markers around him. He barely looked up when they entered the room, as if their arrival was meaningless to him. Wes's comments hung heavy over her, and she looked at the child the way her partner did, wondering if there was something more to him that she was choosing to ignore, something unsettling.

Across from him was a man in his mid-thirties, wearing a maroon ball cap with a stitched Scorpion on the front. He looked familiar, but Margot couldn't put her finger on it. He was pale, and auburn hair stuck out from under his hat, clashing with the maroon. He had a distinctly dad-like quality to him, from the misguided fashion to the gently rounded gut.

"Rog, these are some detectives that wanted to see Mateo."

The man turned and gave them a cold, assessing stare. "Thanks, Jazz."

The girl was already ducking out of the room and heading back to her station at the front desk, or more accurately back to whatever book she was reading.

Alone in the room with Mateo and the man, Wes made the first move, which was fine with Margot, because she wanted to watch. Wes extended his hand to the stranger. All the while Mateo didn't look up, as focused on his drawing as the girl at the desk had been on her reading. It was as if he were so lost in his own world, what was happening in the real one ceased to exist.

Margot recognized the familiar appearance of disassociation. She was no stranger to it herself.

The man stood and shook Wes's hand, looking like he might

be squeezing a bit too hard for a friendly meeting. Wes didn't
flinch. Margot didn't bother to introduce herself, she kept her
focus locked on the little boy in the middle of all this, practically
willing him to do something normal, to prove Wes and her
wrong.

"I'm Roger Davis." The man's initial coldness was beginning to fade away and Margot turned her attention to him as his
tight shoulders loosened and he settled into a more relaxed
stance. She shook his hand, and his grip was loose, palms a little
clammy. She wasn't sure if he was less aggressive with her than
he'd been with Wes because she was a woman, or because his
hostility was dissipating. Either way, she didn't like him.

"Roger, what's your relationship with Mateo Ramirez and
the Ramirez family?" Margot asked.

"I'm Mateo's soccer coach, and our sons have been friends
for a long time."

Recognition clicked, and Margot recalled the photos she
and Wes had been looking at earlier, with one featuring Mateo's
first soccer game. At least that much seemed to check out.

"Is there a reason you're here with him today rather than
him being home with his guardian?" she asked. She meant to
make it sound emotionless, but it came out clipped and cold.

There was an initial flash of defensiveness in his expression,
but he schooled it quickly, his face falling back to a neutral
blank. "I tried to find out where he was staying, in case I could
offer to take him in. He's really close with my son, Jason, and
like I said, our families have known each other a long time. I
thought it would be good for him to see a familiar face right
now. That woman they have him with is a cousin of Evangeline's, he'd never met her before. She seems fine, but still." His
voice drifted off slightly as he looked down at Mateo. "You want
the kid to be with someone they know. Someone who cares."

It didn't escape Margot's notice that he *hadn't* previously
mentioned the families being close, only the boys, but she had

no reason to believe he was making that up. The Ramirez family had obviously had a social structure outside their home. The presence of Emily Potter in the house showed that clearly enough. She did wonder, however, how all these people the family was supposedly so close to managed to miss the signs of what had been happening inside those walls.

"How long did you say you've been close with the family?" Wes asked.

He hadn't.

"Oh, since the boys got into school, probably? Four or five years. We don't live too far from each other."

Wes asked for Roger's address, and the man hesitated only slightly before giving it. Margot wasn't so familiar with the Forest Hill area to know the distance between the Davis and Ramirez homes, but had to assume it wasn't a big gap. Everything here felt like it was its own tight-knit little world, set completely apart from the rest of the city. The more time she spent within the wealthy, polished confines, the more she wanted to be back in her own neighborhood with its dirty sidewalks and air that smelled forever of shrimp from the nearby Chinese restaurant.

"We need to have a quick chat with Mateo," Wes said.

"If you don't mind, I'd like to stay with him. He doesn't have another adult here, and I want to make sure things all stay above board. I'm sure you understand."

Margot and Wes exchanged a quick glance. They didn't particularly want to ask their questions in front of Roger, but they had to talk to him, and if they pushed back against Roger's request, he might try to call in CFS, or demand to have Mateo's legal guardian or lawyer present. Mateo wasn't being questioned as a person of interest, they just needed insight from him to move their investigation forward.

"That's fine, but we'd appreciate it if you don't try to guide him or answer on his behalf," Wes replied.

Roger nodded eagerly, an only-here-to-help expression on his face that reminded Margot of a golden retriever. "Of course, of course, don't let me step on your toes." He turned his attention to the boy, placing a big hand on Mateo's small shoulder. "Mateo, hey buddy, these nice people are here to talk to you."

Mateo continued to color, not glancing up even once to acknowledge their presence or act as if he was aware of what was going on. When they'd interviewed him at the station he'd been a bit withdrawn, but that was to be expected in the circumstances. His behavior now, however, felt different than before, as if he were intentionally shutting things out and ignoring them, rather than being emotionally detached from his surroundings.

"Mateo, do you remember us?" Margot asked.

He nodded, though he remained completely focused on his art. Margot glanced down at the paper beneath his markers and saw that he was drawing a picture of what appeared to be his family: a woman, a man, a girl and boy. But he was vigorously scribbling red over the top of everyone but the boy.

As art went, it was a pretty literal interpretation.

"We need to ask you a few questions, can you put your marker down for a couple of minutes?" Margot pressed on.

The marker went still, and for a long moment Margot wasn't sure if he was going to comply or not. Roger had stepped back to the side of the room with Wes, but she was aware of him hovering, tension radiating from him as if he wanted nothing more than to prove useful in this scenario but couldn't quite figure out how without overstepping, so he did nothing.

Good, he would probably only make things worse.

Finally, after an eternity, Mateo put his red marker down, the tips of his fingers stained from the ink, making it look like he had blood on his hands, and stared up at them.

There was a lost, haunted expression on his face, and his eyes were glassy and barely focused.

Margot pulled out one of the plastic chairs across the table from him and sat down, while Wes and Roger remained standing, confined to the periphery. She wanted all of Mateo's attention on her. "How are you doing, Mateo?" she asked him.

He shrugged, his small bony shoulders lifting almost up to his ears.

"Is everything OK at your... cousin's house?" She wasn't exactly sure what the relationship between him and his guardian was, but cousin seemed the closest fit for someone from an extended family.

"Yeah," he said, his voice coming out for the first time since they'd entered the room. "She's nice. She has a cat."

"You like cats?"

Mateo nodded and started playing with the hem of his shirt. "Yeah. We couldn't have one though."

"Why not?"

"Dad said I was too sick. But I don't think I was. I'm OK now."

Margot resisted the urge to look back over her shoulder at Wes, but she didn't want to break the tenuous connection she'd forged. "You had to take a lot of pills, didn't you?"

Margot was aware of Roger shuffling slightly, but thankfully he stayed quiet. His presence, though, was like a force of vibration coming from the other side of the room and it was starting to make Margot's skin prickle.

Mateo nodded at her question. "Lots."

"This is a tough question, so don't worry if you don't know the answer, OK? But, Mateo, do you know *why* you were taking those pills."

"Dad said I was sick."

"Did you feel sick?"

"Yeah. When I took the pills. Valentina, too. She took them a bunch, but Mom said she stopped being sick when I got older. And then I got sick."

Margot's palms began to sweat. She darted a quick glance over at Roger, really wishing he wasn't in the room right now and wondering how to ask what she needed to without giving him gossip to take back to the neighborhood, or potentially share with the newspapers. She couldn't outright ask Mateo about the handcuffs, not here, but maybe there was still a way she could find out more about them.

"Were your parents very strict?" she asked. "About getting out of bed at night? I know you said you sometimes liked to sneak downstairs."

Mateo, whose attention had been wandering, more focused on the hem of his shirt or his shoelaces, suddenly looked at her dead-on, his expression sharp and piercing. For a moment Margot felt the weight of years' and years' worth of anxiety and pain leveled in that one expression. Her heart hurt for him. "Yes. You can't get out of bed at night. Not for anything." His hand had reflexively gone to his wrist and Margot's stomach churned with bile. What had they put this poor boy through?

"Did you ever tell anyone about what happened at bedtime?"

He stopped touching his wrists and his chin drooped, eyes focused on the table again. "No."

"Do you think Valentina told anyone?"

Mateo shook his head. "She was too afraid."

"Afraid of what?"

"If she said anything, she might get sick again."

Margot gave Wes a quick look and while his face maintained its composure she could see all her own emotions warring in his eyes. Confusion, anger, concern.

"What does that mean, Mateo?"

He had shut down again though, his features masking whatever he was feeling.

"I wish she had just stayed in bed like she was supposed to."

NINETEEN

Margot welcomed the blistering heat once they were outside again, because a chill had spread inside her, clinging to her bones, threatening to keep warmth at bay for the rest of her life. They were silent as they exited the community center and got into Wes's car. It wasn't until he started the engine, and the air conditioning began to blast, that Margot finally shook off her stupor and spoke.

"We need to talk to their family doctor. Evelyn said those drugs were for things like heart disease, kidney issues, serious illnesses that should have put a kid in the hospital." She stopped to make a note on the little notebook she carried. "We should check hospital records for both kids, too. I'm betting they have a laundry list of visits to different places, but not for broken bones. Nothing that would draw attention."

"What are you thinking?"

"I'm not sure yet. It might be a bit of a stretch, but have you ever heard of Munchausen by proxy?"

Wes leaned back in his seat and gave her an incredulous look. "The thing where people pretend their loved ones are sick so they can get sympathy or whatever, get attention?"

Margot nodded. "I'm not an expert or anything, but if they had one sick kid who suddenly started to get better at the same time another one got sick, and now that they're gone, he's not sick anymore? It feels a bit suspicious, doesn't it? And Mateo said if Valentina said anything she might get sick again? What does that even mean?"

"Might be a stretch, but it's certainly worth looking into. It's hard to imagine someone doing that to begin with, let alone to two kids, though. It could also tie in to why they were keeping them chained in bed at night. I think there's a lot of evidence pointing toward straight-up abuse. But the drugs complicate things. And it could all point to motive. What are you thinking, that someone found out what they were doing and wanted to off them? Why kill the girls, then?"

Margot shrugged. "It's only a theory, and maybe not a great one, but I think it's worth exploring. I think talking to the doctor might give us a little more potential insight into whatever the fuck was going on behind closed doors at that house. It doesn't explain why Emily and Valentina were killed—that still feels more like an attack by someone who didn't know the Ramirez family had a son. Like I said, not perfect, but it's a thread and it should be followed."

"Not like we have any other leads to go off."

"We're going to need to put out a call for information, you know that, right?"

Wes shuddered dramatically. "I was hoping we could ignore that, I don't know if I'm up for a million tips from people who are psychic or think their ex-boyfriend probably killed them."

"Well, like you said, it's not as if we have any other leads. And don't forget, Ted Bundy's *current* girlfriend once called in a tip about him, and no one listened to her. They aren't always nutjobs."

"Just mostly."

"Everyone needs a hobby, Wesley."

· · ·

When they returned to the precinct, Leon was on his way out of the building, humming a song Margot couldn't quite catch. He spotted them and made a beeline down the steps in their direction.

"Phalen. Fox." Quick nods of acknowledgment all around.

This close Margot could smell his aftershave, a warm, powdery scent with the faintest edge of spice. It smelled like every nice old man she'd ever met.

"Hey, Leon." Wes nodded.

"Margot, you busy?" Leon asked.

"Oh, you know. Solving murders. Nothing major."

"Well, are you *actively* solving one right now?"

"I have some calls to make, but no, we're not about to go throw some bracelets on someone. What's up?"

"Thought you might like to come back out to the park with me. Ranger Abbott said they found something interesting, might give us a little more to work with on our Jane Doe. Abbott just called me. Didn't give much detail but it seems worth the drive. You coming?"

Margot glanced quickly at Wes, not exactly asking permission, but not wanting to deal with a moody partner when she returned.

"I'll start calling some hospitals," was all he said.

For him to let her go without so much as a snarky comment meant he was trying to be nice. And if he was trying to be nice, it was because he felt bad about the phone calls she'd been getting.

Sorry your serial killer dad is back in your life, go enjoy a stabbing victim to clear your mind.

It was Wes's version of kindness, so she accepted it. "Call me if you find anything," she said sternly.

"Yes, Mom."

Margot didn't bother to give him a proper eat-shit-and-die glare in response, instead she followed Leon as he jogged down the steps and headed toward his parked car. Leon was quick for an old guy and Margot had to hustle to keep up.

"Did Abbott explain what he thinks it is we need to see?" she asked, climbing in the passenger side once the lock was disengaged.

"He was not exactly forthcoming, no. Just said we should get out there. And I gathered there was some sense of urgency on his part, so I decided it might be best to go now rather than mucking about on the phone."

He started the car and as usual an audiobook was playing. This one sounded different from the one he'd been listening to when they originally headed out to the crime scene, making Margot wonder how many of them he got through on a daily basis. Rather than asking him to turn it off, Margot enjoyed the distraction of listening to the unfolding romance between a rakish duke and a quick-tongued dressmaker with a scandalous family history. It was nice to think about something other than her own case for a few minutes.

She could see why Leon liked to listen to these. It might not be her thing under normal circumstances, but there was some-thing genuinely soothing about listening to such frothy and friv-olous problems, given the real-life scenarios she normally found herself in.

"This is a new one," she said, not really asking a question.

Leon nodded. "I'm on a bit of a Loretta Chase kick right now. Historicals aren't normally my thing, but she sure can write."

"Historicals? There's actually a name for these? Aren't they all just bodice-rippers?" Margot chuckled so he'd know she didn't mean any harm by the statement.

"My dear, if there's a niche, the romance world has a subgenre for it. Historical, contemporary, paranormal…"

"Paranormal?"

"Vampires, werewolves."

"Ah yes, nothing more romantic than swooning over monsters."

Leon smirked. "Sports romance, reverse harem romance, billionaire romance. You name it."

"What are your favorites?"

"I'm usually a contemporary guy, but my wife loves a good historical, so she passes the best ones along to me."

"Not paranormal?"

"*Not* paranormal. I see enough monsters in real life, thank you."

Margot smiled to herself and leaned her head back against the seat and closed her eyes, letting the narration drown out the thoughts that had been hounding her all day. For a little while she didn't need to think about Ed or Mateo or anything but a grumpy duke and the scandalous dressmaker who was winning his heart.

They were in the park before Margot knew it, and Leon guided the car to a familiar lot, near the rangers' main building. Since they had removed all but a small tarp covering the primary crime scene further down the path, there was no need to keep the main trail closed to visitors, so the parking lot was bustling with cars as people laced up hiking boots and checked to make sure they had enough water to go on a walk.

It was a mix of city slickers who thought they were about to hike the Pacific Crest Trail, and more realistic walkers who were out in tennis shoes and sunhats, pushing big strollers.

Margot and Leon headed into the ranger station, and Leon greeted the young ranger at the desk with a flash of his badge, his demeanor now more focused and professional. "We're here to speak to Ranger Abbott. I'm Detective Telly, this is Detective Phalen. He called us."

"Yeah, he said to expect you. Follow me." She ducked under the desk and came into the common area, and another ranger appeared from seemingly nowhere to take her place at the desk.

The younger ranger headed toward the exit and Margot and Leon trailed behind her. She was so focused in her movement that she didn't look back over her shoulder to see if they were coming, and Margot didn't want to get lost. Her sense of direction, especially in nature, was borderline terrible. She needed Google Maps to get around San Francisco still, and she'd lived in the city six years.

The ranger headed toward the main walking path, and there was Ranger Abbott, so tall he practically blended in with the trees, waiting at the mouth of the trail. He was shuffling uneasily, and his skin looked pale. Not good signs.

Margot and Leon approached him, and the younger ranger left, heading back toward the office, without so much as a word in parting. She was all business and no bedside manner whatsoever. Margot wondered if park rangers needed to be nice, because if they did, that one wasn't going to make it very far in this line of work.

"Detectives," Abbott said in greeting.

"Good to see you again, Simon," Margot said, hoping he wasn't about to make her regret coming on this excursion.

He nodded grimly and did not return the platitude. *Definitely* a bad sign. She didn't know a lot about Simon, but in her brief exposure to him had found him to be the aw-shucks-please-and-thank-you-ma'am type. Something was up if he was being quick and businesslike with the greetings.

"You mentioned finding something?" Leon urged.

"Yeah, you're going to want to come with me."

Without another word he headed down the trail. Though the parking lot had been filled to the brim with cars, it was clear that the walkers had all departed at staggered times, because the trail itself was relatively devoid of people, giving them some illusion of privacy as they walked. Abbott remained silent and focused, and Margot expected him to stop walking when they got close to where the makeshift tent and caution tape were set up for the original crime scene.

His shoulders tensed as they passed, but he kept walking, his big strides forcing Margot to walk at double speed to keep up. Even Leon seemed to be hustling a bit more than usual.

"Ranger Abbott, could you give us some idea of where we're going?" Leon asked.

"Think it's best you see it for yourself." He faced forward, not turning to look at them, just letting the wind bring the words back as he continued marching.

It took about twenty minutes for them to get to their destination, and Margot had absolutely worn the wrong shoes to go on a hike. By the time Abbott stopped walking, her baby toe was screaming at her. Even the most comfortable heeled booties were not intended to be worn on a backwoods hike. Whatever he had to show them better fucking be worth it.

The first thing she noticed was the blockade that had been placed a short distance from the primary path. It was park-issued, not flashy, basically something official to tell day-hikers that this particular path was closed for repairs or maintenance.

Margot's heart sank.

She didn't think there were any repairs happening down that path.

Abbott began to speak then, his deep voice laced with tension. "Found her on my morning rounds, right before I called you. Didn't want to make a big fuss, just wanted to get you guys out here, then we can call the ambulance. But I thought you ought to see it before we start another circus, y'know?"

Margot didn't need clarification, didn't need him to explain what he meant by *her*. There was another victim.

She and Leon followed Abbott up a steep incline with loose rocks. It was quickly apparent why this might not be as popular a trail. Even though it was well kept by the park staff, the area was more densely wooded, and looked a lot less inviting to casual hikers. Margot focused on keeping her balance and didn't act tough when Leon offered her an arm to steady her. "You found her all the way out here?" Margot asked, trying not to sound like she was struggling for breath. "What time was that?"

"Probably about two hours ago. Was just doing my rounds. Gotta walk all the trails regularly, make sure there's nothing out here that can hurt anyone, make sure no one has gotten lost. It's part of the job. But there's so many trails we sometimes only see the offshoots every couple of weeks." He kept his attention on the walk ahead of them. "Just because a path doesn't get used often doesn't mean it doesn't get used ever, y'know? Over here." He pointed to a place Margot couldn't see yet, but when she got to his level, she spotted the copse of Scots pines, and in the undergrowth was something white. "Was the smell that got me first."

There was another park sign here, closing off the area from the opposite direction.

"What time did you say you found this?" Leon asked.

"About two hours ago," Abbott repeated.

"And it wasn't reported by anyone else?"

Abbott shook his head. "Nah, like I said, this isn't a popular trail. Rock gets really loose after it rains, especially. People prefer the easier paths."

True in life as it was in crime scenes.

Margot followed Abbott off the path and down the hill into the more thickly wooded area where the white form was lying. The closer she got the more evident it became that the lump of clothing on the ground was, as she expected, a body.

Leon was close behind her, and once they were on more solid footing Abbott kept his distance, either because he didn't want to risk contaminating the crime scene, or because he didn't want to get up close and personal with another body.

Might have been a bit of both. Margot wouldn't have blamed him.

The body was already largely decomposed, having passed over the bloat stage and moving onward down the road to skeletonization. The corpse's skin had grown paper thin, entirely eaten away in places by both decay and probably assistance from local wildlife and insects. Bone had begun to show through, with blackened clumps of tissue still clinging to the exposed areas. White teeth grinned out of lips that had peeled back and almost completely vanished, and Margot noted one of the corpse's teeth had a gold crown on it.

Given the tone of what skin was left, it was hard to determine race at first glance, but based on the thick, black hair that remained, tied in a long braid draped over the body's shoulder, Margot was betting the victim was either Asian, or possibly Native American. While the body was in poor condition, there were enough clues left to indicate she had once been a woman. Decaying breast fat and muscle stained the front of her once-white shirt. She no longer had eyeballs or a nose, so distinctive characteristics were hard to come by, but she did still have all her teeth. That, and the gold crown, would hopefully be enough to help them identify her.

Age was also tricky to guess, but there was no gray in the woman's hair, and she was still wearing a pair of Nike Air 1 sneakers, something typically favored by a younger demographic. Margot was no expert, but she'd put money on Evelyn confirming the body was probably in her early to mid-twenties.

Younger than the corpse they'd found the previous night, but close enough they could certainly be related. The general physical appearances of the women were very different as well, the first one being blonde, this one with black hair. Though it would be impossible to guess how much this woman had weighed merely by looking at her now, her frame was slight, she'd been fairly small in life.

When she'd first started working homicide, these scenes had always made her think of Ed. But over time, the crimes all started to look and feel distinct to her, so usually murders didn't chase up any recollections of her father's handiwork.

Today was different.

Today, she couldn't help but think about Ed's supposed seventy-seventh victim, and how she could have been just like this woman in so many ways.

"We'll have to get the ME out to have a look, but seems to me she's been here a few weeks at least, maybe more than a month," Margot said. "But with it being so wet and humid out here, especially with all the heat this week, it's hard to really know."

Leon nodded, leaning over the body but avoiding touching her. His nose wrinkled. Even from where Margot was standing a few feet away the smell of the body radiated out, the stench of liquified organs and rotting flesh.

"Did anyone check this area after we found the initial body?" she asked.

"There was a peripheral search, probably a half mile in each direction," Leon said. "I don't think anyone came this far."

"This one has been here longer. There's always a chance they're unrelated, but seems a lot more likely to me we've potentially found someone's preferred dumping ground." She hefted a sigh, because this would mean lots of extensive searching in the woods, getting in cadaver dogs, and also the inevitable way the press would want to pivot and turn two bodies into a serial killer.

They didn't know that yet. The first victim had been stabbed, and it was impossible to tell how this one had died, there simply wasn't enough left of her to make the assessment without expert help. Evelyn could check for knife scrapes on bone, or see if there were bullet wounds anywhere that Margot wasn't seeing.

Still, two bodies found in as many days, both left in a public space, with no easy way to trace who had been coming and going in the area. It was a fucking nightmare.

Margot crouched, careful to keep her balance on the incline, her gaze drifting over the nearby ground. She hoped, perhaps, to see a wallet, a purse, something that might give her a sense of who this woman had been in life, and how she'd come to be here.

What Margot understood, though, possibly better than anyone else, was that there was rarely a good reason victims like this ended up where they were. Nothing this woman had done in her life should have taken her down this particular path. Maybe she smiled at the wrong man, loved the wrong man, maybe she parted her hair in a way that appealed to him. There were dozens of reasons she could have been singled out, and none of them had been her fault.

Just like Ed's supposed victim seventy-seven.

These women deserved justice, and they deserved answers. Margot wanted that for this woman, and, she knew deep in her gut as she straightened and looked over the body, she wanted it for Seventy-Seven, too.

TWENTY

Hours later, Margot sat at her kitchen counter, a takeout order of dim sum still in a plastic bag beside her, and her cell phone resting on the faux marble. She'd been staring at it for a good fifteen minutes, trying to work up the courage to call Ed's lawyer.

She hadn't mentioned her plan to Wes, not sure if he'd applaud her for it, or try to talk her out of it. She wasn't really sure which way her own internal critic was leaning at this point, if she was being honest with herself. It was easy to be noble and want to fight for justice when there was a literal dead body in front of her, but slightly less so when it was pork buns.

Picking up the phone, she opened the recent calls list, looking at the lawyer's number, labeled SHITTY LAWYER, then switched over to her contact list instead. She scrolled quickly, her fingers working almost entirely on their own, until she stopped, thumb hovering, and hit call.

One ring, two rings. She was about to change her mind and hang up, when a masculine, not-too-deep, voice said, "Meg... Margot?"

Her breath hitched. So few people had known her well

enough as Megan to still use her old name as the default. But one person, and only one, could still get away with calling her that.

"Hi Andrew."

All the tension she'd been carrying, all the fear, worry, and uncertainty, melted away at the sound of his voice. Special Agent Andrew Rhodes had been the man who upended her life, ruined the perfect fairy tale she thought she was living in. He'd also been the man to end the nightmare of Ed Finch and put the Classified Killer behind bars once and for all.

"It has been ages, kid. How are you doing? Is everything OK? Your brother?"

Her brother, Justin, who had become David in his attempt at a fresh start, had never warmed to Andrew the way Margot had. It wasn't so much that Justin had wanted Ed to get away with everything; he'd been younger than Margot when their father was arrested, and the destruction of their family had hit him harder. Margot wasn't sure he ever forgave Andrew, even though he understood the necessity.

She also sometimes got the sense Justin resented her for going into law enforcement, though it was getting harder and harder to know what Justin's specific resentments were, anymore. He had grown from an angry boy into an angry man.

"He's fine. Has a baby now, can you believe it?" Margot wanted to keep the conversation here, in the light airy atmosphere of friends catching up after a long separation, but knew perfectly well it couldn't last. She'd called Andrew for a reason. Try as she might, the decision to see Ed wasn't something she could come to on her own, and if anyone could give her an honest response as to whether or not she should go, it would be the man who knew Ed better than anyone else alive.

"Wow, good for him. And you, you're OK? I haven't talked to you in... a year?" Sounds in the background of his line grew quieter, like he was moving from one room to another to speak with her privately.

"It's been a while," she admitted. Without realizing it, she began to chew on her thumbnail, a bad habit she picked up around the time of Ed's arrest, and something she thought she had stopped doing thanks to years and years of therapy.

At the heart of it, that's why she didn't talk to Andrew often. He'd been so good to her, so lovely through the course of the trial and everything that came after. Even in the book he'd written about Ed, she knew he'd been gentle about descriptions of her family, careful to keep the shadow of blame off her mother.

But he was still a tether to her past, something that kept her connected to Ed and everything he'd done, and whenever they were in the same room, or even speaking over the phone, she was a little girl again, learning the hideous truth about her father.

"Are you really OK, Margot?" he asked, his voice dipping low, secretive.

Margot tried to picture him, in his home in Berkeley. He had kids, she remembered that, but they'd be grown up now, most likely moved out. She realized how little she'd asked him about his own life in their conversations over the years, and now it was much too late to try to be friends with him.

"No. Did you know he was back?" she asked, cutting right to the chase, dissolving the lovely fake atmosphere of small talk.

"Ed?"

"Who else?"

"What do you mean, *back*?"

"He's at San Quentin now. Transferred in this month. Did you know?"

Andrew sighed, "Yes, they told me."

Margot's grip on her phone tightened, a white-hot rage briefly stealing all sense of reason. She wanted to throw the phone across the room, wanted to scream at Andrew, to wrap her hands around his throat and squeeze for keeping something like this from her.

She took a deep breath, then closed her eyes and took another until the anger dissipated enough that she felt she could speak comfortably.

"Didn't you think I might want to know?" Her jaw hurt from being so firmly clenched. In those years following the arrest, he'd been so gracious to her that she had begun to view him as a surrogate father figure in many ways. He sent her gifts at Christmas and on her birthday, checked in with her at least twice a year when she was younger.

He did a lot more for her in those formative years than Ed did, since she and her family remained hidden from Ed's reach.

She couldn't help but feel betrayed now, that he'd known her father was back in California and hadn't done a single thing to warn her about it.

"I'm sorry, Margot. I guess I assumed your lawyer would tell you. I know there wasn't any press on it, they kept things *very* tight-lipped for obvious reasons, but it never occurred to me that you wouldn't have been told. I didn't even think to call you when I heard. If anything, I thought you would have been told before me, considering you're family."

She bristled at the word *family*. Ed didn't feel like family, and hadn't for a long, long time. Just because he was responsible for her life didn't mean he had any claim to be a part of it now, not after what he'd done.

Yet here she was, thinking of opening the door and letting him back in. Remembering why she'd called Andrew in the first place, she set aside her anger once more and took a steadying breath.

"He wants to see me."

Andrew was quiet, his side of the line so completely devoid of sound, even breathing, that she wondered if the call had been disconnected. She glanced at her phone screen to confirm, and they were still active. "Andrew?" she asked finally. "Did you hear me?"

"Yeah. I heard you. Why does he want to see you?"

"According to his lawyer, without saying what he wanted to say, he passed along the request: *Tell her if she says hello, I'll tell her about Seventy-Seven.*" Ed's message was so inked into her brain she could have quoted the lawyer's words verbatim in her sleep. *I'll tell her about Seventy-Seven.* "I think we both know what that means."

Again, Andrew fell silent, but after a moment softly whispered, "Fuck me."

"Yeah. Do you think he's being serious, or does he just want attention?" She returned to chewing on her nail, wanting someone else to give her their read on this situation.

"We always wondered if there had been more. There are lulls in Ed's kill record, places where we couldn't account for him, but didn't have a body or a crime to match. He acknowledged his part in the seventy-six, but he liked to tease us, liked implying there might be things we didn't know, but he never outright told us there were bodies that we hadn't credited him for, and after a while we stopped looking." He took a deep breath, then let out a huff of air like he had just dropped down into a chair. Margot imagined him in a home office, pacing the room until it became too much and then settling into a big leather armchair.

The realistic part of her brain knew enough FBI agents to know they weren't living in the lap of luxury she was picturing, but Andrew had also written three *New York Times* bestsellers detailing his experience tracking the worst of the worst in modern American serial killers. He was probably doing OK financially.

"I have to go. I think you know that," she said, only in that moment really deciding once and for all that she would.

"You *don't* have to go. He's manipulating you, and even if there is another body out there, it's not your responsibility to solve that crime. You don't owe it to this case, and you don't owe him a single second of your life. I'll go."

"No offense, Andrew, but he didn't ask for you, he asked for me, and I think he'll be able to decipher the difference pretty quickly, even if he is getting older. And you forget, I'm not a teenager anymore. I'm a cop, and a damn good one. So, it *is* up to me to solve a murder if there's something I can do to make that happen. It's a visit, that's all. I can manage a visit." Doubt flooded her body, making her limbs feel heavy and useless. She wanted to curl up in her bed and hide from this until it went away, but nothing could be that simple.

"I'm coming with you."

"He wants to see me alone."

"I don't give a flying fuck in hell what Ed Finch *wants*, Margot. If you're going to go speak to him, I'm coming with you. It's not a negotiation. We either go together or you don't go at all."

"You don't get to decide what I do." Her voice was that of a petulant teenager and she hated herself for it. Hadn't she called him to get his approval? She couldn't be mad when she had given him this power and didn't like the outcome.

"No, I can't. You're not a teenager anymore, you said it yourself, but this is *my* case. No one knows Ed and his victim profile like I do, and I think you know that. I'm going to be involved in this one way or another, and it becomes a lot easier for everyone if you just let me come with you. So let me."

Margot hesitated, but she had to be honest with herself, she'd called looking for approval, but hadn't this been what she was hoping for the whole time? A hand to guide her through this ordeal so she wouldn't have to do it alone. That was why she'd called Andrew and not Wes.

"Fine. I'll message you when I confirm a time with his lawyer."

She was about to hang up when Andrew spoke again. "Don't let him control this. It won't be easy to see him, you and I both know that, but you have the power here, not him. Don't let him forget it."

TWENTY-ONE
MAY 16, 1982

Chinatown, San Francisco

Ed chewed on his thumbnail, a bad childhood habit he'd never quite been able to break, and something he loathed seeing others do. His car was parked on Sproule Lane, a little side street not far from Chinatown. The area around him was dark, and in spite of how bustling he knew evening tourist foot traffic would be only a few blocks away, none of it found its way here.

Sproule Lane was practically hidden, the kind of street you only turned on to by accident when you were looking for somewhere else. From where he was parked, he had a perfect view of a row of houses across the street that he knew had been converted into apartments. He'd checked the door a week earlier to confirm numbers, to make sure he was looking at the right one.

Apartment 2A, the one jotted down on the paper in his pocket, had the name Amaro on the buzzer box, which meant it was the place he was looking for. Right now, in the settling dusk, the apartment curtains were open, and one window was cracked to let in the fresh spring air.

*Cece, SWF, 26. Energetic young paralegal seeks single, never
married partner for adventure and excitement. No kids.*

Ed had the paper memorized, both Cece's personal information—Cecilia for her credit card company's purposes—and
the greeting she was hoping to use to lure in a man. *Never
married. No kids.* Those words had ruffled Ed's feathers quite a
lot. Who did these girls think they were these days? Twenty-six
wasn't exactly young and fresh, and Ed himself was only thirty,
yet he wouldn't have made the cut for Cece's potential suitors.

Like it was his fault he'd married Kim. If he'd realized what
a fucking disaster that would turn into, he wouldn't have bothered, but a woman like Cece wouldn't look at it like that.
Married meant used up, meant damaged goods. He was really
bothered by her hubris, that she thought she was so damned
special she would be too good for him.

What did she know about life anyway?

He drummed his fingers on the steering wheel, watching
her window. From where he was, he couldn't tell if it was a
living room or a bedroom, but whatever room it was it had gauzy
white curtains, barely enough to keep prying eyes away if they
were closed, but right now they were pulled wide open.

He froze when she came to the window. He'd been
watching the apartment for a day or two, wanting to make sure
she was the right one, the best fit for him. Cece was pretty and
wore her age well. She didn't have a baby face, but she kept her
makeup minimal, which meant she didn't look too old. Where
other women, Kim included, were favoring shorter hairstyles
with tight perms, Cece was still displaying the more popular
seventies trend, her dark hair worn long and straight.

Sitting on the inside ledge of the window, she opened it
slightly wider, then lit a cigarette. Ed, who had initially felt his
pulse trip with excitement to see her, felt a new wave of revul-
sion. She lifted the cigarette to her lips, painted a red he could

see from even down on the street, and let out a silver-gray plume into the night air.

Ed squirmed in his seat uncomfortably. Reading what she'd written about herself in the ad, he expected her to be health-minded, the kind of woman who went hiking for fun. For some reason he hadn't anticipated that she would be someone who had such a disgusting habit. As he watched her raise the cigarette to her lips again, he could imagine the taste of ash on his tongue, could practically smell the way her skin and hair would stink of stale smoke.

It was almost enough to make him want to start the car and drive away, leave unsatisfied, find someone else who would satisfy his needs more perfectly. But inside him was a hunger, and the gnawing, anxious desire to satisfy that hunger was too much to be denied. He'd already spent so much time following her, learning her habits, making sure she was a good fit.

If he left now, it might take weeks to find someone else who spoke to his desires, who made him want to drive into the city multiple times in a span of weeks. He'd put in work here, and wasn't willing to throw all that away just because she would smell bad. He imagined the stink of smoke and tobacco, but even with that wrinkling his nose, he knew he wouldn't be able to turn back now.

She still called to him, beckoned him forward, demanding his attention, and he knew deep down neither of them could be satisfied until he did what he came here to do. Why else would she sit in the window like that, putting herself on display for him? She wanted to be wanted, and he would show her precisely what that looked like.

Cece retreated from the window, stamping out her cigarette on the wooden ledge before closing the glass. A few moments later most of the other lights inside went off, with a residual glow coming from somewhere within the apartment, an interior room he couldn't see.

Ed stirred in his seat, his erection present but not yet unbearable. It waited, like he did, for the right moment. As he watched the building, the glass front door opened and Cece exited, her long, dark hair swaying hypnotically as she walked. He watched her go, then checked his watch.

This wasn't unexpected, she had a busy social life. Unlike some of his other girls, he knew she wouldn't wait easily for him in the dark of her bedroom. But he also knew that she would return home along the very street where he was parked, and that she was usually drunk enough to not be walking straight.

What was it with girls her age now? They had no sense of decorum or propriety. It was all party, all pleasure. They expected the world to grant their wishes, and not pay any price for the moral indignities along the way. He shook his head and leaned back in the seat, ready to wait a few more hours. The wait would be worthwhile.

His bag sat on the passenger seat, knives ready and singing for blood. Their desperate harmony would be satisfied soon enough. Ed let his eyes half close, and he watched her quiet, dark apartment, imagining the floorplan. The front windows were the living room and kitchen from what he could tell. He wouldn't do it there. He'd go to her bedroom.

He hoped she had fun tonight, because it would be the last night out she ever had.

Hours later, Cece returned, wobbly on her heels and humming a song to herself as she went. As she passed his car, Ed silently got out, his bag in hand, and followed her across the street to her apartment.

It wasn't long after that his knives stopped singing for blood, and he had the relief he had been waiting for all night.

TWENTY-TWO

The chill of air conditioning hit Margot so unexpectedly it stole her breath and immediately caused a full body shiver to run through her. She should have been braced for it, this wasn't her first time at the city morgue, but she was still unprepared.

This stupid fucking heat needed to finish its visit to the city so things could go back to normal, with crisp Bay Area air and the ever-present possibility that fog might roll over the city and leave it a murky, dewy mess.

She couldn't believe she missed the fog. She missed Northern California being *Northern* California. This heat was some pure Los Angeles bullshit, and if she'd wanted L.A.'s weather, she would have moved to L.A.

Waiting in the tiled lobby for Leon to join her, Margot quickly checked her messages. There was a text from Wes that said *Call me* and a message from Andrew that asked *Are you still OK to go tomorrow?*

Hell no, she wasn't, but what choice did she have?

That Andrew was joining her would hopefully make the process a little easier to stomach. He knew better than anyone the horrors Ed had accomplished in his lifetime outside the prison walls, and he understood what had happened to her family as a result. No one else really got that, even if they thought they did. You could know the story beats without understanding it.

No one really understood it, but Andrew came the closest for someone who wasn't in her immediate family.

She was sure Ed wouldn't be thrilled to see the FBI agent, but she really didn't care too much about what pleased Ed. If he wanted to see her, this was the way it was going to happen.

A lump had formed in her throat, something she found was happening more and more frequently these days, especially as the visitation drew nearer. Anxiety was a constant bedfellow for Margot, and she recognized the signs of an anxiety attack when she felt them. The problem with this was that they were coming on daily now, and none of her usual tricks were helping.

She hated the idea of relying on drugs, but reminded herself that if it helped her get through this week, that's what the meds were there for. Anything that might help her sleep, help her breathe. With two active investigations demanding her focus, she couldn't let herself get sloppy now.

Leon came in through the front door wearing a cloak of the outdoor heat around him that dissipated as soon as he reached her.

"Goddamn, did they set the temperature in here to *Antarctic*?" He gave a comically over-emphasized shiver. "And I thought it was bad outside."

"Out of the frying pan, into the freezer. Isn't that the saying?"

"Suppose it might as well be now."

Margot, who had been at the morgue two days earlier, led the way down the basement steps to the dingy, sterile theater that was Evelyn's workspace.

There were two bodies laid out neatly side by side on metal tables, neither of the dead women being given the illusion of modesty for the time being. They were both entirely nude, their skin looking more like plastic than actual human flesh, since even in the chill of the morgue air they had no goosebumps or response to the cold.

Margot often marveled at the little things that surprised her about death, all the tiny details that changed when a person's body became an empty shell.

Evelyn was standing next to the new arrival, the body they'd found in the park yesterday. She was jotting down notes on a metallic clipboard, and while it was evident that she was aware of Leon and Margot's entrance, she didn't look up or say anything in greeting, and simply continued scribbling away. The sound of her pen was heavy and loud in the otherwise totally still room.

After what felt like an eternity, Evelyn slid the clipboard into a slot at the end of the table, adjusted her glasses—these ones a sparkly purple cat-eyed pair—and approached them. She wore a stern expression, which always looked out of place on Evelyn's face, because she was the type of woman who was usually able to crack a joke even if she was elbow-deep in some-one's rib cage.

Now, though, she looked grouchy and unimpressed with their general presence in her lab. Margot might have taken it personally and assumed that the medical examiner was only nice to her otherwise because of Wes, but Evelyn offered the smallest of smiles as she reached them, as if to apologize in advance.

Something was obviously bothering her, but it wasn't the arrival of Leon and Margot.

"You look like someone took a piss in your coffee, Evelyn," Margot noted, trying to lighten the mood.

"I wish, my dear. At least then I could just make a new coffee." She removed her glasses, pinching the bridge to her nose and wrinkling her brow, and Margot could practically feel the headache radiating off her.

"Something specific about our Jane Does?" Leon asked.

"Your Does. Margot and Wes's poor family. The dozen other bodies who have come through here over the last week. I don't know what it is, the weather is certainly to blame in part, but it seems like I barely have time to breathe before someone else is on the slab needing my attention. Margot, you tell that handsome partner of yours to come over and give me a shoulder rub any time he wants." Evelyn, ever a notorious but harmless flirt, hazarded a wink. "Don't report me to HR for that."

Margot smiled for what felt like the first time in ages. "Never. And I'll pass along the message."

"Feeling like chopped liver over here," Leon said with feigned gruffness.

Evelyn patted him on the back. "Oh, angel, you could give me a rubdown any day, just say the word."

Leon chuckled, not bothering to play the wife card. Evelyn did what she did in the name of lightening the mood, not making any genuine advances.

The woman would flirt with a lamp post if she thought it might help ease tension.

"So, I know we've rudely added more to your obviously overflowing plate, but have you been able to get anything useful off our Park Does?" Margot asked.

"Well, would you like the good news or the bad news first?" Evelyn asked, gesturing to the bodies behind her.

"From where I'm standing, I only see bad news, so take your pick," Leon replied.

"A smart man knows when to defer to a lady." Evelyn grinned. Though the dour cloud that had been hanging over her when they arrived was now considerably lighter, Margot noticed some stiffness in Evelyn's body as she led them over to the newest victim. "I have good and bad news for both our young ladies. Our newest victim here, I've had less time with, I'm afraid. I haven't been able to do more than the preliminary examination on her, so no full autopsy yet. That's the bad news. The good news is I can at least give you some pretty solid information to start with."

"We'll take whatever you can give us," said Leon. "Before we came in here, all we had was: Bodies. Park."

"This particular body belongs to Leanne Wu. Thanks to her complete dental we were able to get back identification fairly quick on her. Twenty-five, Chinese descent. And better than that, I can also give you a very good idea of how she was killed."

Evelyn moved to the opposite side of the table and rolled Leanne Wu's decomposing body very carefully onto its side. Here, Margot was clearly able to make out the lividity, the dark pooling and bruising that occurred as blood began to settle after death, which shows how a body was positioned at the time of death. Leanne had clearly been on her back, as the mottled and rotting skin here was considerably darker than the pale flesh of the rest of her body.

There were also wounds here that hadn't been visible through the tattered clothes she wore. *Many* wounds. Now that Evelyn had cleaned the corpse thoroughly, it was evident they were stab wounds, slim, perfect lines in the skin about an inch or an inch and a half long. Margot mentally started counting but her eyes couldn't stay focused.

"Forty-four, I'll save you the effort," Evelyn said. "She was stabbed in the back and on her sides forty-four times, then her killer rolled her onto her back as she bled out. At some point after that, I presume he took her to the dumping ground where you found her. Obviously, exposure to the elements has sped up her decomposition considerably, and I'm going to want to do a complete autopsy before I make any concrete assessments on her time of death, but I'd say she's been in the park about three weeks. There was some postmortem trauma, but from what I can tell most of it is wildlife-related and not intentional mutilation. I'm afraid I can't make any absolute statements on whether or not she experienced sexual trauma prior to or after death, but my initial examination suggests she *was* assaulted in some way. The decomposition means we're very unlikely to find any usable DNA evidence from a perpetrator, but I'll do my best with the remaining hair and whatnot."

Leon was furiously writing on his notepad, while Margot opted to only make one or two key notes. The ME's file would be available to her soon enough for the most vital details.

"All right, want to see what's behind door number two?"

Margot had almost forgotten the blonde, laid out and waiting for them barely six feet away. Strange how you could get so comfortable around the dead that you could turn your back on a corpse and forget it was even in the room with you.

Leon finished what he was writing. As they moved over to the second table, Margot's phone began to buzz in her back pocket. She pulled it out, grimacing an apology to her colleagues, and checked the screen.

Wes.

She'd ignored his texts earlier, but obviously he thought whatever he had to share with her was too vital to wait.

"Hey, I'm in the middle of something, can I call you back?" She lowered her voice to almost a whisper, which was funny because it wasn't like anyone in the room would be offended by a phone conversation. This wasn't a library.

"We're working a case, Phalen, what exactly is so important you can't call me back?"

"I'm at the morgue with Leon and we're reviewing the Park Does with Evelyn." She silently added, *is that important enough for you?* In spite of not saying the words, she knew her tone conveyed sufficient annoyance. She felt bad as a quiet lull filled the line between them. But Wes knew she was working multiple cases, this was hardly the first time.

"I'm sorry, I didn't mean for it to come out like that, and I know you're under... extra pressure right now." The abruptness that had been in his words the first time was gone, replaced with the usual patient Wes she knew was reserved mostly for her and a small handful of others whose opinions he actually cared about.

"It's fine, what's going on?"

"I've got a meeting set up for us to have a chat with Mateo's doctor. He can meet us in about two hours at the hospital, but it's a small window. Think you can make it work?"

Margot glanced back over to the blonde Doe on the table. "Yeah, I think I can do it, do you want to meet there, in case this goes a bit late, then at least one of us will be there for sure?"

A pause, like he didn't even want to humor the idea she wouldn't attend. He probably wanted to remind her which case she had picked up first, and that she wasn't the primary on the Muir Woods case. Margot knew him well enough at this point to hear the arguments without them even being made.

"Sure. It's UCSF Benioff, the children's hospital, and he told me to meet him at the nurses' station on the fifth floor."

Margot jotted all this down on her notepad, cell phone wedged between her shoulder and ear. "I'll be there, Wes. Don't worry."

"Mmhmm. Tell Evelyn I said hi."

"She'll love that."

"I know." He hung up.

"Sorry, sorry," Margot said, hastily stuffing the phone back into her jeans. "Wes sends his love, Evelyn."

"Scoundrel." Evelyn stood at the head of the silver slab, as if the blonde Doe was a grand meal and she was about to say grace. "Detectives, I'd like you to meet Rebecca Watson. While her dental records were not much help to us, thanks to some lovely fresh veneers, I *was* able to get a match off her breast implants."

Leon was scribbling, but Margot couldn't leave that statement hanging. "I'm sorry, did you say her breast implants?"

"Yes, ma'am. All come with a unique serial number on them, just like a shiny new car. Rebecca's 38DDs led us right to her doctor in Los Angeles, who was able to confirm who the implants belonged to."

"What a fucking world," Margot muttered.

"I know. My breasts would be no good in helping ID me," Evelyn said with a shrug.

"Mine either," Leon added, without looking up from his notebook. "What was her doctor's name?"

Evelyn pulled out the metal clipboard attached to the table and flipped it open. "Dr. Bradford Hillman. Hillman of Beverley Hills. What a moniker that is. Wonder if that's his real name."

"I'm sure Dr. Boobjob was already taken," Margot muttered, staring at the nude female body between her and the medical examiner. They now had two named victims, which was good news. Margot looked at the lopsided chest of their first park victim, her body now sewn back up after the autopsy, but one implant obviously never finding its way back in.

"Did she have other work done?" Margot asked. "You mentioned the new veneers, and the implants. We noted on finding her that the blond was obviously not her natural color. I'm curious."

"On our initial examination I noted that she had likely had considerable plastic surgery, based on the implants as well as some other small incision marks we found. You'll be able to confirm the specific surgeries with Dr. Hillman, but I think my preliminary summary indicated a nose job was likely, liposuction probable, though well-healed, and I anticipate Rebecca was a regular user of Botox." Evelyn ran a gloved thumb over Rebecca's baby-smooth forehead. "She's forty-six. I don't care how good you are with your sunscreen regimen, you don't have a forehead that looks like this, pushing fifty, without a little help."

Margot had nothing to add to that particular assessment, and neither did Leon, as they both stood quietly and waited for Evelyn to continue. Seeing that the stage was still hers, Evelyn withdrew her hand from Rebecca's forehead and continued with her speech. "You can see the lividity for Ms. Watson is on her front left side, which I believe is the position you found her in?"

"She was flat on her front in the park," Margot corrected.

"Then she likely lay somewhere else for quite some time before being moved there, as you can tell the pooling is considerably darker on her left, so I believe she was probably leaning up against something, as it's not a usual angle for a body to lie in naturally."

Both Margot and Leon noted that, and Margot's mind raced, wondering where Rebecca had been before the park.

"When rigor set in, she was stretched out like this?" Margot asked, indicating the relatively natural pose Rebecca was in.

When they'd found her in the park her body had looked much like that, only face down, no awkward bends or angles.

"Yes, she was lying quite straight."

"So pretty unlikely she was being stashed in a trunk or other small storage space. Wherever our perp had her, she was able to lay stretched out, just... on an angle?" Margot tipped her hand to the side to demonstrate what an angle looked like, to two people who knew precisely what she was talking about without visual aid.

"I'd agree with that," Evelyn replied. "Had she been in a trunk or similar I think we would have seen the lividity settling much more on the side of the body rather than toward the front, and she would have likely been folded into more of a fetal position for ease of transport."

"Unless the perp had a covered truck bed," Leon noted.

"Or a van," Margot added.

"Guess you've managed to rule out compact cars. Well done, Detectives."

Evelyn could joke, but it *did* help give them at least something small to go on when they finally were able to narrow down a potential list of suspects.

"As for cause of death, you'll find it to be very similar indeed to our poor friend Leanne over there." Again, Evelyn went to the far side of the body and rolled Rebecca toward her, exposing the cleaned skin of her back, and similar-looking cuts, though these looked smaller.

As if reading Margot's mind, Evelyn said, "I believe the weapons used in each of these murders are the same *size* of blade, though I obviously can't say they came from the same knife. In the case of Ms. Wu, you might have noticed some of the cuts looked larger, but that's due in part to the more advanced stage of decomposition. What I did notice with Ms. Watson was that her wounds are more ragged, more violent. I believe that whoever did this felt a personal sense of anger toward her, and that the wounds demonstrate a level of viciousness not present in Ms. Wu."

"There are fewer wounds here, though," Leon noted.

"Yes, only fifteen," Evelyn confirmed. "But don't let that fool you. I think these attacks, if they are related, demonstrate a potential development from our killer. Again, it's not for me to tell you if the same killer murdered both these women, but I see enough similarity in the wounds I would not rule it out. With Ms. Wu it was all about getting a job done. Those wounds are very much in and out, like this." She picked up a nearby scalpel and raised it up, dropping it in an abrupt stabbing motion downwards, over Rebecca's body, which made Margot flinch. Evelyn repeated the gesture twice more. "In the case of Ms. Watson here, what we're seeing looks much more like this." She lowered the scalpel blade again, but then mimed a shoving and dragging motion that definitely looked much more aggressive than the first.

"He might have known the second victim," Margot offered to Leon. "Might have been more personal?"

"We have to go on the assumption—if we assume these *are* related, which I'm still not completely convinced they are—that the killer might have been personally connected to both women." Leon made a few more notes, and Evelyn returned her faux murder weapon to the table beside her. "I think our best course at the moment is to assume that what we're looking at is two unrelated homicides. We have to be careful about lumping them together simply because of the location of death. I think there's a distinct enough difference in the quantity and style of the stab wounds to suggest we might have entirely different perpetrators here."

Margot went to interrupt him, but Leon quickly raised his hand to stop her, a small smile crossing his lips.

"Don't panic on me, Margot. I *know* what it looks like. But if you and I immediately leap to thinking it's a potential repeat killer, you know how that's going to go with the press, and the last thing we need is anyone starting a serial killer klaxon in the media just yet."

Well, if he was going to go and make a perfectly valid point about things, then so be it. Margot was, after all, probably more inclined to see serial killers in her victims than others might be. Still, this case very much felt as if it had the potential to lean in that direction, and she didn't want Leon to overlook the obvious simply because he wanted to do things by the book.

"But we can keep it in the back of our mind, right?" Margot said.

"We would be foolish not to, my dear."

Margot nodded, soothed at least for the time being that her temporary partner knew what he was doing. This wasn't

Leon's first rodeo, and he *was* the primary on this investigation. She was only along for the ride and to lend a hand if he needed it, which he probably didn't. Of everyone in their department, Leon had one of the best case closure rates, and managed to do that without the regular aid of a partner. He was also one of the few that the captain allowed to go partnerless for so long.

It tended to work out beautifully, as the newbies would get assigned to Leon and absorb his knowledge for a few months, then get partnered up with someone more permanent once they were settled.

Homicide wasn't a lifetime gig for most cops. It got to be too much to handle for most people's mental health. Being a homicide detective was usually a stepping stone on someone's career path to bigger things, or to a post they wanted more but needed major crimes experience for. For Leon, though, homicide was it, this was where the train of his career stopped. And Margot knew this was probably all she'd ever do, as well. She couldn't see herself working narcotics or robbery. She wanted to keep doing what she was doing.

She glanced down at her watch and swore softly. Though Wes had given her a two-hour window, things here had taken longer than she anticipated, and it was also nearing rush hour, meaning both time and traffic would be against her.

"I've got to go meet Wes at the children's hospital, can you handle it from here?" she asked Leon.

"I think we're pretty much finished here?" He asked this as a question directed at Evelyn.

"Yes, thank God. Get out of my morgue so I can confirm the cause of death on some obvious elderly heatstroke victims. Something *easy* for once. Don't bring me another one of these for at least a week." She gestured to the women in front of her.

"Would love to never bring you another one again," Margot muttered from the door.

"As lovely as that would be," Evelyn said with a sigh, "I remain a realist."

"Realism is a miserable business," Leon said.

Margot took those words with her as she left the morgue and headed back out into the oppressive heat of the evening, heading in the direction of her car. The statement followed her even as she pulled into traffic and pointed herself in the direction of the hospital, keeping an eye on the car's clock to make sure she was still on time to make it.

Realism is a miserable business.

All too often, she knew, so was life.

TWENTY-THREE

Margot pulled into the hospital's crowded parking lot with a good fifteen minutes to spare, and a newfound loathing for rush-hour traffic in San Francisco. How could an area so small condense so many terrible drivers into just one city?

It was like there was an unspoken competition to see who could push other drivers to the brink of insanity on a daily basis.

Margot locked her car and jogged across the lot, checking her notes to see where she was meant to meet Wes. Instead of having to find him, though, he had evidently found her.

His entirely too-tall frame was leaned up against the front pillar of the hospital entrance as he scrolled through his phone, looking every ounce as casual and cool as he was likely trying to. If a man who looked that good were to suggest she sell her soul, she might have to give it a long consideration.

"Stop trying to pick up nurses," she told him.

"I simply exist and look good, it's not my fault if people are drawn to that, Margot. Don't hate the player."

He needed to get new lines. "I will never speak to you again if you finish that sentence."

"You're no fun."

"The buzziest of buzzkills, don't you know that's why they put us together. Cap said there was only so much ego they could fit into the office and asked if I could poke a hole in yours every so often. Keep you modest."

Wes huffed. "Don't have to keep my modesty *quite* so in check, you know. A man needs to feel like he's appealing."

"You don't need to appeal to me for validation, Fox."

"What if I want to?" He gave her a grin that was probably usually reserved for women on dating apps, one of those sinful, promising smiles that was best viewed in dim bedroom lighting and not harsh hospital fluorescents.

Whoa.

Margot had been in full-on banter mode, which was a nice change of pace from her recent trip to the morgue, and also her *very* recent snippy phone conversation with this same man. And while Wes's tone was still very much fun and games, she hadn't been prepared for what sounded to be a completely frank question.

What if he *did* want to appeal to her? And what would that even mean?

Her head was swimming with the precise best way to answer that question, when he grinned broadly. "You couldn't handle it. Look at you, cat got your tongue and everything." Wes winked, making the whole thing a joke, which Margot was more than happy to play along with.

Had she considered it? Considered Wes?

She would have to be blind not to, he was so handsome he should be used to sell suits and watches, not solve crime, and not to mention the worst of it all, he was her *partner.*

No, absolutely nothing under this sun could convince her that this was a notion she should dwell on even a second longer, let alone circle back on later.

There were other options, if that was an itch she felt a

particular need to scratch, and those options didn't have the ability to completely upend her life.

Margot followed Wes into the hospital, where he led them toward the elevators with the distinct air of a man who knew precisely where he was going. Margot had been to this hospital once or twice, but couldn't have told you the lobby from the cafeteria. In their line of work it wasn't uncommon to have to meet witnesses, perps, or even soon-to-be-victims in the hospital, so she had seen the inside of every single one in the city at least once. But telling them apart from each other after all this time was too much to ask.

Wes had no such difficulty, and soon they were on the elevator heading to the fifth floor. When they arrived, a stocky man with thick black glasses was standing at the nurses' station, as if waiting for them, which Margot quickly realized he was.

He smiled warmly as they approached, which was something she was unaccustomed to as a homicide detective. People usually looked at her with either horror or guilt. It was a rare day indeed that someone was happy to see her and Wes.

Still, the stocky man shook their hands like old friends, the faint scent of fading Old Spice radiating from him as he greeted them.

The man, who introduced himself as Dr. Daniel "Call me Dr. Dan" McRae, was about fifty-five years old with hair as dark as his glasses, showing surprisingly few grays for his age and occupation. He had an olive complexion and dark brown eyes, and when he smiled there was a sparkle in his eyes that immediately made Margot want to trust him. He was probably wonderful with the kids in his care. At least at first meeting he had the right bedside manner for pediatrics.

Calling him Dr. Dan was completely out of the question, however.

"Dr. McRae, as I explained on the phone, we wanted to ask

you a few questions about a patient of yours." Wes had pulled out his notepad already.

"And as I explained to *you* on the phone, I cannot share any information about a patient."

"Is there somewhere we could speak privately?" Margot asked, not liking how completely exposed they were at the moment.

Dr. McRae nodded and led them down the hall to a small office that had no personal effects decorating it, and appeared to be for general staff use rather than a private office. The walls, however, had a cheery mural of green frogs and rainbows, making it an inviting if wildly inappropriate space to talk about what they had come to discuss.

Margot and Wes took the two available plastic chairs across from the desk, and rather than sitting, Dr. McRae leaned against the desk instead. His expression remained warm, but he was obviously resolute in his HIPAA stance.

"Sir, we are investigating the murders of the Ramirez family. We have good reason to believe, based on years' worth of prescriptions, as well as documents found among the Ramirezes' belongings, that you have been seeing both Valentina and Mateo Ramirez for quite some time."

Margot wasn't sure how much Wes had explained on the phone before they arrived, but he'd obviously failed to mention the annihilation of the whole Ramirez family. Dr. McRae's entire expression and stance changed. Gone was the friendly but defiant smile. Now his shoulders sagged and his whole body seemed to fold in on itself.

"Evangeline?"

Funny, how he didn't mention Hector.

"The whole family, and a family friend. All but Mateo."

"Good God in heaven." He circled behind the desk, deciding perhaps that it would be best to take a seat after all. "I saw Evangeline and Mateo only last month. This is impossible, it doesn't seem real."

Instead of looking at them he looked down at his own clenched hands, his focus now glassy and far away.

"Would you say you were close to the Ramirez family?" Margot asked, trying to guide him gently back to the topic. "It's obvious this news is hitting you very hard. I'm sorry."

Dr. McRae cleared his throat and tried to regroup, sitting up a bit straighter, but Margot didn't miss the glint of tears in his eyes, or the way his whole demeanor had become depressed in mere moments.

"I'm not sure *close* is the right way to put it. I knew them, of course, and yes, I was familiar with both Valentina and Mateo. Those poor children, so many health problems over such a long time. And Valentina had begun to show such improvement."

Margot looked sideways toward Wes, wondering if he was also thinking about the absence of cuffs or chains on Valentina's bed. When he didn't look back at her, she returned her focus to Dr. McRae.

"Doctor, do you mind explaining—and you can avoid the specifics of the children if you must—but generally explaining what brought them to you so frequently? You have to understand why we'd be concerned, there were a *lot* of bottles with the children's names on them, and with Mateo now staying with an unfamiliar family member, we're worried there may be a condition he has that's going untreated." She ended there, on the unspoken guilt, hoping he would be more amenable to opening up to them.

The doctor nodded, again looking down at his hands. "Evangeline..." His voice hitched, and he took a moment before starting again. "Evangeline had difficult pregnancies, both times. She really struggled through the whole duration. I wasn't her doctor then, I'm not a delivery doctor, you see, but she explained to me that with Valentina, the doctors told her she shouldn't try again, but she got pregnant with Mateo, and he was her miracle baby. That's what she called him, her little miracle. Except, she very nearly died giving birth to him, and this time I believe her doctors made it quite clear that another pregnancy would kill her. She loved those children with every ounce of her being. Every time she was here you could see it, how much she cared about them, how much she worried. She was such an angel."

"And Hector?" Wes asked.

Dr. McRae huffed, then said, "He worked quite a bit."

"So, he wasn't here with them as often?" Margot asked.

"If ever."

Margot and Wes scribbled notes in unison and the doctor continued. "I met Valentina first. She started getting sick right before Mateo was born. And it was so unclear what was wrong with her. We'd treat her for asthma, then she'd start showing signs of heart trouble. We'd treat that, then skin issues would appear. It was one thing after the other with that poor girl. And then Mateo, when he turned about two, it was the same thing. We ruled out issues in the house after they moved, ruled out environmental concerns, but they just kept coming back, and every single time we'd treat one problem and thought we'd gotten it under control, they'd be right back again. Evangeline was beside herself, as I'm sure you can imagine."

"I'm sure," Wes said, in a way that let Margot know they were on precisely the same page.

She didn't want to do it, but it seemed absolutely necessary she ask. "Dr. McRae, did you and Evangeline Ramirez have a romantic relationship?"

This took him entirely off guard and he sputtered a few times before saying, "I imagine the way I'm speaking about her might lead you to ask that. I was incredibly fond of her, and she *was* a beautiful woman, but I'm a married man, Detective."

"That doesn't typically stop people."

"Well, it stopped me."

"So you're suggesting the opportunity was there?" Wes asked.

Dr. McRae paused, sighed heavily, then spoke again. "Yes. I'm not proud of myself for it, but during all the time she and I spent together we did become quite close, and I felt so deeply for her, and for the clear lack of care her husband had. It was disgusting, really. Never around for his wife, for those poor children. But it was just a kiss, and only once. We both knew it was wrong."

"You saw a lot of the Ramirez children over the years. Did you have any reason to believe there was any abuse happening?"

He seemed more offended by this question than he had the implication of an affair. "Of course not. And I take umbrage with the question. As a doctor I'm a mandated reporter, I'm required by law to report potential abuse if I see it. I never did; those kids were sick, nothing more. Evangeline would never hurt her children, they were her entire world."

Ignoring his obvious bias, Margot sat back, her plastic chair creaking. "Dr. McRae, are you familiar with the concept of Munchausen by proxy?"

The air around them was so still it crackled. Margot could hear voices in the hallway passing by, chatter between nurses, it sounded like, but for the most part it was only the soft drone of two female voices. The tone was too light, too friendly for the frigid stillness that had settled around them in the office.

"I don't think I like what you're implying, Detective."

"I just asked a question. Are you familiar with the concept?"

"I am familiar with the syndrome, yes."

"And I expect that you, as a medical professional who works with children, would be trained to look for signs of something *like* Munchausen, correct?" Margot set her notebook down on her lap.

"Of course. But this isn't some fanciful television series we're in, Detectives. Munchausen, and Munchausen by proxy, are both exceedingly rare, and I can assure you we would be able to spot a situation like that in its infancy. We would never let harm come to children in our care."

"Do no harm is the adage, I suppose, isn't it?" Margot asked.

"It is. Now, if we're done here, I need to return to my rounds." He stood up, bracing himself behind the desk for a moment, as if not totally trusting his own balance.

"Oh, one more thing, Doctor," Wes interjected, rising himself so his full imposing height towered over the doctor. "Where were you last Thursday evening at around eleven o'clock at night?"

TWENTY-FOUR

"He looked like he was going to shit his pants when you asked for his alibi." Margot dumped a load of deluxe fried rice out onto a clean white plate, using her spoon to create a little basin in the middle. She then repeated the process on a second plate.

"Not sure that alone makes him guilty." Wes had laid out several files on Margot's dining room table, a piece of furniture she owned solely for evenings such as this, and not because she ever actually ate her own dinner at it.

No, Margot's idea of dinner generally eschewed plates entirely and was eaten from takeout containers as she melted her brain with TV until she was so full and so desensitized she thought it might be safe to go to bed.

With Wes here, she would be fancy and put her takeout on the nicest Target plates she owned.

As he sorted through a few of their files, which he'd brought from the station in a cardboard banker's box, Margot added sweet and sour pork, beef with vegetables, and BBQ duck to each of their plates.

"Margot, I don't know how to tell you this, but there is a

world of delicious food in this city that isn't limited to the Chinese place down the block from the station."

Sure, and that world could now be delivered right to her front door, which certainly made people wonder about her unusual takeout habits. But how could she explain *why*. Why she didn't want anyone to know her address. Why she never took an Uber alone. Why she didn't create any habits that could trace back to where she lived?

Telling people her reasons would make it too clear who she'd once been.

Never let a stranger know too much about you, Megan. Never make yourself a target.

The best advice on personal safety that Margot had ever received came from a man who stole credit card slips from the newspaper where he worked to track down women who paid for their classified ads.

Ed had been a genius to give his daughter the wisdom to avoid men like him, but it had ultimately made her afraid of absolutely everything that left a trail. She'd resisted getting a credit card until she was in her twenties for fear that someone out there might have the same way of thinking that Ed did.

Ordering things on the internet still made her nauseous.

Margot brought the still steaming-hot plates of food over to the dining room table and set them next to the already open bottle of white wine she'd left a few minutes earlier. Wes, in his efforts to put their homework together, had taken the time to pour them each a glass.

What a gentleman.

He'd also graciously waited to put out any of the crime scene photos with bodies in them until after they ate.

Still, an array of images from the Ramirez house were sprayed across the table, along with Wes's handwritten notes, and printed copies of the notes he had taken the time to type up. They had copies of Evelyn's reports on each victim, and an itemized list of things found in the Ramirez house.

Margot's gaze drifted across the entirety of their accrued knowledge of the case, wishing it might form a sign that pointed them directly at their killer.

"Do think the doctor could be our guy?" she asked.

Wes shrugged. "I'm not married to the idea, but he'd be a good fit. We still need to check out his alibi, and I'm not convinced *I was at the hospital* is the foolproof cover he thinks it is, but we'll check on it tomorrow. Still, he had motive. He was clearly in love with the wife, hated the husband. Maybe it was an *if I can't have her no one will* scenario."

"I don't love it, though. He'd have known Mateo wasn't one of the victims, and killing Emily just to go through with a plan seems like overkill. Besides, if you love the wife, why kill Hector first? And why kill Evangeline in such a grisly way? It doesn't fit."

"Like I said, I'm not suggesting he's the only option. But he's the only one we can really put a name on right now. I like that a lot more than suggesting it was some random psycho who might be lying in wait out there to do this to another unsuspecting family."

Margot shook her head. "I don't get that vibe here. This felt really personal to me. Maybe the doctor killed them all because he figured out Evangeline and Hector were hurting their own kids. Maybe he felt betrayed because she'd played him for a fool all those years."

Wes nodded. "It could fit, would certainly explain her being a victim the same as Hector. I'm still not sure where the kids fit in though. Why kill Valentina and Emily if you're mad at the parents? Valentina was as much a victim as Mateo, and Emily was completely innocent."

Margot chewed thoughtfully on a piece of duck, spitting the bone onto her plate as an idea came to mind. "What if

Valentina was in on it *with* her parents? Maybe she graduated from abused to abuser and that's why there weren't any more chains on her bed, why the doctor suddenly started to see her improving." Margot lifted her brows at Wes.

"Poor fucking Emily," he grumbled.

"I think no matter what we conclude, Emily's story is going to be *wrong place, wrong time*."

"I wish I could tell her parents something different, something meaningful. Instead, they're going to go the rest of their lives blaming themselves for letting their kid go to a fucking sleepover."

"Not that this will make you feel better, but I'm pretty sure they were going to find a way to blame themselves for this no matter what explanation we gave them. That's how survivors deal with the trauma."

Wes took a long look at her, then said, "Do you have any soy sauce?"

"This shit isn't salty enough for you already?"

He wagged a finger at her. "Don't judge me, Phalen, just tell me where the sauce is."

Margot directed him to her pantry, and before she could register why she *shouldn't*, he had already opened it.

"Wes—"

Too late, though. He had the door open and the red and yellow bottle of soy sauce in one hand, and in the other he had a prescription bottle. He put the one prescription down and shuffled through the dozen others.

She couldn't see the pantry from where she was sitting, but she knew perfectly well that next to all the neatly ordered bottles of pills there were other bottles. Wine. Whiskey. Gin. She loved gin the most because of how much Ed had hated it. She remembered him being so mad at her mother once for getting gin instead of vodka by mistake. It was the closest Margot had ever seen Ed get to hitting Kim.

He hadn't, but she remembered how scared she'd been of him that night.

"Jesus, Margot."

The dining room chair squeaked as she pushed herself away from the table and stood next to him, gently pushing the pantry door closed. "I guess this is why most people put them in the bathroom, so they don't know when friends snoop."

"I wasn't snooping."

"I know, Wes, it's fine."

"That's a *lot* of pills."

"Yeah, well, I don't take them all at once. They're for varying levels of mental disfunction. Sometimes I'm just a little fucked up. Other days..."

"A lot fucked up," he finished.

"A lot fucked up."

He put the soy sauce on the counter and turned to face her. "And now? How fucked up are you now?"

"You worried about me?"

Wes didn't smile, he didn't change his stance, he just stood leaning against the counter and staring at her, expecting a response.

"A bit more fucked up than usual."

"Is it the case?"

Margot shook her head. "No."

He placed a hand on her shoulder and the sudden warmth of it was a beautiful and unexpected thing. He had such lovely, big hands.

"You can tell me if it's too much."

That made her laugh. "No, Wes, it's not the case. It's almost never the case. I wouldn't still be doing the job after all these years if dead bodies sent me off my mental game, y'know?"

In spite of her assurances his hand did not leave; instead it moved up her shoulder to her neck, the roughness of his palm tickling her throat. He rubbed his thumb along her jawline and

Margot felt her knees turn to Jell-O. Oh why, why did that have to feel so good, so safe?

She thought about pushing his hand away, but didn't want to, and let herself lean into it for a moment longer. The smell of him was so wonderful this close up, expensive cologne and cheap deodorant.

"You can tell me anything, Margot," he said.

There were a lot of *shoulds* in this scenario, things Margot knew she ought to do, ways she was meant to respond, but right then logic was long gone, and her body was telling her that it had been months since anyone touched her, and being touched like she was a fragile, breakable thing felt so incredibly good she had no interest in telling him to stop.

"I'm OK," she said.

"Are you, though?" His thumb was under her chin now, and she wasn't sure how it was he was able to maintain a train of thought when all she could think about was how close his thumb was to her mouth.

Multitasking had never been one of Margot's strong suits.

"I will be."

"Is it about your father?"

One minute Margot was thinking about subtle ways she might take his finger into her mouth, and then there it was, the ice-cold bath in the form of a question, sucking all the breath from her lungs, and with it the red-hot ember of desire that had been building low, low down in her belly.

She pushed his hand away. Not an angry shove, but rather softly, taking it away from her face, putting a period at the end of the sentence this moment had been.

"Please don't."

"Margot..."

"It's going to be hard enough without you giving me pity eyes about it, OK? I'm going to see him, and yes, I am taking more meds because the idea of seeing him makes it impossible to sleep and gives me panic attacks. Was that what you wanted to hear? How fucked up I am about a face-to-face with my serial killer dad?"

"I didn't mean—"

"No, I *know* you didn't mean it, Wes. I know you were trying to help, but this isn't like a scrape you can put a Band-Aid on. It's not something you can *fix*. There's a really good reason I don't share this part of my life with people, because they go into this mode where they want to tell me I'm not him, and the things he did don't define me, and blah, blah, blah. I've heard it all, from friends, from therapists, you name it. But he's still there. He's still in my blood, and I can't *ever* get rid of him."

"I'm sorry."

Margot hefted a sigh, then let out a little laugh. "I really wish you'd just kissed me before you said too much and fucked it all up, you idiot."

"Shit, if that was an option let's do that," he said quickly.

"Ah, too late for that now. I've come to my senses." She shook off the discomfort of the tension between them and grabbed the soy sauce off the counter. "Let's look at this shit again from the top."

TWENTY-FIVE
OCTOBER 12, 1982

San Francisco, California

"Don't move. Don't say a fucking word. If you're a good little girl this will all be over before you know it and you'll never see me again. Do you understand?"

A muffled sob, and the woman's head bobbed up and down.

Ed could feel her heart hammering, the pulse vibrating through her back. Her fear made him harder than he thought humanly possible. It was thick in the air and tasted like sweet candy at the back of his throat. This was his favorite part. He liked all of the stages of his art, but there was something special about drawing the fear out as long as he could.

Sometimes, when he had them tied up, he would leave the room. He'd go away long enough that they thought he was really gone, and he'd hear the telltale sounds of struggle. They'd try to work their bindings free, and sometimes he'd wait long enough to hear a body thump to the floor before raging back into the room, *I thought I told you not to move.*

He liked the way he could menace them in nothing more than a whisper, the way they yielded to his strength and understood his power. Pretty little girls who did exactly what he told them to, and if they didn't, he showed them what a mistake they had made.

This one, Amy, he'd been watching her on and off for weeks, whenever he was able to find an excuse to go into the city. She was sparky, wild. She drank too much and spent more time than she ought to out of the house going to bars and parties. On weekends she was almost never home. That's why he picked a Tuesday night.

No nightlife on a Tuesday. Amy had work in the morning.

She wasn't so wild now, though, between his thighs, his weight pinning her to the mattress. He finished tying her hands, and she cried harder, so he knew they were tight enough. Soon she'd start to lose circulation to her fingers, and he might give her a tiny taste of hope by loosening the rope.

If he was making her more comfortable, surely that meant he was going to let her live, right?

They always tasted better when they got that euphoric hit of hope.

That's when he'd cut them open.

With Amy, though, he liked the way she wriggled and squirmed. He ran the blade of his knife along her inner thigh, and she bucked under him, squealing into the piece of fabric he'd tied around her mouth. Old bedsheets Kim had thrown out. He'd sliced them to ribbons and put in his kit.

Turned out she was helpful to him sometimes after all.

"What if I stuck this knife inside you?" he whispered into her ear, trailing the blade all the way up to where her thigh met her panties, putting sharp pressure on the cotton seam.

Amy cried.

"No? Not the knife. Something else then. Don't you worry, Amy, be that good little girl I know you can be, and this will all be over soon. I promise."

Ed undid his belt, making sure to do it nice and close to her ear so she could hear the tension of the leather, the sigh as it passed through each belt loop. When he undid his zipper, she began to hyperventilate.

Yes, tonight was going to be a very good night.

When he was done, and Amy's crying had been silenced at last, Ed took his time in her apartment. He stripped off the remainder of his clothes and bundled them up in a paper bag he'd brought with him, then headed into her cramped bathroom.

Her whole apartment was small, barely more than a studio, but given the illusion of being a one-bedroom because the bed technically had its own area. Still, he could barely swing his dick in the place without bumping into her secondhand furniture and the piles of shit she had lying everywhere.

"Not a very clean girl, were you, Amy?" He lazily kicked a pile of used towels out of his way as he climbed into her shower. At this time of night there wasn't much competition for hot water, so he was able to take his time, clean the smears of fresh red blood from his skin and hair, though he was sad to see them go.

He should have sat around longer, enjoying the blood as it turned tacky on his skin, but he'd learned from past experience that as it dried it got harder and harder to get it all off.

While Kim had never noticed any on him before, she was starting to pay sharper attention to him when he came home from the city. He'd learned to ensure his backup clothes were the ones he left the house in, and changed to secondhand items before entering the girls' homes. Clothes Kim wouldn't notice were missing because she never knew he had them.

Ed rested his head against the warm tile of the shower and thought about Amy, about the way her voice had gone ragged when he'd finally cut her open, and the way he'd silenced her animal braying by slitting her throat.

He'd let her twitch under him a few moments more after that, but when she went well and truly still he was done, and it was time to move on.

Still, she was fresh in his mind's eye now, a memory that would sit with him for weeks, keep him calm and present. He'd be quiet, normal, at least for a little while. Long enough for Kim to stop hovering. Long enough to be the father Megan needed.

Long enough.

Until the next time.

TWENTY-SIX

The drive from Margot's apartment in North Beach to the San Quentin State Prison would take less than an hour. If not for the outcrop of Richardson Bay, she could have probably seen the prison on a clear day, settled in along the water like a fancy spa getaway.

What was it with prisons in the Bay Area getting such prime real estate?

She hadn't visited Alcatraz since middle school, and understood its location was entirely a matter of isolating prisoners from the heavily populated mainland, but still, pretty sweet spot right in the middle of the Bay.

San Quentin, she knew, was no spa, in spite of its relatively lovely location. Much like Alcatraz it was isolated, or as isolated as it could be when surrounded by one of the most populous cities in America. She'd never been to the prison, having had no reason to visit until now, but she knew what the interior would look like. Cold, impersonal, multiple levels of cells where prisoners would spend the majority of their days.

She wouldn't see any of that when she arrived, though. Ed Finch wasn't being kept in the general population, and meetings between outsiders and death row inmates were carefully orchestrated, to say the least. They would meet privately, with only her, Andrew, and Ed's lawyer.

And the guards. Of course, the guards.

Andrew had offered to drive up with her, but she didn't need to share this experience with him. Just getting there was going to be difficult, and every few minutes she thought about turning her car around and heading home. She had to laugh at the idea of pulling an illegal and impossible U-turn on the Golden Gate Bridge to back down from what she had agreed to do today.

No, she needed these forty-five minutes alone to prepare herself; not that this was a scenario anyone could really *prepare* for. She hadn't seen her father in over twenty years, hadn't really thought of him as her *dad* for that entire time.

Ed was a bad dream she couldn't ever fully awaken from, and today she would be entering that nightmare willingly. She got off the bridge and quickly realized she was heading back in the direction of Muir Woods, which sent a prickle down her spine.

Death was inescapable here, it was like no matter where she looked or where she was going, the memory of the place was stained in death. She should have been taking this road to drive home to Petaluma, to visit her parents on a break from work, maybe meet a nice girl Justin had brought home. Instead, Justin and Megan were gone, they might as well be dead, because they had been erased from the memory of the world.

And Ed, well Ed was sitting there waiting for her to come to him, to present herself like the good little daughter she was. *Daddy's girl.* His voice echoed in her head, something she hadn't heard in decades, but was as crisp and real as it would have been if they spoke daily. She remembered acutely the way words rasped at the back of his throat like he was a smoker, but Ed actually abhorred smoking. He always sounded a little like he was rolling a mouthful of marbles in his cheeks when he spoke, not quite with a lisp, but something that kept his words from being crisp or elegant.

She used to love listening to him talk, the lurching uneven quality of it, it was so uniquely him that she could have recognized him from across a dark room on the cadence of his words alone.

Now she was so bone-scared of hearing him say her name that she wished she'd never agreed to this.

Margot passed the exit for Muir Woods, an urge to pull off there and walk deep into the trees, possibly to never return, so intense that her palms prickled, her fingers itching to hit the turn signal.

Coward.

But that wasn't wholly fair to her either. She'd been fifteen when she lost her father, and that's usually how she phrased it to people. *I lost my father when I was fifteen.* It gave the impression of a tragic passing, of a beloved paternal figure shuffling free of his mortal coil and leaving his family without him. The image it conjured for most people was half-true, which was true enough for Margot's purposes. It wasn't a lie in saying that she'd never known her father, or he'd gone out to get milk one day and simply never returned. She *had* lost her father when she was fifteen, by his own hand, and his own choices.

The day Andrew, the FBI task force, and the local Petaluma police department had shown up on their front lawn, guns drawn and voices elevated, still haunted her. The image of Ed being led away in handcuffs, a gaggle of officers watching his every step, practically begging him to step out of line and give them an opportunity. Let them pull the trigger.

There were days Margot wished Ed had fought, had given them the excuse.

She wished he was truly dead, and not just dead to her, because then she wouldn't have to know he was out there, practically walking in her shadow now, breathing the same Bay air as her, so close she was sure he'd give away all her secrets and ruin her life yet again.

The man she was going to see today wasn't her father. He was a killer, a prisoner, and as far as she was concerned, was a means to an end. If visiting him today would mean closure for some unknown family, then she had to do it. She had to give them that much, and bring another lost daughter home.

As she drove, the radio DJs chatted inanely about the newest superhero film coming to theaters in a few weeks, and whether comic movies were only for nerds, and Margot watched the lush greenery of Muir Woods give way to a split vision. On the left side of the highway were exits that would take her to various hiking trails, like the unoriginally named Engagement Hill where lovers could propose in the most Insta-grammable way possible, the Bay and Golden Gate Bridge as an idyllic backdrop for the moment.

On the right-hand side of the road things were more settled, modern, with Marin City approaching and the signs of industry and settlement everywhere. It was an unusual juxtaposition, the beautiful, lush greenery of the woods, and then the day-to-day living of a bustling city area.

Soon she was angling away from the verdant, inviting views and heading toward a wide-open space, sunbaked with the shimmering Bay behind. Passing through the charmingly anointed Strawberry, she knew it wouldn't be long before the prison would be visible, and before she was quite comfortable accepting it, there would be signs guiding her to turn off for San Quentin.

Margot had been sure, in spite of her misgivings, that she was ready for this, but she was now profoundly aware of why it was she'd really told Andrew she wanted to come on her own.

She pulled off to the side of the road just past Strawberry, her pulse hammering and blood throbbing in her ears. The background swishing sounds of traffic were nothing but a hum behind the dull roar of her own heartbeat. Her temples hammering in rhythm, a sharp, aggressive headache coming on almost out of nowhere, making the bright morning light all but unbearable.

Turning off her car entirely, she engaged her blinkers and rested her forehead against the steering wheel, trying to remember what her therapist told her, trying to maintain some sense of calm in the onslaught of panic. The car felt both incredibly small, and also like it was comforting her, a metal shell keeping the world outside at bay.

She cracked a window, and squeezed her eyes closed tightly, blotting out the sunlight as best she could. Margot ground the heels of her palms into her eye sockets, too aggressively and certainly managing to smudge her mascara to shit, but the pressure felt good.

"One." A deep breath in through the nose, held, and released in a long sigh. "Two." She repeated the process again and again, focusing only on counting and on the in and out of her breath. It was only her and her breath in the car, no expectations, no plans; she had nowhere to go and nothing to do except sit in this car and *be*.

"Twenty."

Her skin prickled, covered in goosebumps, but her forehead and neck were beaded with sweat. It was too hot to be sitting in the car without air conditioning on, even with the window fully open. Once she was sure she could breathe on her own and open her eyes without unease, she let her head slump back against the driver's seat headrest, and turned the key in the ignition before finally letting her eyelids flutter apart.

It was day, the sun was high in the sky and there wasn't a cloud to be seen. This wasn't a scary back alley somewhere, and no one was lurking in the darkness, waiting to show her just how fragile, fleeting, and terrifying life was. She was, at least for this moment, alive and untouched, and she could do this.

She *had* to do this, because it was the right thing. Too bad that, no matter how many times she told herself all of the good and valid reasons she was making this drive, there was a deeper calling that made her get in the car that morning, and it had nothing to do with the moral white area of playing the hero to some family she'd never met.

The truth of the matter was, she hadn't seen her father in twenty-odd years and she was... curious.

She started the engine, turned off her blinkers and waited for a gap in traffic before easing back onto the highway.

Margot didn't miss him, not the man he really was. The man she missed had died a long time ago, if he had ever truly existed at all. She had a hard time trusting her own memories when it came to her childhood experiences with Ed. How much of that was real, and how much had been the mask worn by a psychopath who was only pretending to be a human?

The hugs, the gifts, the love, the guidance. Ed had taught her to ride a bike, and had taught her how to be wary on dates in terms of boys who might try to push her for more. He had spent years teaching her to protect herself, and what she understood now, better than anything, was that he was teaching her to protect herself from men like him.

No, Margot wasn't curious about her father, but she *was* curious about Ed, about what he looked like and if his voice sounded the same. She wondered if he might show signs of repentance for what he'd done, not that he'd ever indicated a sense of guilt in the past.

She wanted to know if he was an old man now. Surely, he must be, but she couldn't picture him as fragile or infirm. She was almost forty herself, now, and Ed was in his mid-sixties, which was ancient compared to her memory of him when she was fifteen. Margot wanted to know who he was now. She didn't have any lingering dreams of telling him off or trying to make him feel sorry for what she'd been through. She wasn't Megan Finch anymore.

But the fifteen-year-old girl she'd been couldn't help but wonder if she might be able to catch a glimpse of the man who had been her father, sneaking glances somewhere under the surface of the monster he'd become.

The monster he always was.

TWENTY-SEVEN

The rules of visiting a death row inmate at San Quentin were made very clear to Margot well in advance of her arrival. Ed, while notorious, was hardly special within the walls of the prison, and wasn't the only serial killer in there either.

Margot had been given all sorts of direction on what to wear, what she could bring, and how to prepare herself for the visit. Her gun, naturally, had been left at home, and she locked her badge in her glove compartment when she parked in the visitor lot.

She couldn't wear jeans—too close to prison-issue pant colors—and had opted instead for black slacks and a butter-yellow shirt with three-quarter length sleeves. Anything form-fitting was a no-go, so she'd picked the most modest clothing she had. She wore plain black slip-on flats, and had skipped an underwire bra. No jewelry, and her hair was pulled up in a top knot bun. She was about as muted as she could make herself.

Condemned. That's what they called the men on death row here, and there were different places they were housed, and different designations of their visitation levels. Condemned prisoners of the A grade were those who behaved themselves and were allowed contact visits. B grade prisoners had to sit in isolation cages for in-person meetings.

Ed was considered A grade, meaning he was quiet and polite to the guards and didn't throw shit at anyone. Good for him. But he was also a serial killer, one of the worst in American history, and was housed in the worst of the three death row wards at San Quentin, the Adjustment Center, or A/C as she'd heard it called.

From Margot's peripheral understanding of the sections of the prison, the A/C was basically a prison *within* the prison; those who stayed there were either in solitary confinement or intended to be kept away from the general population. These guys were, to put it lightly, the absolute biggest pieces of shit in the entire place. Murderers, rapists. The Adjustment Center was where Charles Manson had been housed when he was still alive.

And now, it was where her father lived.

She was grateful she wouldn't see Ed in his cell, that wasn't something guests were privy to, even those attending on police visits. She didn't need to know what he did in his spare time, how he decorated it, if he had a TV. The fewer things that could potentially humanize Ed, the better, frankly.

Margot followed all the instructions she'd been given in advance, heading to the visitor center, where she met with Ford Rosenthal and Andrew, both of whom were already waiting. She registered at the desk and was surprised that the person she spoke to showed no reaction to the name Ed Finch. Given there were over seven hundred death row inmates and almost four thousand prisoners in one building, it was probably hard to single out any one as being the actual *worst*, she had to admit. She also knew there were guys there in the general population who definitely didn't deserve to be lumped into the same category as her father.

As they waited for their escort, she sat down on a long

bench next to Andrew and gave him a once-over. "You got old," she whispered.

He chuckled. "You're not fifteen anymore, either, you know."

His appearance was still a surprise to her. He'd been in his mid-thirties when they'd arrested Ed, which meant he was now pushing sixty. But despite Margot's teasing, the years had been kind to Andrew. Instead of the fresh-faced, clean-shaved young man he'd been when she first met him, his hair had gone almost fully silver, and he was sporting a tidy salt-and-pepper beard. Lines had deepened in the creases around his eyes and mouth, but they just made him look like a man who was still able to laugh, in spite of the horrors of his day-to-day life.

He looked good. Handsome.

Rosenthal was precisely how Margot had imagined him from their conversations on the phone. He was young, but going prematurely bald at the back of his head, and he was a little thick around the middle. He wore silver-framed glasses and appeared, to her, to be a man who knew what a hedge fund was and wouldn't mind talking to you about it at length during a dinner party.

Margot and Rosenthal were never going to be friends, and she resented him on a personal level for forcing her to be here.

After being checked and briefed once again on the rules, Margot, Andrew, and Rosenthal were escorted into the prison itself, through a maze of locked doors and gates, and finally led into what looked like a small cafeteria.

Margot took a deep steadying breath as she entered the sterile gray room, which was filled with about a half dozen white circular tables with bench seats built in. Margot wasn't sure what she'd imagined in terms of how she would meet Ed after all these years, but she had expected it to be a bit more... distant. Phones through a glass window, perhaps? She would have been fine with an isolation meeting where he was kept in a cage and couldn't touch her.

The guard guided them to one of the tables, where she and Rosenthal sat down. Andrew remained hovering in the background, his hand frequently going to where his belt should have been, but he'd had to remove it in the visitor center. She knew exactly what he was feeling. She, too, kept wanting to touch her gun to assure herself she was still protected.

Instead, she needed to depend on the two guards standing in the corner of the room, each carrying a large automatic weapon, and while the guards looked detached and uninterested, she knew they'd be watching the interview the entire time.

As soon as they were settled at the table, an electronic buzzing sound drew their attention to the back of the room where one of the guards was standing. Two other guards entered, and sandwiched between them, shuffling along in his joined wrist and ankle restraints, was Ed Finch.

For a moment, Margot completely forgot how to breathe. However she had expected today to go, she already knew she wasn't going to be able to control what came next. She wanted to cry and throw up in equal measure, but more than anything she desperately wanted to run out of the room.

Ed wore the prison-issued uniform for condemned inmates: navy blue sweatpants with yellow letters that said CDCR PRISONER down one leg, and a plain blue short-sleeved shirt that looked an awful lot like scrubs. His shoes, from what she could tell, looked like Converse.

He was older, much like Andrew, but because she had avoided any news or information about Ed through her adulthood, his appearance was almost startling.

For one thing, he'd lost weight. Not in a gaunt, hungry way, but the man she remembered had always been a bit on the pudgy side, an early classic case of "dad bod." Now Ed, even in his mid-sixties, looked like he worked out with some regularity and had shed much of that extra fat he once carried around.

He looked tired though, his skin a sallow, pale shade, his ginger beard flecked through with white hairs, and silver at his temples as well. Bags creased the skin under his eyes, dark, bruise-like circles making the blue-green irises of his eyes pop.

Those eyes were now locked on her.

Ed and the guards shuffled closer, and they helped guide him onto one of the benches before undoing the chains around his wrists and ankles. Margot bit back the sudden urge to ask them to re-chain him.

You're safe, she reminded herself.

The threat Ed had posed in the outside world had never been a threat to her. Still, a knot had formed between her throat and chest, making it hard to swallow or breathe as he put his hands on the white Formica tabletop and reached across to her, smiling.

Margot physically recoiled, pulling her hands away even as his rough fingertips brushed her skin. She felt cold, and wanted to wash herself immediately.

Andrew, who had taken a step forward when Ed moved, was censured by a guard. "I don't care who you are, bud, you're going to sit down when you're in my house." He jerked his chin toward an open seat at a nearby table, and Andrew complied, but Margot could tell he didn't like it.

She folded her hands in her lap and focused on her breathing for one second, then two, surprised and almost grateful that Ed didn't speak until she did.

"Ed." The single syllable was all but impossible to say calmly, and she was sure he could hear the venom dripping off her tongue even as she tried to act calm and unaffected.

"I'm glad you came." There it was, the same voice she had been imagining in the car, but this time all too real and present, not the making of her memories but the real Ed, licking gravel from the back of his cheeks with each consonant. He sounded, she realized then, like he was always a little drunk.

"You didn't give me much choice, did you?" She wanted to hold on to her anger, because it was the only thing keeping the fear and nausea at bay. If she could simply stay mad, she might get through this. She could even look at him now, taking in his face, marked with purple-brown age spots. His skin sagged in places, and unlike Andrew, the lines Ed had developed over time were between his brows and in the downward turn of his mouth.

Frown lines.

For some reason that made Margot feel better. Laugh lines on this man would have been such a cruel joke to the universe.

"Now, Megan, you don't need to be like that. This is friendly, this is bonding time."

Margot opened her mouth to correct him, but quickly stopped herself; she didn't want to tell him her new name. All the better he not get to touch that part of her life, and what she had built in the years he'd been away. It seemed like Rosenthal hadn't shared what he knew about her, much to her relief.

"We both know the only reason I'm here is because you said 'Seventy-Seven.' You knew perfectly well I'd come, because what choice would I have?"

"I see you brought a friend." Ed glanced over Margot's shoulder, his blue eyes locked on Andrew and any faux semblance of kindness draining away like he had exchanged one mask for another. "Special Agent Rhodes," he greeted coldly.

"Ed."

"How do you like the finery of my living arrangements? So nice of you to pick the nicest hole to bury me in."

Andrew wasn't playing, and shook his head. "You're here because you want to be. You could have stayed in New York and no one would have bothered you."

Ed rolled his eyes. "Because Clinton was such a day on the beach."

"At least Clinton doesn't have death row anymore, Ed. Not sure why you volunteered to come back to the Bay."

"I missed home." His eyes glistened, and for a moment it looked as if he was remembering something fondly, and Margot highly doubted it was her family. "I'm back where I belong now." This time his gaze landed on her, and the masks shifted again, and he was Ed, the man she remembered.

Too bad she had seen the magic act as it happened. The way his expressions had moved so fluidly from her to Andrew and back again was more than unnerving, it was genuinely terrifying. Was that what his victims had seen? First a smiling man, coercing his way into their homes asking for a phone, asking for help, anything to gain their trust.

And then what... the mask dropped? Jovial Ed vanished and was replaced by the Classified Killer. Had the women all known what was coming when they saw that change?

They must have.

Margot wondered how she could have ignored who he really for such a long time when she was younger. Had she excused his behavior, his outbursts of rage, as being something normal that every dad did sometimes? Had she simply not wanted to know?

Digging her fingernails into the tender flesh of her palm, she steadied herself and met Ed's gaze, though she didn't smile back at him.

"Now that you're home, let's do what you came back for."

"I came to see you." Again, the quick uptick at the corner of his mouth, the wrinkling around his eyes. It was a well-rehearsed fiction that a child inside her almost dared to believe in. "How are you, Megan? Really?"

"Please don't call me that," she whispered.

"Well, Ford won't tell me your *new* name," he spat, his tone suddenly acidic. "And Megan was the name I chose for you. It's a good name, it's *your* name."

Margot shook her head, fingernails piercing the skin on her hand, and she eased up so as not to cut herself too deeply. "You know what, you can call me whatever you want if it will make this easier. You can have this one."

Ed didn't boast, he didn't smile. If he felt like he'd won something it didn't show in his face.

"You look really grown up, Buddy," he said, lancing her with a nickname she hadn't heard in decades.

She steeled herself, in spite of the struggle to breathe.

"Yeah, well you got really fucking old."

TWENTY-EIGHT

Ed chuckled, but the laughter faded quickly, as if he counted to three and then stopped. "You should be nicer to me, if you want what I'm going to give you."

"You want people to know what you did, Ed, don't pretend otherwise. You're mad because there are other people out there taking lives and getting press. You're mad because Ted Bundy has fancy documentaries on TV and you don't. You think people are forgetting you, *that's* why you're here. And you're only going to get that with our help, so don't pretend you were homesick, and just talk." When Margot was done the air felt electric, as if the faintest spark of static off someone's shirt might set the room alight.

The hair on the back of her neck stood on end as Ed leveled her with a careful and cold glance, not as hateful as the one he'd reserved for Andrew, but definitely no longer faking for Father of the Year, either. There he was, then, the real Ed Finch. Not happy-go-lucky, not full of jokes and charm. Just ice cold, with an empty room behind his eyes where most people kept a soul.

"Who taught you to speak like that? It was your mother, wasn't it?"

"No, she killed herself before she could teach me things like that." Margot watched him, trying to gauge if there was any reaction. He would have known about Kim's suicide, of course; despite any barriers between him and her family, that was the sort of news that got around. Still, there was no emotion whatsoever on his face. "Nothing to say to that?"

"Your mother gave me the best thing in my life when she gave me you, and after that I'm not sure I had any more need for her and her abysmal attitude."

Margot was glad Justin wasn't around to hear how little Ed thought of him that his only son didn't bear mention in this conversation.

"Tell me about Seventy-Seven," Margot said.

"You sound very official, Megan, have you done this before?"

She was realizing, now, he was weaponizing her name against her because he knew she didn't want him to use it. He was doing whatever he could, in his limited capacity, to get the upper hand, and that only succeeded in pissing her off.

"I can tell you want me to share something, and you know what, let's do that, it'll be fun. I'm a police officer now. A detective. I catch men like you."

Ed leaned forward, resting his chin on his tented hands, and gave her a serious look, like if he stared at her for a long enough time, he might be able to read the secrets hidden inside her.

"Are you any good at it?"

"I think so."

"Are you working a case right now?"

"Yes."

"Was the victim a woman?" His head tilted to the side and for a moment his eyes half-closed as he drifted away from her, from this room, and off to somewhere she didn't want to imagine. When he focused on her again there was the faintest flush to his cheeks.

Her skin crawled.

"Yes."

Ed smiled. "Tell me her name and I'll tell *you* a name."

"I could make up a name, you wouldn't know."

"You wouldn't do that, Megan. That would be cheating, and I think I raised you right. To play by the rules."

Margot bit back what she wanted to say. Antagonism couldn't be a two-player game in here. If she wanted to know the victim's name, then perhaps she could give him what he wanted. What was the harm, it was public record anyway. She thought first of the Ramirez family, of the three women, their heads in foggy plastic bags, their blood flowing so thickly it had come right through the floor.

It felt wrong to give Evangeline, Emily, or Valentina to him.

While there wasn't a victim who deserved to be a bartering chip, she couldn't use those little girls.

She went, instead, to the most recent Muir Woods victim. The one who had made up Margot's mind for her. The reason she was here at all. "Leanne Wu," she said.

Ed's eyes closed completely. "Asian?"

"Chinese," Margot confirmed.

"How old?"

Margot's tongue was thick and sour in her mouth as she spoke again. "Twenty-five."

Ed smiled to himself, his eyes still closed. "How did she die?"

"That's more than name for a name. If I tell you how she died, you're going to tell me *exactly* where to find Seventy-Seven, am I clear?"

Ed's eyes fluttered open, as if waking from the best dream he'd ever had. "You tell me what I want to know, I'll tell you."

"Blunt force trauma." She tapped the place on the back of her own head. It was the first lie she'd told since arriving, but she'd done it for good reason. Her answer must not have been helpful to Ed's fantasy process, because he watched her make the motion, and his smile became a grimace.

He didn't approve of blunt force trauma.

Ed had always been a knives kind of guy.

"Now it's your turn," Margot said flatly.

For a long minute she thought he might not do it. It's not like it would be a shocking plot twist for the psychopath to go back on his promises. They didn't feel remorse about things, after all, so lying was as easy as breathing, something she knew all too well about her father at this point.

"You're right, you know, about one thing."

Margot didn't want to keep playing games with him, but it was her own damn fault for putting up with his requests up until this point. Had she just told him to fuck off right from the get-go he would have known she couldn't be manipulated. Instead, he'd played her, and he'd won, and as a result he was going to keep right on pushing her buttons until he found her limit.

She had no idea what that limit was, because she desperately wanted to find this last victim, and if that meant dealing with his bullshit, she was going to need to do it.

"What's that?" she asked.

"You're not Megan anymore."

Margot sat back as best she could, considered the seat had no backing, and met Ed's gaze with as much intensity as he was giving her. She didn't say a single thing more, and crossed her arms over her chest. Her palm was throbbing from where she'd dug her nails in.

"I do think I'd like to get to know this person better, though." He smiled to himself, but it was almost sad, and she wasn't able to tell if that was faked like everything else, or if he really was mourning something lost between them.

"Tell me her name," Margot insisted.

"Tell me yours."

"Absofuckinglutely not," Andrew interjected, moving like he might stand up.

The nearby guard clucked his tongue once, and Andrew froze, settling back onto his bench. Margot lifted her hand to the FBI agent, hoping to appease him, but never taking her eyes off Ed.

"That wasn't the deal. The only name of mine you ever need to know is the one you gave me. End of story."

"We'll see." He nodded to himself, his gaze briefly drifting over to Rosenthal for the first time since he'd sat down. It was almost as if he'd forgotten the other two men were present.

"Let's say there *is* a seventy-seventh," Ed said after a long pause.

"We *are* saying that."

"Allegedly," interjected Rosenthal.

"Oh, fuck right off with your *allegedly*," Margot growled.

Ed grinned and took a pause to chew on a hanging bit of cuticle and the corner of his thumbnail, working the hard bit of tissue between his teeth. When he realized what he was doing he stopped immediately, putting his palm flat on the table.

"*If* there was a seventy-seventh, you know, it would be so hard for me to keep track of them all at that point."

Margot stood, and both guards still in the room moved in unison, coming toward the table.

"Ma'am," said a younger one, his finger trembling near the trigger of his weapon. "I'm going to need you to sit down, or this visitation is over."

"Maybe it should be," Margot said, glaring at Ed.

"Sit down," Ed said.

"Maybe you never intended to tell me anything."

"Sit *down*," he snarled, and a chill shot down Margot's spine.

She thought she'd seen the monster earlier when his fake friendly veneer was chipped away, but no. There he was, in front of her now. Blood drained from her face and though her whole body resisted, and her brain screamed at her not to give in, she sat.

The guards hovered a moment longer before retreating slowly back to where they'd been standing before.

Ed's entire body was trembling, but it was so subtle she doubted anyone but her could see the way he shook. Anything resembling humanity was gone from his eyes, replaced with an empty blackness in the pupils that made him look like a shark.

"Tell me her name, Ed, or I'm leaving this place and I'll never, *ever* come back." She had no intention of setting foot in this prison again after they were done here, but she had to hope that his desire to see her, the thing that had brought him all the way back to California, was enough to make him cave now.

"Theresa. Her name was Theresa. I don't remember her last name, she was a hitchhiker I met on the road in September 1993. I left her body in the woods off a service road near Old Mill Road, off the one-sixteen."

Margot stared at him for a long time, waiting for her voice to work. "Between Petaluma and Sonoma?" she asked.

Ed nodded, as if waiting for her to put the pieces together.

"In September 1993?" Margot had been thirteen at the time, and a friend of hers lived in Sonoma, the small city nearest Petaluma. She frequently had Ed drive her there on Friday nights so she and Lucy could spend a weekend together playing Barbies and watching forbidden horror movies after Lucy's parents went to bed.

Margot swallowed hard. "Seriously? Dropping off or picking up?" The question wouldn't make sense to anyone else in the room.

"That time?" Ed asked.

TWENTY-NINE
SEPTEMBER 13, 1993

Highway 116, near Sonoma, California

The sun was still hanging on the mid-horizon as Ed steered the car back toward Petaluma. The weather that week had been blistering hot. Some might have called it Indian summer, but to Ed it still felt like the peak of summer proper, and Megan and Justin had insisted on having the backyard inflatable pool filled up again.

For Ed, summer had felt like something of a gift. He'd enjoyed spending time with the kids, and Kim had picked up a new job at the local library that kept her busy several evenings a week, leaving Ed at home to do house-husband duty after work.

What he'd discovered in those torrid summer months was that he *liked* the distraction. He was beginning to know his children more, as they started their journey to becoming little adults, and Megan especially was becoming a sidekick to him.

She was thirteen, and starting to show signs of becoming a woman, something Ed knew was inevitable, but had hoped he might ignore a few years longer. But she was beginning to blossom. From Kim's motherly intel he knew she'd started her period a year earlier, and had begun developing little breasts, but now he noticed the way her cheeks flushed when she saw boys at the store.

She'd started to become more independent, too, taking her bike out on her own to meet friends and staying out to play until the sun began to drop.

The little cul-de-sac they lived on had plenty of families with kids Megan and Justin's ages, making Ed's job of keeping them amused a lot easier. In an unspoken arrangement between the block's parents, each day someone new would put out a sprinkler on their front lawn, and all the local children would merge on that property, splashing and screaming as the cold water pelted them.

In those months, with his focus on the kids and being a dad, with enough distance between himself and Kim that she didn't push his buttons on a daily basis and her mood was boosted by the new job, he felt a temporary peace within him.

For a little while, the hunger inside was quiet.

He wasn't sure how long it would last, and if perhaps it was a permanent shift, but he didn't spend his time at the store looking for potential options. He didn't listen to the voice messages left by women and decide based on the way they sounded and how they described themselves if he was going to go look for them.

It had been over two months since he'd jotted down a name and address.

The knives were all safely stored in his shed, and he rarely dreamed these days of blood and fear. The kids were happy. Kim was happy. Ed felt like this was the life he had intended to have. He would spend evenings while Kim was at work, after the kids had been fed, watching TV with them, or sometimes he'd let Megan stay up late and they'd sit on the back deck together and talk.

He liked getting to know her as a person, seeing the parts of himself that had gone into making her. She was funny in the same sarcastic way he was, and he liked that he caught her smiling proudly whenever she made him laugh.

She was smart, too. So smart. She had been using her summer hours not just in play, but had built her own summer reading list and took her bike to the library two or three times a week to return old books and take out new ones. A little spot under the tree in their backyard had a patch where grass wouldn't grow anymore because Megan hauled the deckchair cushions out there to sit and read for hours.

Then the end of August came on, still sticky-hot and brilliant blue, but the sprinklers were soon just for lawn maintenance, and the sound of shrieking laughter died away. Megan, Justin, and the other local children returned to school, and each morning after he walked them to the bus stop at the end of the road, a nagging emptiness began to build inside him.

Kim was still working evenings, and Ed had his work at the paper to keep him busy during the day, but when the kids came home there was homework to do, bedtime hours to be observed, and Ed no longer felt as needed as he had over the summertime.

He started to notice names more. Brenda. Kylie. Patricia. Their voices followed him to bed at night. *Hi, I'd like to place a personal ad. Single white female, twenty-five. Slim, pretty, seeking man twenty-five to forty. Serious commitments only. Must love cats.*

Ed did not care for cats.

He imagined Patricia's apartment, a thin layer of cat dander covering everything. He'd encountered women with pets before and they made him nervous. Inevitably the hair of the animal always came with him, sticking to his clothes, the fabric inside his car. It took weeks to get rid of that hair, and he could never be entirely certain he got it all.

Not that anyone would ask questions about a few dog or cat hairs. Those could come from anywhere.

Still, pets made him nervous. Animals were unpredictable, sometimes defensive. Cats didn't care for humans much one way or the other, but dogs? He'd left a woman alive and untouched once because she had a big German Shepherd dog that looked at him the second he got to her apartment door with a face that said *I know what you're thinking of doing.*

Ed wouldn't say he was afraid of dogs, but he didn't like the looks of that one. That night he'd gone to a nearby park where a handful of homeless people camped together. He'd watched them from his car for a good hour, trying to determine if there was an opportunity among them to feed his hunger, but they were all too close, too aware of each other and outsiders.

They would have noticed if someone had come into their midst.

He'd gone home unsatisfied, and swore from then on, he would be aware of dogs ahead of time.

Cats he plain didn't like.

So, Patricia was a non-starter.

But he was thinking about them again, about the girls. He was listening for one with a voice he thought might sound good when it cried, when it begged. *Please, please don't, I'll do anything, just don't hurt me. Must love dogs.*

Ed wanted something, and he no longer felt fully satisfied at home. But things weren't bad, he didn't feel like Kim was pushing, nagging, wearing him down. He didn't feel like the raw, frayed nerve he usually was when he decided it was time to pick a girl.

Still, that evening on the highway, as he drove home from taking Megan to her friend's house, he saw the girl on the side of the road. Her shape beckoned to him like a crooked finger, calling him to the shoulder of the highway.

She was young, maybe sixteen or seventeen. Usually, Ed didn't like them that young, he preferred them a bit older, with their own routines and spaces. He liked women, their fully formed bodies, little bellies he could cut into. Girls were all angles and sharp edges.

This one looked well-built, though, even under the green military surplus jacket she wore. Her hair was blond, worn in a high ponytail with teased bangs that stuck out two inches above her forehead. The sleeves of her jacket were pushed up to her elbows, and on each wrist was a stack of at least fifteen bracelets in every color of the rainbow. They looked like the beaded friendship bracelets Megan had been obsessed with making earlier in the summer, forcing Ed to endure many trips to the local craft store for shimmery plastic junk.

He pushed Megan from his mind, trying not to think of his daughter as he assessed this girl on the road. Her hips and chest were fully developed, giving her a womanly hourglass figure. He would have thought her older if not for the roundness and baby fat still filling out her cheeks. Her thumb was out to the road, and she pouted as if personally affronted by every car that wouldn't slow down for her.

Ed pulled up, pausing a few feet away. The girl lowered her sunglasses and squinted at him, trying to make out his features through the glaring sun on the car's windshield. Ed put on his friendliest dad face and waved. As she jogged over, he leaned across the passenger seat to roll down the window, giving her an aw-shucks shit-eating grin as he did.

"Hey there. Dangerous to be out here alone, you know? Where are you headed?"

"Going to San Fran," she said.

Not a local, then. He eyed her big backpack, the thick layers of dust on her clothes, and wondered how long she'd been on the road.

"Well, I'm headed to Petaluma, that'll get you to the one-oh-one. Maybe you can catch a bus from there."

The girl snorted. "Mister, if I could afford a bus, you think I'd be standing out here talking to you?"

Ed unlocked the door and pushed it open. "No, I don't suppose you would."

She got in, giving him another assessing once-over as she did. Whatever she was looking for in terms of red flags, she obviously didn't see any. Ed knew what she saw. A man in a button-down short-sleeved shirt and khaki shorts. Socks and sandals. The back seat had a bunch of Justin's toys on the seat, and one of Megan's favorite Barbies, which it now occurred to him she would be missing this weekend.

Too late to turn back now.

The car door clicked shut in a satisfying way. The girl smelled sweet, faintly of sweat and suntan lotion, but also of a perfume he vaguely recognized, soft and childlike, the lingering scent of baby powder.

That was something else he liked about women, real women. They smelled of more expensive things: flowers and vanilla, perfumes with French names. Sometimes he'd spray their perfumes on something they owned, underwear, a scarf, and take it with him. Keep it until the scent had faded away completely.

Once he'd taken a full bottle of Oscar de la Renta perfume, unopened, that one girl had obviously bought recently, or been waiting for a special occasion to use, and gave it to Kim. It still gave him a thrill every time she wore it.

Baby powder, though, felt different, maybe a little wrong.

Oh well.

He started the car, watching from the corner of his eye as she glanced around, getting her bearings.

"You got kids?" she asked.

"Two. Boy and a girl."

"Cool." She did up her seat belt, and Ed steered the car back onto the highway. The girl left her window down, the windy air from the open road ruffling her sky-high blond bangs.

"What's your name?" he asked, keeping his tone light and friendly.

"What's yours?" she countered.

"Ed."

"Hoo boy. Ed. That's a real dad name, ain't it. Wow. Never Eddie? Ed. Woof, what a bummer."

"You can call me Eddie if you want to." He shrugged. "Ed never bothered me, though."

"Well, Eddie, I'm Theresa. Mom called me Tessie sometimes."

"What do you like?" He kept his eyes glued to the road, but his palms were starting to sweat, and a familiar gnawing sensation grew in his belly.

"I think I like Theresa."

"Theresa it is." He turned on his signal, angling the car onto a dirt road that disappeared into thick trees.

"Where are you going?" Her voice was nervous, though she tried to hide it.

"Don't worry. I've done this before." He glanced over at her and smiled, his biggest, friendliest smile.

Theresa didn't look convinced.

"Like a shortcut?"

"Mmhmm."

He realized, then, he didn't have his knives with him. They were all neatly locked away in his shed. Ed gripped the steering wheel, leather creaking under his damp palms.

Too late to turn back now.

THIRTY

Margot made a beeline from the visitor center to her car, but before she was even halfway across the parking lot, she bent double and threw up on the scorched gray concrete.

She had nothing in her stomach but coffee, and the acidic burn of it at the back of her throat made her retch a second time. She stayed bent at the waist, staring at the brown puddle in front of her shoes, until she was positive she was done, then she spit once, wiped her chin on the back of her hand, and straightened up.

Andrew Rhodes stood in front of her, allowing a few feet of distance between himself and the vomit.

"I was going to ask if you were OK, but I don't think I need to anymore," he said.

"If we're being brutally honest here, Andrew—and I feel like I can be in this particular moment of disgusting vulnerability—I'm not sure I could tell you the last time I was *OK*."

"Fair."

Margot sidestepped the puddle, wishing she had a water bottle or something, not just to clear out the burnt coffee taste in her mouth, but also to wash away the evidence of her weakness.

That's what it felt like: weakness. At least she'd waited until she was outside the prison before it happened, which was about the closest thing to a victory she could imagine today.

"You think he was telling the truth?" she asked, continuing in the direction of her car. Andrew followed behind her, falling into step as they walked down the rows of visitor cars.

"We're going to look for missing women that fit the name and description, but yeah, I think he was being genuine. You want to tell me what that last little bit was about? 'Dropping off or picking up?'"

They were at Margot's car now, and she had the key fob in her hand. "The road he was talking about, it was how he would take me to a friend's place in Sonoma. When he killed her, Theresa, whoever she was, he had just dropped me off. He wouldn't have been there if it wasn't for me." She stared vacantly at the shiny window of the driver's side door. "She might..."

"You can't think like that, Margot. What's done is done, and it's not your fault, you need to remember that. None of this is your fault."

Margot scoffed. "What a fucking stupid sentiment. I'm sorry, look, I know you mean well, and truly I know I'm not the one who killed her, but the truth is he wouldn't have been on that road on that day if it hadn't been for me. I didn't kill her, but I put him in the literal position to be there *to* kill her. The time, the place. He's to blame, but *opportunity* is part of any crime, and I gave him that."

Andrew stared at her, unblinking. "Does it help you, to put some of the blame on yourself? Do you feel like you're carrying some of his burden that way?"

"Don't you start with that psycho-babbly shit on me today, OK? I'm not in the mood. I have a therapist for that, and she's already going to have a field day with this."

"I'm not a therapist."

"No, but I've seen your book blurb bio, haven't I? I know you have a Masters in psychology."

"Abnormal psychology."

Margot laughed, a short, humorless hiccup of a sound. "Perfect." She wanted to get into her car and have a nervous breakdown in peace. Was that too much to ask?

"Do you want to come with us?" Andrew asked.

The question was unexpected, and she didn't have an immediate retort handy. She stopped playing with her car key and looked him directly in the face, as opposed to shouting at his reflection in her window.

"To find the girl?"

Andrew nodded. "He didn't give us too much to go on, it'll probably take a few days to find her, once we get access to some cadaver dogs. I think it might help you a bit, to be there when we find her."

Margot thought about it for a minute, then a minute more. She knew her father's crimes almost by heart. She'd seen the late-night TV specials, she'd read Andrew's book. She knew the names of the seventy-six women he'd killed probably better than Ed or Andrew did. But she'd never been in a position to see one of them, to *find* one of them.

It was bittersweet, and she felt almost guilty for how badly she wanted to go. Since finding the right words was a struggle, she simply nodded.

"In a professional capacity, of course. Some of my team will need to know, just to understand why it is Ed would share the details with some random cop after all these years. And obviously the Bureau has a record of your name change if anyone wanted to go digging—it's not like you're in Witness Protection. But I think the fewer people on the local team who know, the better."

"That's generally my rule of thumb in life, yes."

"All right. Well, give me a few days to put something

together, get the dogs called in, and I'll let you know when we're ready to head north. When was the last time you were in Petaluma?"

Margot rested her hip against her car. "When we left. Twenty-two years? I haven't wanted to go up there since. There's nothing for me there anymore."

Andrew placed a big hand on her shoulder, his brown eyes warm. "Well, I guess now there is."

Nothing quite like a good old-fashioned body search to prove that you *can* indeed go home again.

THIRTY-ONE

The last thing in the world Margot wanted right then was to go home.

She thought about calling Wes, thought she might just throw common sense to the wind and show up at his house with a take-it-or-leave-it offer for a one-night stand, but unfortunately for her it was only one o'clock in the afternoon, and there was no way to make a mid-afternoon booty call with your work partner not look like a cry for help.

Which is exactly what it would have been.

The very notion of it sobered her up relatively quickly as she got back onto the highway heading home.

She'd booked the day off for this, which meant neither Wes nor Leon would be expecting her presence at the station. Part of her wanted to go in anyway, give her mind something to focus on other than what had just played out with Ed. But that, too, seemed like a bad idea that would lead to others asking too many questions rather than giving her the space she needed.

Not that she had any idea *what* she really needed right then.

A drink sounded great, but again, it was one in the afternoon, and she wasn't quite so dedicated to her alcoholism that she wanted to go down that path yet awhile.

No, she needed something less destructive and more focused, something to keep her mind busy before she let herself spiral into another panic attack. One of those per day was quite enough, and she'd already met her quota.

Later, *later* she could hide her phone to avoid drunk-texting her partner, and polish off an entire bottle of Sauvignon Blanc by herself. But in daylight hours, there were better ways to use her time.

In less than an hour she was back in the heart of the city and parking on a dangerously uphill slope near the offices of the *San Francisco Sentinel*. The old building had art deco flair with a white exterior that had aged to a creamy finish over its decades in the fog and sea air.

Margot locked her car behind her and made the uphill climb to the newspaper office. Once inside she could almost immediately smell paper and ink suffusing the air, a scent that was all at once foreign and familiar. She breathed deeply, feeling a modicum of comfort inside these walls.

At the front desk she was greeted by a handsome man with deep red-brown skin and dark hair, who was already smiling at her before she even uttered a word.

"Good afternoon, ma'am, welcome to the *Sentinel*. How can I help you today?"

Jesus, there were people in the world who could be this peppy? Terrifying.

"I need to speak to Sebastian Klein," Margot said. "Tell him it's Detective Phalen."

The receptionist's smile faltered the tiniest bit at the word *detective*, but he bounced back with gusto, blasting her once again with the mouthful of pearly whites. There was no way his teeth were that white naturally. No one reached adulthood without some kind of staining.

She thought briefly of Rebecca Watson, whose fresh veneers had made it impossible to identify her body at first. What a world.

One phone call and a few minutes later, Sebastian Klein had deigned to grace Margot with his presence. She'd once thought of him as an attractive option to periodically scratch her sexual itches, but quickly learned he was out on two counts. First, he'd figured out who she really was. Second, she was definitely not Sebastian's type.

Sebastian's type was more Captain America than Wonder Woman, though he'd told her once over drinks that he wouldn't be averse to giving it a try sometime if she was in dire straits.

As of yet her straits had not been that dire.

Sebastian was almost too attractive for his own good. Much like Wes, his handsomeness was at odds with what he did for a living. Surely there was a cologne ad somewhere that needed these men's faces on it. Instead, the only print marketing Sebastian's face ever saw was the little black-and-white photo that went next to his bylines in the newspaper.

He was a few inches under six feet and had the lean physique of someone who could eat whatever they wanted without gaining a pound. He was currently sporting a nice summer tan, which made his thick, perfectly styled black hair look all the darker for it.

Wearing thick-framed black glasses that he did not need, but wore to protect him from "blue light"—she actually believed it was to make him look smarter, which was wholly unnecessary —he was now staring her down through those same glasses.

"Margot Phalen, to what do I owe the dubious pleasure?"

"What if I told you it was purely social and I was here to take you to lunch?" she offered.

"I'd call you a lying harlot, but would still say yes to lunch."

.   .   .

Outside, Sebastian wrinkled his face at the sun, as if wanting to let it know how personally affronted he was by the heat. He was wearing a sweater that was probably made of cashmere, and perfectly tailored linen pants. He could have waltzed into a yacht club later and not looked a hair out of place among the upper elite of the city.

It was how he managed to get all the best dirt on people, because he *looked* like someone you wanted to share dirty little secrets with.

In Margot's case, she hadn't been given much choice, since he'd dug hers up without her knowing.

They walked up the block to a little sushi restaurant, somewhere they'd been together a handful of times before. He liked it because it was close to work, she liked it because it was nowhere near any other part of her life. After they placed their orders, Sebastian leaned back in his chair and gave her an all-too-knowing look.

"When were you going to tell me?" he asked.

"You're fishing. Don't be coy."

"That means you have more than one secret you're keeping from me, Margot, and you know I'll get them all eventually."

She snorted and sipped the green tea that had been delivered to them by their waitress. It tasted, to Margot, like steeped grass clippings, but she still kind of liked it.

"Tell me what you *know* first, and then I'll tell you one you don't," Margot offered.

Sebastian squinted at her. "Something story-worthy?"

"Probably."

He let out a little *harumph*, then finally gave in. Leaning across the table and lowering his voice to a conspiratorial whisper, he said, "When were you going to tell me Daddy was home?"

Oh, how she hated him for phrasing it like that. It was so lurid and gross, and made her skin crawl. "How did *you* find out?"

"It's not like prison transfers are top secret. Reporter friend of mine in New York told me earlier today. Brace yourself, because it's going in the paper tomorrow."

Margot swore under her breath. She'd really hoped no one would notice the quiet return of Ed Finch, but she supposed this was what *he* wanted. And as soon as she and Andrew found Seventy-Seven he'd become a national news spectacle again anyway. This was just sooner than she'd hoped. When Ed was the focus of media attention it always put her on edge, because it brought up unanswered questions about him.

Questions like, *Where are his kids now?*

It made her feel vulnerable.

"Could you please not mention my family?" she asked.

"Not planning to, don't worry."

"Thank you."

Sebastian shrugged, but she knew he'd done it for her, eased the burden of the news a little bit. She should be grateful, at least, she'd learned about Ed's return from his lawyer and not the local newspaper. That was one small silver lining in all of this shit.

"So, you know about that one, how would you feel about an exclusive?"

Sebastian leaned forward again, eyes gleaming, and Margot knew she'd chosen her words poorly. "No, not with me."

"Such a tease."

Margot debated how best to proceed. "Seb, the *Sentinel* still has Ed's old letters, don't they? The ones he started sending in the late eighties?"

"Yes." The affirmation was long and drawn out, more a question or concern than an actual answer. "They're not the originals, those were handed over to the FBI. We have copies of them all, though. Why?"

"I want to see them."

"So go talk to your BFFBI or whatever and get the originals."

Margot gave him a look. "Please give me this evidence on a long-closed case which I am not currently working because I'm *curious* and definitely not the killer's daughter. Come on, man."

"Like it's going to sound any less nuts when I ask for them out of the archives. *You* come on, man."

"What if you had a good reason to want to look at them?"

"Do I have a good reason?"

Margot knew she should wait until they had recovered Theresa's body before giving this information to Seb, but she also desperately wanted to go through those letters, to see if Ed had ever given any clues or indications that pointed not only to Theresa, but to potential others that they'd never pinned on him.

"What if there was a seventy-seventh victim?"

THIRTY-TWO

Sebastian had copies of the Ed Finch letters made and couriered to her apartment by that evening. While she'd had to swear on her life that she wasn't lying about the victim, Seb had needed to swear on his that he wouldn't leak information about Theresa before Margot gave him the go-ahead.

In order to make it worth his while, she had promised she'd give him the heads-up when she knew that Andrew's team was headed north to look for the body.

For the time being, Seb was satisfied to break the news of Ed's return, knowing they could do a highlight reel of Ed's past misdeeds for a few days, perhaps another in-depth focus on the monsters who had called San Quentin home, and then, just as things started to settle down again, he'd be able to break the biggest story of the year.

Ed Finch wasn't done.

Her stomach churned, knowing she'd used her inside knowledge of the case for her own benefit, but there was nothing she could do about that now. She had a thick envelope sitting on her dining room table waiting for her.

Some of the letters were already in the public domain, the

ones the paper had chosen to print, and a handful that Andrew had included in the back matter of his book about Ed. But Margot knew there'd been more. Not only had Seb told her so, but Andrew had intimated the same. Dozens of letters bragging about his kills, talking about who he'd kill next, and mocking the paper and the police for not being able to see what was right under their noses.

He really meant it in the case of the newspaper. Ed might not have worked for the *Sentinel* directly, but his work appeared on their pages. Both literally and metaphorically. Literally in that he handled classified recording for multiple different papers, including the *Sentinel*, and metaphoric in that they'd been splashing his misdeeds all over their front page for *years*.

This was before he was the Classified Killer. Back then they still called him the Bay Area Killer, but it wasn't until the mid-nineties that they were able to piece together how he'd found most of his victims.

Margot slid the stack of papers out of the envelope, the scent of fresh photocopier ink still clinging to the crisp, white pages. They were copies of copies of messily handwritten letters, meaning they weren't the easiest to read, but as she laid the pages out in front of her, she could only stare at them for a long time.

The handwriting, while not perfectly Ed's, bore enough telltale similarities she knew immediately it was his. The squat *o*, the *d*s all in upper case. She'd seen them on a dozen birthday cards. *Love, DaD*.

Unlike those cards, though, the writing here was slapdash and manic, none of the letters or words were uniform. In hindsight, she knew there had to be an element of intention to this wild writing, to make it less likely anyone would immediately recognize the style as his, but it looked like the penmanship of a lunatic.

*Hello editors (idiots), I see you've once again run a story about
me, but you continue to get all the details wrong. If you're going
to continue to make a mockery of journalism, let me give you
some insider tips. The girl in the gutter downtown wasn't me,
and I marvel at your simplicity for thinking it was. Really, you
think I'm capable of such an ugly, sloppy crime? Give me more
credit. Just look at the one I left in her home last week. No one
even heard her scream.*

Margot absorbed the words, the way he tried to make
himself sound polished and educated. It definitely reeked of the
self-satisfied gloating opinion Ed had of himself.

But he had never gone to college, and barely graduated high
school. He'd married her mother when they were both only
nineteen years old, and had been working since he was a
teenager. Ed might think himself a student of the world, but he
was not the man he projected onto those letters.

Good for him, though, because early profilers on the case
had a hell of a time pinning him down. They assumed he was
older, educated, had a reason to feel superior. They thought he
lived alone, or perhaps as the caretaker of an elderly relative,
someone he resented.

She'd learned a lot about the mistakes of the police and FBI
from reading Andrew's book, which had been very candid
about the shortcomings in the investigation. The police then
didn't have the same tools they did now, so it was hard to blame
them. When you couldn't check DNA samples for more than a
simple blood type, let alone match someone directly, it made
things incredibly difficult. Not to mention her father hadn't
been a career criminal. He'd never been fingerprinted or
entered into a database in his life until he was arrested for
seventy-six murders.

Science eventually caught up to Ed, but for the longest time
he was right to believe he was the smartest man in the room.

Margot flipped through several more of the letters, her stomach turning with the way he preened over his killings and mocked the press and police for their mistakes. He was vague about the details of his murders though, not letting much stand out that could tie to specific victims.

She found a letter from late 1993, however, that made her sit up straighter in her chair.

I've been quiet too long, you relaxed, you let your guard down. Now at an old mill there's a girl who won't ever make it to the big city. Never become complacent. I'm always there, waiting in plain sight. Even the light of day couldn't save her. Didn't need my knives, I am a killer without them.

Margot grabbed her laptop and opened up a maps site to show her the road between Petaluma and Sonoma. There, about halfway in between the two, was an offshoot called Old Mill Road, just like Ed had mentioned in their interview. Anyone reading Ed's letter would have assumed a literal mill, or that he was using a metaphor. Or perhaps he was simply lying.

But there it was, exactly where he told them Theresa's body would be found. He'd given this to them decades earlier, but no one made the connection, no one understood.

She snapped a photo of the letter and texted it to Andrew along with the message: *We need to keep digging.*

What else had they missed in all the clues Ed had given them over the years?

What other girls like Theresa were still out there waiting to be found?

THIRTY-THREE

Andrew Rhodes kicked at the dry patch of dirt and grass at his feet and adjusted his sunglasses, the piercing light beating down on him and the area around him. Margot stood next to him, her aviators covered in a fine coat of dust, giving the world a hazy, surreal quality.

"You know," Andrew began, "it's not often we understand the full scope of a killer's work at the time of arrest. Gary Ridgway, you know Gary Ridgway?" He glanced over at her.

"I am acutely aware of who the Green River Killer is, Andrew."

"OK, OK. Well, he was only convicted of forty-nine homicides."

"Only," Margot scoffed, as if the number wasn't disgustingly high on its own.

"Anyway, thing is that the police always thought he had way more victims, upwards of ninety."

"I'm not sure what you're trying to say."

Below them, a team of men and women in lightweight navy windbreakers with bright yellow letters spelling FBI were milling around between trees and underbrush. Some were squatted in place, scouring the ground for clues, while the majority were following behind two trained cadaver dogs, watching the pups as they nosed their way through the trees. One was a yellow lab named Buster, the other, a coonhound named Arnold. Margot had been formally introduced to the dogs and their handlers earlier that day, but she'd already forgotten the humans' names.

She had wondered, briefly, if it might be worth taking those dogs out to Muir Woods to see if there were any more surprises waiting for her and Leon on the hiking trails.

Putting a pin in that, and trying to remind herself that two bodies did not a serial killer make, she drew her attention back to the work of one already bona fide serial killer looking to add a name to his notorious tally.

Andrew continued on his train of thought. "I'm only saying that it's not all that uncommon to find out about new victims long after a killer is caught. Bundy sure tried to convince anyone who would listen that he had more, but he was trying to save his own ass."

"Doesn't mean he didn't have more."

"Suppose it doesn't, but he won't be the one to tell us about them. And you know it's always been my theory Ed must have started killing—or at least victimizing people— before Laura."

Margot wanted to point out that he was assuming she had read his book, because that was where he'd shared that theory in detail, but instead she gave a tight nod.

Andrew dabbed at the back of his neck with a handkerchief, sweat beading at his temples and around his mustache. Margot, who had opted for a plain white T-shirt with her jeans, was warm, but he looked especially hot.

"Do they require you to wear those stupid jackets even in the middle of summer?" she asked.

"It's strongly recommended, yes."

"You know Ridgway wasn't even the most prolific American serial killer, right?"

Andrew smirked at her. "I am, as you would say, acutely aware of the statistics. Ed sure made a push for number one, though, didn't he?"

Margot chewed on the inside of her cheek, glad he couldn't see her expression darken under her sunglasses. "Well, we're not done here yet, are we?"

She didn't wait for him to reply, just marched down the slope away from the road and into the thin tree line, listening for sounds from the dogs. Arnold, the coonhound, was the more vocal of the pair, letting out *awoos* and grunts as he worked, mostly out of excitement. Based on the sounds from the human audience in tow, they still hadn't found Theresa.

A wasp buzzed lazily around Margot's head, too hot to be bothered with proper aggression. She didn't swat it away so much as nudge it off by waving her hand in the air nearby. She had no interest in getting stung today. Thankfully the wasp had no interest in stinging.

Stopping a few feet away from one of the kneeling agents, she glanced back over her shoulder to the road. Even from this distance it was hard to see the cars, and she knew if she went in a little ways further Andrew would disappear from sight as well.

She tried to imagine it as it would have been on a September day almost twenty-four years earlier. The road wasn't frequently used now and they were on an offshoot from Old Mill Road itself, making it even less used than the already barely traversed main road.

Ed would have had plenty of time and privacy to do what he wanted to do with Theresa and then drag her body away from the car and into the woods. Or maybe he brought her into the woods first and killed her out here, away from the road entirely.

This wasn't his usual pattern. No wonder they hadn't known about her, or thought to connect her victim profile to him. Andrew had found the twenty-five-year-old missing person's report for Theresa Milotti and shown it to Margot before they'd come out. She'd originally been from Illinois and told her parents she was coming out to California to find work and live the sun and fun life she imagined. The last time they spoke to her she told them she was headed toward San Francisco and would tell them when she arrived.

They'd told her not to hitchhike, and offered to send her money for a bus, but Theresa had dismissed their concerns, saying everyone in California was nice and she was only traveling in the daylight.

She assured them she was safe.

Now she was somewhere in the woods.

Still, aside from a handful of outliers, everyone else Ed had killed fit a certain pattern. He broke into their homes and killed them over the course of hours, drawing out his torture. Again, Andrew's book had been very enlightening when it came to Ed's pattern of rape, psychological abuse, and murder. He'd often linger in the homes of victims long after they were dead, eating their food, using their showers. He would visit the bodies repeatedly over the course of a night, though he was adamant he never had sex with them once they were dead.

Ed wanted it to be known he wasn't a freak.

He didn't rape corpses, he just sat on the couches of dead women and watched TV, drinking beer from their fridge.

He also had a signature weapon. Ed was a knife guy. He stabbed, he gutted. While choking was present on some victims, knives were a constant.

Theresa's victim profile actually reminded Margot a lot of Ed's first victim, Laura Welsh. They were young, younger than the type he usually preferred. Most of Ed's victims had been in their mid-twenties to early forties, women who lived alone and followed a distinct routine. Lonely women who put ads in the paper looking for love.

Laura had been seventeen. Theresa nineteen.

These girls had truly been victims of circumstance. Ed had admitted that in Laura's case he'd decided to kill her simply because she'd been *there*. He had thought about killing women for months, maybe years, but it wasn't until he saw Laura standing on the side of the road in the middle of the night that he decided to make his move for the first time.

If Margot understood the timeline of events, Theresa was Ed's first killing in almost eight months by the time he brought her out here. Margot envisioned it: he would have dropped her off in Sonoma, was headed back to Petaluma and saw a girl on the side of the road with her thumb in the air.

Theresa thought she was going to get a little closer to San Francisco and whatever dream awaited her there.

Now they were hoping two dogs could unearth her skeleton, which had lain alone in the dirt and debris for decades, no one knowing where she was or what had become of her.

Margot took a deep breath.

Out of sight, deep in the trees, Arnold began to bay loudly, his distinct howl filling the air. Buster's howls soon followed, and excited human voices joined the chorus. Margot looked back up the hill and met Andrew's eyes.

It was time to bring Theresa Milotti home.

THIRTY-FOUR

Hours later the sun was down, the heat of the air was gone, and Margot had stopped mocking the navy windbreakers and had borrowed one for herself. Dozens of agents swarmed like worker ants around the crime scene that the dogs had pointed them to, with yellow tape cordoning off the area and spotlights set up, plugged into portable generators that buzzed loudly.

A forensic anthropologist team was hard at work digging up the ground in the designated zone. Margot knew how rare it was to have such skilled specialists on hand at the first sign of a grave, it was usually unheard of. There weren't a lot of forensic anthropologists out there, but having the FBI leading the case meant they'd been on call for when the dig site was located.

Twenty-four years in the ground, bones were all that would be left of Theresa now, and making sure the team found as many of those bones as possible was up to Dr. Bradbury and her team.

They wore matching white jumpsuits that made them stick out like ghosts in the darkness, and were busy sifting dirt through metal trays, separating the harder material from dust, hoping to find more bone fragments. What had been located right away was pretty impressive. An intact human skull, most of Theresa's spine, and the larger bones of her arms and legs.

What the forensic team was looking for now were smaller bones or bone fragments, that might bring them a more complete skeleton of their victim. While unlikely, they might even be able to find Theresa's hyoid, the bone in the neck that most frequently helped indicate whether or not a victim had been choked.

Margot wasn't holding her breath that they'd be able to find that, not after all this time, but she'd been amazed by all the little pieces they were amassing on a nearby table.

Of course, Margot was assuming the body was Theresa's. There were already plans to give the dogs another pass of the area in the morning, in case this had been a frequent burial site for Ed or anyone else. It was a perfect location to bury the dead, honestly. Who would come looking out here for anyone? It made her wonder about her Muir Woods victims, and why the killer hadn't opted for a location like this.

He'd *wanted* their bodies to be found almost as much as Ed hadn't wanted anyone to find Theresa.

Theresa had been in a fairly shallow grave, quite a bit of debris and broken tree limbs strewn on top of her. Because of the depth at which she'd been buried, it was likely scavengers had still picked away at her corpse as it decayed, taking away some things they would never find. The ribs, for example, were mostly gone, as were the fingers.

Extremities were easy to chew off.

Margot's phone buzzed in her pocket, and she turned away from the crime scene, following the road lights that had been left on the ground to guide agents to and from the scene. When she was within sight of the makeshift command center on the main drag, she pulled her phone out.

"Phalen."

"Margot." Leon's voice came through clear as a bell, in spite of how deep into the middle of nowhere Margot was. "Did I get you at a bad time?"

"As good a time as any." She glanced back over her shoulder to where the crime scene was lit up like a beacon almost a half mile into the trees. Branches snapped around her as agents and officers she couldn't see continued to mill around, either moving toward the body or away from it.

It never occurred to her she could stand in a darkened wood with the sound of footsteps around her and not feel afraid.

She just felt tired and sad.

"Wesley told me you were up north, helping the FBI with a case?"

"Mmhmm." She didn't offer anything beyond that, though she could tell Leon was hoping she might give him a bit more detail.

When she said nothing, Leon continued. "I've spoken to both Leanne and Rebecca's families. Both women had recently been reported as missing, neither family could offer much in the way of help when it came to pinning down potential suspects, I'm afraid, but I did get names of boyfriends, frequent contacts, work associates. I'll continue to make calls. Do you think you'll be back tomorrow?"

Margot continued to stare at the light off in the distance, barely registering what Leon was telling her. "Tomorrow?"

"Yes, will you be back in the city tomorrow?"

Since Margot wasn't actually part of Theresa's investigation, and only here as a favor from Andrew, she could technically leave whenever she wanted to. And she felt like she'd been back in the past long enough at this point.

"Yeah, I'll be heading back first thing."

"I'd like to go back to the woods," Leon said.

Margot would like nothing more than to get *out* of the woods. "Why, do you think we're missing something?"

"It's hard to say. We did manage to miss an entire body the first time around."

Margot gave a humorless chuckle. Lot of that going around right now.

"Wesley offered to come along, give some extra insight. I thought we might walk the path from the parking lot, try to determine how our killer—or killers—brought the women to their final resting places."

Margot, her mind freshly buzzing with the atrocities of her father's legacy, was all for a little field trip to distract her. Focusing on a case that had nothing to do with Ed was precisely what the doctor ordered. "All right. It's an hour from here to get back home. I'll load up tonight and come back so we can get started early. If Wes is offering to help it's because he thinks he can speed things up and steal my time back for himself. He's not the most altruistic person."

"I think you might be a bit unfair about Detective Fox," Leon chided.

"I think I'm the *most* fair about Detective Fox," she said, laughing genuinely this time. "You tell him I'll be expecting the biggest coffee money can buy when I see him tomorrow."

"Tell her to buy her own damn coffee," Wes grumbled in the background after Leon immediately passed the message along.

Margot knew there would be a fresh coffee in her hand the next morning.

She disconnected from Leon and headed back up the hill. A big FBI cube truck sat with its back doors open, Andrew inside at a makeshift desk, furiously typing on his laptop. When he looked up at her, he seemed to have aged a good five years since that morning.

"Rough day," she said.

"Good day, though. In a sense." More agents buzzed around

them up here, everyone doing a job, none of which were entirely clear to Margot.

"If you want to look at it that way."

"Of course I do. We found a body out there today, Margot. If it's Theresa, that's a family who finally knows what happened to their daughter after twenty-four years. If it's not, well, we go looking for someone else's family."

Margot took off the loaned windbreaker and placed it at the back of the truck's doors. "Thank you for letting me be part of this."

"Did it help?" He'd closed his laptop so he could give her his full attention, a level of hyperfocused scrutiny she was unprepared for. Andrew was a man who noticed things, and she really didn't need him to notice how totally *not* OK she was.

She was pretty sure the next time she saw her therapist this was going to be discussed at great length. *And why did you think going to see one of your father's crime scenes would help you?*

Why, indeed.

"As much as anything can, I suppose. It's been a weird week."

"No doubt."

"Does it ever get easier?" She crossed her arms over her chest, suddenly cold in the windy nighttime chill.

"What part?"

"You've helped bring in so many monsters, men who have done the unthinkable. Do they ever stop looking like monsters? Can you ever just look at them and say *What a sad, broken person that is?*"

Andrew got up from his little makeshift table and moved toward the back of the truck, crouching down by the exit so he was at her eye level. "You want to know if I ever stop being afraid of them?"

Margot nodded, feeling for all the world like the fifteen-year-old girl she'd been the first time she met him.

"I think if I ever stop being afraid of them, that means I need to step away from this job. No. I'm not scared of them in a check-under-the-bed way, but what I've seen them do to people haunts me. This." He jerked his head in the direction of the lights out in the trees. "This will follow me to sleep."

"He's always going to be there, isn't he?"

Andrew shrugged. "In a sense, I guess. But he doesn't dictate who you are. You have done so much good, helped so many people. Maybe you don't see it that way, but I hope you know that he doesn't get to define you."

Margot's shoulders sagged. She couldn't decide if this was exactly what she'd wanted to hear, or the worst possible thing he could have said. It cut too close to home either way.

"Thanks again, Andrew. Really."

"You're leaving." It wasn't a question, really. He glanced over at the jacket she'd left behind.

"You don't need me here. I was only a tourist in this whole thing anyway."

"Are you staying the night? It's late. I could arrange a place for you at the motel."

"I can't sleep well away from home." She gave him a small smile. "At least I know what monsters are under that bed."

She had intended to head right back to San Francisco.

A left off the 116 and she would be going south, back toward her apartment and whatever fitful sleep awaited her. Instead, guided by an invisible hand, she turned right, and headed into Petaluma proper.

It was late, but there were still signs of life in the city, though not quite as bustling as her new hometown. She took East Washington, memory taking over and guiding her to a place she hadn't been in ages. She had driven this way before, her father in the seat next to her, trying to give her patient wisdom about turn signals and using the brake.

He'd been teaching her to drive the day they came for him. When they turned on to Clairmont Court the street had been lined with black SUVs and police cars. Their neighbors spilled out onto the sidewalk to see what was happening.

Ed had tried to run.

He'd gotten out of the car while Margot had still been driving, slowly rolling up toward their house at the end of the cul-de-sac. She turned onto that street now, and could practically see the scene unfolding in front of her. He got out, stumbling, running in the direction of the main road. A dozen police officers and FBI agents in bulletproof vests with guns drawn went after him, screaming, shouting commands.

A man with a gun had come to Margot's window and demanded she stop the car, but she couldn't remember how to do it, not with a handgun pointed at her face and a man in dark sunglasses screaming at her.

That was when she first met Andrew. Special Agent Rhodes had climbed in the open passenger door, placed a hand over hers on the wheel and said, "Megan? Your name is Megan, right? Can you put your foot on the brake? You know which one the brake is."

Through choking tears Margot braked, sending them both lurching forward.

Andrew had eased the gear stick into the Park position.

"Can you turn it off for me?"

She did as she was told, staring straight through the windshield to where her mother was collapsed on the front lawn, screaming and crying, and Justin sat at the end of the driveway with his knees pulled up to his chest.

The angry police officer at her window was gone, and it was just her and Andrew in the car together.

Somewhere outside she heard someone scream, "*Got him, got him, got him!*"

"Is my dad in trouble?" she whispered.

Andrew gave her shoulder a gentle squeeze. "Yes, hon. I'm afraid he is."

Now, twenty-two years later, Margot stopped her car in front of her old house, shocked that it was still there. It amazed her it hadn't been torn down in an attempt to chase away the ghosts of the past.

It looked different than she remembered. The new owners had painted it a cheerful sky blue, instead of the brown it had been when the Finches lived there. They were also clearly avid gardeners, as Ed's plain grassy lawn now had a lovely cactus garden in it, and planters overflowing with petunias. In the dark she couldn't make out too many details, but it was obvious this family had turned her old house into a home.

She wondered if they knew who had lived there before. It must have come up at some point, you couldn't really sell a property without explaining why people might periodically show up on your front lawn to pose for pictures.

The weird subset of true crime rubberneckers who wanted to touch something close to a serial killer. And for what? A thrill? A safe sense of fear?

Margot looked at the house, the window in the front corner where her bedroom had been, and all she felt was sad. A deep, unrelenting sense of sadness.

For fifteen years she'd lived there thinking it was how normal, mostly happy families lived.

Now she had no idea what a normal family was.

THIRTY-FIVE

Wes brought her coffee.

A piping hot paper cup of Philz, exactly the way she liked it, placed directly in her eager hands as she got out of her car in the Muir Woods parking lot.

"Did you ever know that you're my hero?" she sang softly to him.

"Yeah, yeah. Wind. Wings." But his smirk told her that it hadn't really been a hardship.

Leon, who had driven both him and Wes, leaned against his own car, cleaning the lenses of his glasses. Margot sipped her coffee, the caffeine an immediate balm to her bone-tired body.

After her little detour down bad-memory lane last night, she hadn't gotten back to North Beach until after two o'clock in the morning, pushing closer to three. It was now shortly after eight, and she hadn't been able to sleep much at all. She was going to be a bag of shit today, so Wes had truly saved everyone, because without coffee she would have been a *cranky* bag of shit, so this was at least a minor improvement.

Thanks to valuable lessons learned from her last hike out here, Margot had opted to wear the same worn-in hiking boots she'd taken with her to Petaluma the previous day. If they were going to be traipsing through the brush and up rocky trails, she was going to be better prepared this time.

She was about to make fun of Wes for poor life choices when she saw that he, too, had opted for a pair of beat-up running shoes.

"Leon warned me," he chuckled. "You thought I'd be out here in my best Ted Baker brogues?"

"I really wanted to see you try to hike in fancy clothes. I didn't even know you owned sneakers. What the hell do you use them for?"

Wes raised an eyebrow at her. "Running, Detective."

"Oh, so you finally admit the hot bod doesn't come naturally."

"I will take that as a compliment."

"If you two are done flirting with each other, I'd like to get through this before noon. It's supposed to be another scorcher today." Leon, his glasses now suitably clean, had joined them.

"Lead the way," Margot said, gesturing to the path.

The trail itself was once again open to hikers, though the parking lot only had two other cars in it and one of them was parked in front of the ranger station. Margot had to believe that news of the bodies found in the woods had put a bit of a damper on hiker interest in the trails, but that was all the better for the three of them.

"Did you see the paper this morning?" Wes asked, his voice low but with an edge of caution to it.

"I did not," Margot replied.

Leon cleared his throat, almost as if warning Wes against this topic, but then he was the one who spoke next. "Up around Petaluma yesterday, were you?"

Margot shot a look at Wes. She hadn't hidden the fact that she was helping the FBI, and it also wasn't a giant secret where she was going, but something about Leon's tone made his question feel especially loaded.

"What was in the paper this morning?"

"Seems like the FBI pulled a very old body out of the woods yesterday. A body which they are suggesting might be a victim of the Classified Killer," Leon went on.

"So, they did identify her." This, Margot said mostly to herself, surprised she hadn't gotten a text from Andrew.

Wes shook his head. "No, they haven't given a name or any more specific detail, but the story indicated that Ed Finch had shared the details with the FBI."

"Just the FBI?" Margot would murder Sebastian if he'd let it slip that Ed had actually given the information specifically to her. She thought she could trust him, but reporters were a tricky lot. Story first, friendship later.

"Yeah, just the FBI."

"Funny how a man like that suddenly decided to grow a conscience all these years later," Leon said.

"Yes. Hilarious." Margot fell into step with Leon, letting the older man set their pace. She didn't want to talk about this, to give any more information on what she'd been doing at the scene. As it was, Leon's tone and demeanor suggested he knew she was hiding something, but she wasn't sure how much he suspected.

The three of them walked in silence together for a good ten minutes before they arrived at the first crime scene. The tent and lights were now gone, but the yellow police tape remained, although part of it had come off its tether and was dragging on the ground, occasionally flicking upward in the breeze.

The scene looked abandoned, like no one cared about it anymore.

There was now a distinct footpath connecting the main trail to the crime scene, enough so that the park had needed to post a sign reminding visitors to remain on the main path, as this little offshoot did present an enticing invitation to step over the railing.

Which was precisely what Leon did.

"Wesley, can you lift Margot over the railing?"

"I can lift myself over the railing just fine," Margot protested, clutching her coffee cup to her chest and taking a step back from them.

Leon shook his head. "It's not an act of chivalry, my dear. While you're not exactly the same build as our victim, I'm curious to see how difficult it is to pull a body over those railings without damaging them."

"He could pull *you* over the railing," she suggested.

"I weigh quite a bit more than our victim."

Margot glanced at Wes, hoping he would step in to say she didn't have to do it, but he shrugged and said, "Promise to make it as painless as possible."

"I hate you."

She put her coffee on the ground near the railing and took a sidestep away to ensure she wouldn't accidentally kick it over when she turned herself into a human anchor.

"Leon, I see now why you wanted me to come along this morning, and I'm definitely taking you off my Christmas card list for this year."

"Oh no," Leon replied in a deadpan. "Wesley, if you would be so kind?"

Wes came back to Margot's side of the fence and stood a few inches away from her. He moved, as if to grab her, then paused. "Are you OK with this?"

"I mean I'm not in *love* with this, but yes, I'm fine."

He must have remembered her meltdown in the car the previous week. It was sweet, in a subtle way, that he didn't want to upset her.

Margot steeled herself, and said, "You better not fucking drop me."

"I'll do my best."

He stepped behind her and wrapped his arms under hers, doing his best to avoid her breasts, and failing entirely. "Sorry," he muttered.

In response, Margot let her legs give out under her, all her weight dropping, giving him absolutely no help in keeping her upright. Dead weight.

He grunted, struggling for a moment to hold her, and adjusting his grip until he had a firmer grasp. He gritted his teeth, not even pretending to be a strong, tough man's man. "Dammit woman, you're heavy."

She rolled her eyes. "Sweet talker."

Wes dragged her toward the railing, managing to get his legs over one at a time while still maintaining his vicelike grip on her. He tried, valiantly, to lift her over the railing by tugging at her roughly under the arms, but it was no use, and when Margot finally said, "Dude, ow," he stopped that effort. The railing had rocked several times during the process.

"Well, if he did it that way, he probably would have taken part of the fence down," Leon noted. "Though the body he was dragging would have complained a lot less, I'm sure."

"Again, I say, we could use you as the *prop* in this exercise," Margot shot back.

Wes, still motivated to get the job done, turned Margot and, to her surprise, hoisted her in one swift motion over his shoulder into a fireman's carry. One moment she was looking at his face, and the next she was looking at his ass in bewilderment.

He was able to easily get her over the railing this way, and he then started walking her over to the crime scene itself.

"You can put me down now," she told his butt. "Point has been proven."

Wes stopped and helped her down from his shoulder and back onto solid ground. Flustered, and tidying her ponytail which had been thrown askew, Margot made her way back to the main trail to grab her coffee.

"So, there's definitely a way one person could have gotten her over here." Leon gave a nod, pleased that his experiment had given him an answer.

Margot sipped her coffee and remained next to the railings. "I'm sure it wouldn't have been comfortable to haul dead weight over his shoulder a long way, though." She glanced over at Wes, who nodded his agreement. "We need to take into account the distance he would have to move her from the parking lot here. And before you ask, no, I will not be reenacting that. I think we can all assume that dragging the dead weight of a human body almost a mile into the woods without assistance would be impossible. Not to mention the woman up the hill was even further in."

Leon scratched his dark beard contemplatively. "He either needed help from a person, or some kind of equipment, then."

"All that presupposes they were killed elsewhere. What if he brought them here under their own power and then killed them once he had them where he wanted?" Wes asked.

Margot shook her head. "It doesn't quite line up with the evidence we've found. For Leanne Wu, she had over forty stab wounds and then lay on her back for a good long time after death. Where we found her, she was sitting up against a tree, and there wasn't a significant amount of dried blood in the area."

"Blood washes away," Wes noted. "And there's also something else to consider: maybe he killed them here and came back several times to visit them, or move them around into different poses."

Margot grimaced at this all-too-plausible suggestion. She glanced over at Leon. "Someone could have killed them further off the trails and left them. Then he came back to see if they'd been found. He might have kept moving them until it became obvious."

"Could explain why we didn't see Leanne the first time officers searched the area. Maybe he was annoyed that he'd hidden her too well, wanted the notoriety. Or, if it was two killers, maybe Leanne's killer was frustrated that Rebecca's body was getting all the attention." He started to scribble things down.

"You're thinking the killings might not be connected?" Wes asked. "They sure *look* connected."

"And I'm sure you know what they say about those who assume things, Wesley," Leon reminded him.

Not wanting to walk into the insult left hanging, Wes held his hands apart in a *help me out here* gesture. "You're considering the option that they're connected, though?"

"Of course," Margot answered for Leon. "We'd be idiots not to. But Leon is right, the victims have nothing in common at a surface level aside from being women. They didn't work in similar fields, they were from different socioeconomic groups. As far as we can tell, their paths never crossed before, so to assume the same man— person, killed them... it's too early; we need a bit more time."

Wes rolled his eyes and let out an exasperated sigh. "You guys just don't want to say *serial killer* when news about Ed Finch is already in the paper."

Margot bit her tongue and tried not to let her face react to that name being said out loud, while silently cursing Wes for bringing it up. "If and when it's time for people to be concerned about that, we'll make the appropriate decisions."

Leon smiled the tiniest bit, probably pleased to hear his own rationale coming out of Margot's lips. "Let's go to the other scene, shall we?"

"Are you going to make him drag me up that rocky hill? Because if so, I think I'll head back to the car right now."

"No, I think we're done with experimenting for today,

Margot. I want to get a sense of the space between the two sites when we don't have anyone hovering nearby."

Leon and Wes returned to the main trail, and they continued their trek deeper into the woods. It really was a pretty walk, but also quite a solid distance away from the parking lot, making it all the more difficult to imagine someone hauling a body down the path all by their lonesome, no matter what time of night they'd done it.

As they walked, they passed a young mother heading their direction, two snoozing toddlers bumping along in the wagon she pulled behind her. The three detectives smiled at her, but she must have found their presence a bit off-putting because she picked up her pace, the wheels of the wagon crunching as they sped down the trail until she was completely out of site. Margot watched the dark head of one of the children bob precariously, and thought briefly about Mateo and Valentina.

Her focus then shifted to the wagon itself and her hand flew to Leon's arm, squeezing tightly.

Margot, Wes, and Leon all exchanged glances.

"You think one of those things could pull a human body?" Margot asked.

"I think it's certainly an option. And we already know the perp was likely driving a truck or a van. Plenty of room in the back for a wagon as well," Leon said. "Friends, I feel like perhaps this visit has been very educational for us after all."

THIRTY-SIX

They made their trek up to the second crime scene and scoured through the underbrush, looking for any clues that might have been left behind, or any additional insights to the murder itself. But, coming up empty-handed, they returned to their cars and headed back to the precinct.

Wes was already back in their office when Margot got to the station, arriving a few minutes after the others got back, but Leon cut her off before she could join her partner. "Can I speak to you for a minute?"

Her pulse hammered and instinct told her to run for the door. To Margot, there were few more frightening sentences in the English language than *Can we talk.*

Leon guided them to an open interrogation room, which didn't do much to help Margot's growing sense of guilt and panic. This wasn't a fancy interrogation room with a giant mirror on one wall, but rather a small space, little more than a modified storage closet with a small table and two wooden chairs inside. They recorded interrogations in here with the camera mounted on the ceiling, but the red record light was currently off.

Margot sat in the chair usually reserved for detectives and Leon took the opposite seat. In some of the other rooms, a single leg on one chair would be filed down slightly, so that a perp could never quite get comfortable as the chair listed to one side, but in here they relied more on the fact that the chairs were exceptionally old and unpleasant to sit in.

With the door closed the room felt especially claustrophobic, and Margot began to sweat even before Leon spoke.

"I want to know why you didn't tell me about your family," he said quietly.

Margot froze. Despite the side-eyed glances and the hints, she hadn't really believed that Leon knew the truth about her. The captain certainly hadn't told him, and she believed Wes wouldn't sell her out like that.

"How did you know?"

Leon leaned forward, his forearms resting on his thighs, and it was a gesture she recognized from dozens of moments where she had needed to be gentle with the family of a victim, or a sensitive witness. It was a gesture that said *You can trust me I only want to help.* "I wasn't totally sure until yesterday. I always knew there was something you were hiding, but I assumed it was an abusive ex-husband, perhaps, or some other reason a woman might choose to leave her past behind. It wasn't until Wesley mentioned you were helping the FBI that I wondered why they would need you, specifically, in an area so far out of our jurisdiction. There were no cases I could recall having a tie to the area, but then I saw the paper from a few days ago, with the splashy headline about Ed Finch returning to the Bay, and it mentioned that he'd lived in that area. Google did the rest, though I must admit unless someone knew you well, you don't look much like you did when you were young."

Margot touched her nose. "Not all of me is the same as it was back then."

"You kept the red, though."

She nervously twirled a piece of hair around her finger, looking at the copper locks which looked almost dull in the harsh yellow light of this room. "I wanted to keep at least one thing that was mine. I gave up my name, my home, my entire life. This, I kept."

She'd lost a lot of weight, too. In her youth she'd always been quite pudgy, giving her a round baby-face. Hitting a late-teen growth spurt helped spread a lot of that out, and the added height, plus her nose job, really did make her look almost wholly unrecognizable to the full-cheeked teen with acne and braces she'd been.

That was probably one of the reasons most armchair sleuths hadn't been able to find her quite so easily. But Leon was a real detective, and he'd done it.

"You didn't say anything to anyone else, did you?" she asked.

"No. But I do wish you'd told me yourself. I'm assuming Wesley is aware?"

Margot nodded. "The captain decided to tell him when he paired us up together. All secrets on the table sort of thing. I think he thought it would help bond us, but I was so mad at him for telling Wes I think it almost ruined the whole damned thing. There's a reason I don't share it with a lot of people, and I'm sorry if you feel hurt by that, but I'm trying to keep it where it belongs. Buried."

"Except you were out there with the FBI yesterday, literally digging it up."

She let out an exhausted sigh, sitting back in the chair before remembering that the rigid wooden back made it impossible to relax or feel comfortable. "I needed to see it for myself. To see that she got taken out of the ground, so she can go home, you know?"

"I can't honestly say that I do, Margot. This is something

not many people can pretend to understand. But did it help you find some kind of closure?"

Margot stared at him, his brown eyes warm and open, showing that he cared. "No. I don't think this is something I'll ever be able to find closure for."

THIRTY-SEVEN

Needing a break from the station, and from Leon's watchful, too-knowing gaze, Margot suggested she and Wes head back to the Ramirez house. The forensics team was mostly finished combing through everything at this point, but the little field trip they'd taken to Muir Woods had her wanting to walk the house one more time before things got turned over to professional cleaners.

Wes dug his sunglasses out of his blazer pocket before they headed back into the bright afternoon. "I'm not sure what you're hoping to find in there, Margot, we've been through the place three times ourselves, and they've pretty much combed every inch of it since then. If there was something to find, we would have found it."

"Humor me, OK? I don't know if I'm looking for anything tangible, or just hoping something clicks when I see it, you know? But whatever it is, I feel like we need to go back."

Wes drove, giving Margot ample time to sit with her thoughts and ruminate over the last two days. The last week, really. The quiet, safe little sphere she had built around her life had started to crack from every conceivable angle, and it was sending her completely into a tailspin. But here, this case, this was something untouched by Ed. It didn't remind her of her father at all, and she really believed the answer was sitting right in front of her.

This was solvable. There was an answer in her grasp if only she could find the missing piece to the puzzle.

What broke her heart was that there was almost no one waiting for her to find the answer. Mateo would finally know who took his family from him, but she doubted he'd be able to appreciate that closed chapter until much later in his life, if ever. She briefly thought about her brother in that moment, knowing that sometimes answers weren't the same thing as closure, and sometimes you *never* get better. Like for Emily's parents, what good would the knowledge do them? Emily was never supposed to be there, never meant to be a target, but now she was dead. Did putting a name to the randomness of that crime really help them?

Maybe. Maybe not.

Wes pulled up in front of the Ramirez house. There weren't any crime scene vans outside today, nothing to indicate on the surface that the place was an empty shell that had once held something happy. The family would never again awaken to Christmas gifts beneath a tree, or gather together for a Thanksgiving dinner. There was a very finite period at the end of their sentence.

She wondered in a vague way what would happen to the house. It probably belonged to Mateo now, along with whatever Hector and Evangeline had in their estate. They had to be doing pretty well to maintain this address. The kid would probably never want for anything in his life except the one thing money couldn't bring him.

Maybe the one thing he'd never had to begin with.

Margot had a hard time imagining the family would keep the house. Who would want to move into a place where a loved one had died, and so brutally? No matter how good the cleaning crew was, the place would be forever tainted.

No, they would probably sell it. That's what Margot would do.

Inside, the air in the house was so still and quiet it felt like it was closing in around her, a hand squeezing and squeezing until her lungs were empty and she had nothing left to give.

She counted slowly to five in her head before moving past the front entrance, wishing they could crack a window or turn on the air conditioning. The house was stiflingly hot, and Margot wondered how the forensics team had been able to focus here the last week, wearing their white jumpsuits, spending most of the day upstairs. It must have been unbearable.

In the living room, the stained white carpet had been cut away, leaving only the untouched white border, and the stained hardwood beneath. Likewise, they had cut away the drywall in the ceiling where the blood had steadily dripped down from the study above.

Margot looked up into the exposed ceiling, but it was stripped back to wood beams and the floorboards above, mixed with bits of insulation and wiring. There was no blood to be seen, nothing sinister, except for the way the empty space looked like a wound in the otherwise unmarked ceiling. It gave her the heebie-jeebies.

Still, she decided to start in the sitting room.

Wes was right, they'd already spent a lot of time here, had access to literally thousands of photos captured by the forensics team, as well as boxes and boxes of physical evidence. There wasn't much left in the house that could pertain to their case.

And yet she felt compelled to keep looking.

Margot sat on the floral sofa in the sitting room, staring first at the space in the carpet, then the hole in the ceiling, letting her eyes then drift around the room. It was an exceptionally formal space, a room where you'd be surprised to learn its owners had children. Everything was neat as a pin and, were it not for the new layers of dust forming, it would have been spotless.

This was not a family space. She couldn't imagine Mateo sitting on this couch with a Game Boy in hand, or Valentina painting her nails on the coffee table. This room felt like it had already been a museum before the family had died. She glanced quickly around, seeing only neatly folded newspapers tucked into a magazine stand at the end of the couch. All of them the *New York Times*. There were a few copies of *Good House-keeping* and *Architectural Digest* but otherwise nothing that seemed to belong to the kids.

They were the bland magazines you might find in a doctor's office, and they barely said anything about who had lived here. This whole place felt devoid of any real personality. Who had these people *been*?

Margot pulled out one of the newspapers. It was several months old and folded to the crossword, all the answers complete save for one.

"Five letters. Strips in a club. Ends in *n*, has a *c*," she said out loud.

"Strips in a club?" Wes asked, giving her a befuddled expression. "What are you talking about?"

She waved the newspaper at him. "It's going to bother me."

He paused, looking at the photos over the mantel on the fireplace, all stylish black-and-white pictures of the Ramirez family and their children. None of them were taken on vacation, or candid. They were all done in a professional photo studio.

The pictures were as sterile as the room.

Wes snapped his fingers excitedly. "Bacon," he said, a ring of triumph in his tone. He gave a little fist pump in the air.

"Bacon?"

"Strips in a club. They mean a club sandwich, not a strip club."

Margot glanced down at the paper, and sure enough, *bacon* fit. "I hate these things." She got up from the couch, putting the newspaper back with its fellows, the final clue incomplete, but solved. She passed through the dining room, which was equally rigid. Everything from the cherry-wood china cabinet on one wall with beautiful plates and cups positioned on display and a row of lovely teapots on the upper part of the shelf, all angled in the exact same way.

The only thing that gave the room the tiniest ounce of personality was a wall-hanging that took up almost the entire wall at the head of the table.

It was a black piece of fabric about the size of a tablecloth, that had been embroidered all over with brightly colored thread, to depict flowers and birds. It reminded Margot of traditional Mexican dresses, and she wondered if it was a family heirloom from either Hector or Evangeline's family.

Nothing else in the house really spoke to them having a connection to their Latin heritage, but this certainly stood out, being the only really vibrant thing in the entire house.

The dining room itself offered her nothing. She opened and closed drawers, but all she found were extra napkins, the fancy silverware, and a drawer filled with old art from the kids. Dates and ages had been carefully scrawled onto the bottom corner of each piece of construction paper.

The flow of the house brought Margot into the kitchen next. The back door was positively festooned with fingerprint dust, where the team had done their best to lift anything that might have belonged to the perp. The big boot mark on the outside had been measured, photographed and captured for posterity to within an inch of its life. If it washed away in the rain now, it wouldn't matter.

Nevertheless, Margot still unlocked the back door and looked at it. The mud, long-dried, had started to crumble away, but the outline of the print was still perfectly visible. The guy had big feet. Forensics was running the print through a database that helped match prints to shoes, so they would have a close match to what he wore soon enough. They looked like work boots, though, or something with a substantial tread.

She stepped outside and sat on the back steps of the house, scanning the backyard. There were plenty of places the guy could have come in. The back fence had a gate. There was another gate leading up to the front of the house, and the fence between the Ramirez family and their neighbors was a low, chain-link number that wouldn't have been very difficult for an adult man to climb over. No special equipment needed, no real advanced knowledge of the house and family needed. Anyone could have come in the back gate, walked quietly across the lawn, and kicked in the back door.

Not that kicking in a door was *easy*, but the rear entrance to the Ramirez house was definitely older and less well maintained than the front. It wasn't impossible.

Again, back here things were impersonal. No swing set or play structure for the kids. No soccer goal, or sign of any toys. Sure, Valentina was a bit old for toys, but Mateo certainly wasn't. When Margot's brother had been his age there was always a bike fallen on its side in the backyard, deflated sports balls of every conceivable variety, lost baseballs, plastic junk from the dollar store that was left out in the rain too many times.

Kids left shit everywhere, so why not here?

It was as if the Ramirezes wanted the perfect on-paper family, but didn't want any of the messy or unappealing things that went along with it. Their kids were like accessories to them, one more thing they used when it served them and then locked away when it didn't.

Margot's stomach churned.

Those kids had never really had a childhood, had they?

There was a small shed at the back of the yard, which had been scoured top to bottom, and while there were a few things in there belonging to the Ramirez children, it didn't feel like enough. Where was their fingerprint on this place?

"You have siblings, right, Wes?"

He answered from where he stood in the doorway. "Two sisters."

"And they have kids?" She looked over her shoulder at him in time to catch the beaming smile.

"Yeah. Libby has two boys and Katherine has a girl and a boy." His obvious love of his siblings shone through. Margot had a hard time imagining Wes as a father, at least a father on purpose, but he was clearly a very committed uncle.

"You ever see a house where kids live that looks this... clean?" she asked, gesturing to the empty yard. "Like not a single thing out here says *children* to me."

"I dunno, it's hard to say. I think it's obvious from the interior they were trying to project a certain image, and that image wasn't a busy, bustling family one." He shrugged. His thoughts had echoed her own perfectly, but there was something they were both missing. "Plus, given what we've learned about the Ramirez parents, I'm not sure we should expect them to have behaved in a typical way when they were alive."

"See, I thought that, too. But I think, based on what we've learned, that they'd want to appear as normal as possible to anyone on the outside looking in. This shit is weird." She gestured toward the empty yard. "It's like they didn't want anyone to know they had kids."

"Except the pictures." He jerked his chin back toward the living room.

Margot nodded. "The perfect, stylish pictures. Yeah."

"I think if we were trying to put together a case against the Ramirezes themselves, you might be on to something, but don't get distracted. Remember why we're here. Someone killed *them*." He came close, bumping his shoulder against hers.

"Maybe it was someone who saw what we're seeing, though." When Wes made a face, she went on. "Someone knew, or suspected, what was going on in this fake perfect dream house they had. *Someone* knew they were fucked up. I think that's what got them killed."

"I still think the doctor is a good fit for it. Hospital confirms he was at work that night, but doctors and nurses come and go from that building all the time without having to badge in places. He wasn't in surgery or doing anything specific at the time of the murders, and it strikes me as more than a little suspicious that a pediatric doctor who normally works days would opt to pull an all-night double without having a *reason* for it. A treatment, a procedure, something that meant he needed to be there after eleven at night. Something about that doesn't sit right with me."

"I agree, and we know he had a complicated relationship with more than one of the victims, but that doesn't mean we know for sure he's our guy. Something about him still feels wrong to me. Why kill Valentina, for starters. And Emily. God, why kill Emily?"

"Do you honestly think the idea of a random killer makes more sense?"

Margot got up from the back step and returned to the house, careful to lock the door behind her. "No, random killer is almost never the answer, especially not with this many red flags. And it doesn't fit my theory that this was motivated by someone who had learned the family's dirty little secret. Maybe the doctor hired someone, though?" She raised a brow at Wes. "Here's ten grand, go kill these parents. And the guy panicked when he saw the girls, killed them both. Didn't know the family well enough to know there was a son, too. We should check Dr. McRae's bank records, see if there were any sizable withdrawals recently that might align with him hiring someone."

"That's almost as out there as random killer," Wes replied.

"Almost but not *quite* as out there. Wealthy doctor, reason to feel slighted by the parents for making up diseases for their children. Concern over their wellbeing? Not to mention Evangeline emotionally manipulated him for years. I've seen men do worse for a lot less."

"Phalen, we've seen people take nine rounds to the face over a baggie of crack, so respectfully, let's not start comparing the validity of motives. People don't need a lot of reasons."

Margot opened the basement door, the air smelling stale and a little mildewy. "I like it better when they have a reason."

"Don't we all?"

As she descended, Wes remained at the top step, blocking out most of the natural light coming in from the kitchen. "You know what I don't like about the hired killer angle?" he asked.

"Everything? No one ever wants it to be a hired killer, feels too clichéd."

"Aside from that."

"No, what?" She pulled out her flashlight, aiding the weak overhead bulb with a little extra light for the darker corners of the space.

"That killing felt personal. Whoever did it wanted them to suffer, he wanted it to be terrifying and painful. He made the girls watch while Hector killed himself. You don't do things that way for a couple thousand bucks. A professional would come in while they were asleep and put two in the back of everyone's heads while they slept. They'd use a silencer. This was…"

"It was overkill."

She swept the flashlight beam in between stacks of cardboard boxes, not really sure what she was looking for. This was where she'd found Mateo, but it wasn't really part of the crime scene. The likelihood of finding anything here was so slim she felt like she was wasting her time.

Yet a voice at the back of her head, one she couldn't manage to ignore, said *keep looking*.

So, she kept looking.

She ducked under the stairs to where she'd found the boy, she looked at the boxes stacked, the ones that had protected him.

One was marked Halloween, and it sat on top of one labeled Summer.

Shouldn't Summer be on top?

It was such a weird thought, but when Margot had been young, they'd stored all the holiday items in the garage, and her mother had been meticulous about making sure they were packed away so that the next holiday on the list was the easiest to get to. That way at Christmas you weren't digging behind boxes marked Easter or Clothes for Donation.

Margot couldn't expect every parent on the planet to behave like Kim, but she thought about the way Evangeline kept her house, and the way each box down here was neatly labeled, not with pen, but with properly printed labels. There were even notes, again on label paper, to indicate what was in each box or bin.

The kind of person who did that didn't store her boxes out of order.

Maybe Mateo had moved them when he'd hidden under the stairs, stacking whatever was nearby in hopes it would protect him. Maybe the crime scene techs hadn't put them back in the right order.

Her flashlight lingered on the two boxes until she finally decided to look closer. She moved Halloween to the floor, penlight sweeping over it. Nothing looked out of place. It was an orange plastic bin and apparently contained old costumes, a pumpkin carving kit, and decals for the windows. Margot had a hard time imagining decal clings up in the windows upstairs.

She pushed the box to the side and looked closer at the Summer box. This one, according to the label, had an inflatable water slide, water wings, and water balloons in it. It was a large cardboard box that had been sealed with packing tape, but at one corner, the tape was roughly lifted.

"Wes, come down here for a minute."

"You actually find something?"

"I don't know yet, just come down here."

When he joined her, she handed him the flashlight, and pulled the Summer box away from the wall to get a better look at it. From this angle it was more evident that not only had the tape been pulled back, but one of the box's corners was folded over. Ever so slightly. Not something that would normally stand out, and certainly not something that would have raised any alarms with the forensics team, but still, it felt completely wrong.

"You have any gloves?" she asked.

Wes pulled out a pair of blue gloves from his back pocket and handed them to her. Leave it to the former Eagle Scout to always come prepared. Margot should have thought to have a pair with her, but her mind had been pulled in a million different directions before they arrived. She hadn't thought about it.

Slipping the gloves on, she peeled the tape back further and lifted the bent flap of the box so she could see inside. Part of her expected a body part, or bloody stash of clothes. But at first glance the contents of the box were precisely what the outside label told her she would find. Plastic bags filled with water balloons, a cardboard box for a Slip-N-Slide, and a few bright beach towels stored in rolls.

"Wes, can you bring the flashlight closer?"

He did as he was asked and positioned the flashlight right

above the box, his leg pressed to her thigh so he could be close enough to give her the full beam of the small light.

There, on one of the towels, was a smear of dried blood, like someone had hastily wiped it off their hand. And as Margot reached into the box to pull the towel out, something clattered to the floor at her feet. She dropped the towel back in the box and took a shuffling step back. There, right where her feet had been, was a fancy black pen, with the name of Hector's construction business written on the side.

She held it up, so it fell in the flashlight's beam, and there, unmistakably, was a thick smear of blood around the point of the pen.

Margot looked up at Wes. "Guess there was something to find, after all."

THIRTY-EIGHT

Back in the morgue, Margot looked at Hector Ramirez's mottled, naked body, which lay on a table in the middle of the room. Once more, in the span of a little over a week, Margot was sharing a room with a cold, dead body, and while it was an integral and normal part of her job, it wasn't something she'd ever get used to.

Her gaze briefly flicked to the empty tables nearby, anxiety gnawing at her stomach over the two dead women who had so recently been laid out there. She and Leon were still working through theories, but they had no real leads to speak of and all their tips were coming up on dead ends. She didn't like to be stuck in a position where the next step was to wait for another body to show up.

But she had a body in front of her to deal with first. One where the killer seemed much closer at hand.

Evelyn was standing opposite them, with a plastic evidence baggie in her hand. "You know, Detectives, it's really quite unusual I find myself stumped, and honestly I wasn't sure what to make of this when you gave it to me. A bloody pen does not really fit with the cause of death I had for any of our victims, and yet, a bloody pen you have given me."

"Are you saying it doesn't match up to any of our victims?" Wes asked.

"Now, now, I hope you know me better than to think I would bring you all the way down here just to let you know your hunch was wrong. That's not really my style."

Under normal circumstances, Margot might have made a joke about Evelyn wanting to see Wes in person, but right now she only wanted answers. She thought there was something in the house that would guide her and Wes to their killer, and now she had *something* but she didn't know what it meant.

She had a good hunch about where the pen had come from, a memory jogged by the incomplete crossword puzzle in the living room. When they'd searched the house shortly after the murders she'd found a crossword on Hector's bedside table, but no pen.

No pen, until now.

Now they knew where the pen had likely come from, and they could confirm if need be by matching the ink to that on the crossword, but she still didn't know what it meant.

"I believe the pen *was* used on Mr. Ramirez, though in spite of the bloody exterior, I don't think it actually left any notable damage, which is why I didn't notice it in my first investigation of the body. That, I'll admit, is entirely my fault, but you'll excuse me for saying that the cause of death in his case looked rather obvious. And was the gunshot wound to his head.

"However if you look here." She hovered over Ramirez and pointed to some very minor indents on the skin on his chest. "I pretty much ignored these originally. They don't break the skin, there's no bruising in the area, they're very easy to miss. But then I decided to take another look at his shirt."

She went to a plastic bin sitting on a nearby cabinet, and with gloved hands removed the polo shirt Hector had been wearing. It was cut down the middle for removal, but left other-wise intact so they could use it for evidence at trial, if necessary.

Evelyn laid the shirt out on a wheeled metal tray next to the body that would normally carry her surgical tools. At first, Margot didn't see what Evelyn was trying to point out, until the medical examiner pointed a gloved finger in the general area of Hector's heart.

There, bled into the cotton but barely visible because of all the blood on the shirt, were a half dozen black marks. One or two were deep enough there was a tiny hole in the cotton.

"What is that?" Margot asked.

With the pen still in its plastic evidence bag, Evelyn wrapped her hand around it and mimed a stabbing motion into the shirt.

"You're saying he was stabbed with the pen?" Wes asked.

Evelyn shook her head. "No, I'm saying someone *tried* to stab him with a pen, but they barely got through his shirt. The blood on here isn't from a wound created *by* the pen, the force of the assault was much too weak to break the skin, but it's Hector's blood. I think whoever tried to stab him with the pen must have given up because they got too much blood on the pen to continue. Blood from the wound that actually killed him."

Margot straightened up, staring from the body to the pen, then her gaze drifted to Wes.

The pieces were now together, even if the picture still didn't make sense.

Margot knew where they had to go next.

THIRTY-NINE

Wes parked the car in a nearly full lot behind the community center. As they got out, a general din greeted them in the air. Children's voices shouting, laughing, parents and coaches adding to the chorus. Whistles blew, and the hollow *twang* of cleats on soccer balls made up the multi-layered orchestra of the playing field.

Margot waited a moment, watching the familiar scene, recalling a time when it had been Ed sitting on the sidelines, invariably arguing with whichever poor local father had been roped into coaching her soccer team that year about how best to utilize the players.

Ed craved confrontation in the most peculiar ways.

She tried to spot Mateo from the car but couldn't. Before Wes could open his door, she said, "He's just a kid... I mean..."

"Yeah, Phalen, I know. We'll be gentle."

She shook her head. "That's not what I meant. Well, yes, by all means let's not tackle the literal *child*. What I mean is there's no way a nine-year-old did this by himself. So who else was it? Another kid? The doctor?" Margot scanned the fields again, trying to pick out one familiar face in a sea of strangers, and wondering how they hadn't seen this sooner.

His strangeness, his coolness. She hadn't wanted to read that behavior as a sign of guilt. She hadn't *wanted* him to be involved like this.

Something he had said to her earlier haunted her now, because she had completely misunderstood it at the time.

She should have stayed in bed like she was supposed to.

Now, with a sick sensation in her gut, she knew his words had nothing to do with the abuses they'd experienced at the hands of his parents, but rather that Valentina had probably not been a part of his original plan.

"He's just a kid, like you said. He'll tell us."

Margot wasn't so sure, since he'd managed to keep them from the truth for days at this point, but maybe it would be different now that they knew he was involved.

She had never felt this *bad* about learning someone was responsible for a murder.

Well, at least not since she'd been fifteen.

They crested a low hill and the expanse of various active soccer games unfolded around them. Four different games were happening, each with a group of parents settled into folding lawn chairs, or chasing their children down the field on the sidelines, screaming more directions than the coaches.

One group was easy to eliminate at first glance, the kids no older than five, and barely able to focus on which goal was theirs as they ran into each other and tripped over the ball in an effort to get it anywhere. One little girl had sat down in the middle of the field and was loading her bright orange team T-shirt with every dandelion she could reach.

"Hazel, you have to get *up*," shrieked a harried man with graying hair from the sidelines.

Hazel did not appear to agree with his assessment and went on picking flowers.

Since that group was too young, Wes and Margot continued in a clockwise direction, able to oversee most of the games from their place on the hilltop. Another group was teenagers, a bit rougher and more invested in the game, and all obviously too old to be Mateo's teammates. This left the two games being played on the middle fields, which had children about Mateo's age, and a mix of male and female players in each game.

Margot blocked the sun with her hand, trying to see if she could recognize him from this distance. Instead, she spotted Roger, the too-friendly soccer coach who had insisted on sitting in on their questioning of the boy the week previous.

She was in no great hurry to speak to him again, but he was probably their best target if they were looking for Mateo.

They headed down the hill in his direction, Margot more focused on seeing if she could spot Mateo among the kids on the field, but they were all moving so quickly and so many were little boys with dark hair, it was hard for her to single him out.

As she got within about fifty yards of Roger, she pulled out her badge, waving it in his general direction, in case he didn't remember them, which seemed unlikely.

All around them children were screaming delightedly and laughing, while parents huddled together in private chatter. The air smelled of suntan lotion and orange slices.

It was so idyllic and suburban, and Margot's guard was so far down, that she didn't immediately register the expression on Roger's face. She thought the pinch of his brow was due to squinting at them with the sun in his eyes.

She was about to make a comment about needing his help when he dropped the clipboard he'd been holding. It bounced off the shoulder of a little girl sitting in the grass next to him and she let out a dramatic, over-enunciated, "*Ouch.*"

Roger didn't seem to hear her.

One minute Margot was clipping her badge back on her

jeans with a smile on her face, and the next minute Roger was running. At first, she didn't understand what was happening, because he was standing only a short distance away, and then all of a sudden he was sprinting across the field while the game was still live, practically tripping over kids in his hurry to put distance between himself and them.

Margot was stuck standing there, hand still on her badge, stupidly trying to process what the hell was happening.

Why was he running?

Her brain finally caught up, and while the whole incident had only taken a second or two, she couldn't believe she had been foolish enough to simply stand there and watch him go.

In a split second, she thought anew about his overattentive focus, the way he'd pushed his way back into Mateo's life after the murders, and the myriad unnamed reasons she hadn't liked him, and the puzzle pieces all fell into place.

"Son of a bitch," she snarled. As she took off after Roger, she yelled back to Wes, "Get the kid."

The game had stopped amid the commotion, and parents were scrambling onto the field to get their children out of the way, even though they couldn't have possibly understood what was happening. Margot barely understood herself, but she knew one thing with absolute certainty.

Innocent men didn't run.

Roger was cutting across the field with the littlest kids now, barely looking where he was going as he wove through their tiny bodies and toward the parking lot.

"Roger, *stop*," Margot shouted, her lungs reminding her that she wasn't nearly fit enough to be on a foot chase, and as soon as this was over she would buy a treadmill for her apartment. "SFPD, get out of the way," she demanded of the growing crowds.

She really didn't want to pull her gun out on a field full of children. Roger headed up the hill and Margot was hot on his heels. She might not run regularly, but she did have the genetic gift of long legs, and had wisely chosen to wear boots without a heel today.

Roger hit the parking lot, and her initial fear that he might get to a car vanished when he bypassed all the vehicles in the lot, heading right for the main building and the road beyond it.

"*Stop*," she yelled again.

He was no more interested in stopping this time than he had been on the grass, and she still couldn't draw her weapon safely. Margot kicked up her pace, her shins screaming, her lungs aflame, and knew in that exact moment she was going to catch him.

Just as he passed the main complex of the community center she lunged, throwing her entire body weight against him. Since he'd been running, he already had forward momentum, which brought him crashing easily to the ground.

He began to squirm under her, but she dug her knee into his back and wrenched his arms out from beneath his body, pinning them behind him. Running might not be her forte, but she had plenty of practice in jujitsu and Krav Maga. "I fucking *dare* you," she snapped as he continued to buck.

She was able to cuff him as the patrol car they had requested earlier pulled into the lot. A moment later Wes arrived with Mateo in tow. The boy wasn't cuffed, and didn't seem to be too fazed by what was happening.

"You Mirandize him?" Margot asked.

"Mmhmm."

"Well, *you*"—she got off Roger's back as a pair of officers helped get him off the ground—"have the right to remain silent..."

She continued the well-practiced spiel, following him all the way to the car. As one of the uniformed officers pushed Roger's head down to avoid bumping it on the car, Margot couldn't help but add, "We weren't even here for you, you stupid son of a bitch."

The door shut tightly as she limped her way back toward Wes's car.

Now they had not one but two suspects, and she didn't feel good about either one of them.

FORTY

Roger Davis was not a tough man.

He was not a cold-blooded killer.

He pissed his pants three minutes into the interrogation.

As the smell of hot urine permeated the larger interrogation room, Wes and Margot were at something of a loss. They had to pause their recording and be thankful, at least, that there was no rolling momentum that had been interrupted by the unfortunate incident.

In all her years of doing the job, Margot had dealt with just about every possible response from criminals put under pressure. This wasn't even her first time dealing with someone who wet themselves, though usually that came as the result of too much booze or drugs.

All it had taken in Roger's case was Wes asking, "Why did you do it?"

Margot and Wes watched as the man completely unraveled. He hadn't asked for a lawyer, hadn't bothered to deny anything. He'd simply started to sob so loudly that a snot bubble emerged from his nose, and then... he pissed.

Wes and a uniformed officer guided Roger to the bathroom, where a pair of sweatpants from the lost and found were procured and the man had a chance to clean himself up for a few minutes. A janitor was called to deal with the mess in the original interrogation room, and Margot, Wes, and Roger moved on to a new space.

Roger continued to choke out sobs, and his nose continued to run, but at least this time Margot felt confident there wouldn't be any further accidents.

"I didn't want to kill those girls," he said finally, between hiccups. "They weren't supposed to be a part of it."

"Are you saying you *did* kill Valentina Ramirez and Emily Potter?" Wes confirmed. There was a camera mounted in the corner of this room recording every word. Always best to get the confessions clarified, though. Since Roger had waived his right to an attorney, which probably had more to do with shock than with him thinking he could get away with it, they needed to ensure everything he said here could be admissible in court.

Margot wasn't about to let this shithead get away on a technicality.

"Y-yes," he stammered. "They weren't supposed to be there, though, you need to understand. He told me they wouldn't be there."

"Who told you?" Margot asked, not willing to play the pronoun game when his answer could make or break their case. She needed to know her suspicions about what had happened that night were correct.

"M-Mateo."

"Mateo Ramirez."

"Yes."

"Roger, can you explain for us how a nine-year-old boy was involved in the murder of four fully grown adults?" Wes had the same information as Margot, had seen the pen, and shared the same suspicions, she believed. Still, he was playing it coy for Roger.

Margot fought the urge to lean forward. She needed to know what happened. She still had trouble believing that Mateo had been a participant in his family's murder. Four lives.

Roger wiped his snotty nose on the back of his sleeve. His eyes were bloodshot and puffy from crying. Margot had seen violent crime victims less pitiful than Roger looked right now. She wanted to slap him.

"You have to understand."

"Help us understand," Wes urged.

"He told me about what his parents had done to him. When I was coaching him, I noticed he had bruises on his wrists, and at first they were minor, you could write them off as kids being kids. Bruises happen." He stared imploringly at Margot, as if the only woman in the room might understand the nuances of children's behavior better than anyone else. She looked back at him blankly. "But after the second or third time I noticed them, I pulled him aside. I wanted to know if he was OK. He didn't want to talk about it at first, but eventually he told me that his parents made him stay in bed because he was so sick. His parents, they'd told me about his asthma, his heart issues. They told me he was special, and I should go easy on him. He was such a small kid for his age, you know? I took him under my wing, I really cared about him. And when he told me *how* his parents made him stay in bed, I couldn't believe it."

Wes waited a beat and then asked, "Why didn't you call Child Protective Services? You're a kids' sports coach, I'm sure you had access to that information from the community center. Or Google." He dropped the last line in like a lead anchor, hanging it around Roger's neck.

"He told me I couldn't say anything. If someone showed up at his house they would know why, and his parents would hurt him. Or Valentina."

"Roger, he's *nine*." Margot could hear the exasperation in Wes's voice. "It was your job to tell him that wouldn't happen."

"But what if it had? I believed the Ramirez family were good people, I believed they loved their children. I was wrong. Maybe they would have done it. I had to help him."

"How did this help him?" Margot asked, completely unable to comprehend the logic that had gotten Roger to the point of violently butchering four people.

"I got him away from them." His eyes gleamed, and he appeared almost proud of himself for a moment, before remembering where he was and why. He folded inward on himself, then, his shoulders slumping, and the glimmer leaving his eyes.

"You killed four people. Two of them teenage girls." Margot slid photos of Emily and Valentina across the table. Happy photos of the girls when they'd been alive, that she'd taken off their social media feeds. Roger winced to look at them.

"They weren't supposed to be there. Mateo told me they would be at Emily's." He shook his head. "Valentina walked in when I was tying up Hector. She screamed, and I just... I had no choice. She'd seen my face. They tried to hide in her room but I couldn't leave them alive."

Margot thought about Mateo's story, about him being in the basement when he heard Valentina and Emily screaming. Even if he *had* believed the girls would be away that night, surely he'd had an opportunity to tell Roger things had changed before the events of that night had unfolded.

Margot's blood felt cold and thick.

"Roger, did Mateo ask you to kill his parents?"

His head nodded as if controlled by some separate part of his brain, and when he realized what he was doing he said, "No. No, he only asked me to help. He was so scared."

Looking sideways at Wes, Margot then asked, "Why did you do it the way you did? It was so violent. There's a term we use for crimes like that, Roger. It's called *overkill*. When a crime is personal. Why make the women watch while Hector killed himself? How did you get him to do that?"

When Roger spoke again the tremor was gone from his voice, and it had become cold and level, like he was a completely different person now. "I told him they'd be spared if he showed those he loved how guilty he was. They needed to see what happens to men like that. Men who abuse their power. Men who hurt their children. Hector Ramirez was not a good man."

"Are you a good man?" Wes asked.

"I'm a righteous man," Roger replied.

"Did you know that there was so much blood on the floor after you slit their throats that it leaked through to the floor below?" Margot leaned back in her chair, trying to determine how this would make Roger feel. "Do you know how long it takes a human being to die from exsanguination?"

"What's that?" Roger asked.

"Bleeding to death."

"I think it's quick? Isn't it? From the throat?"

Margot stared at him and leaned forward again. "Wouldn't you know?" An uneasy thought was emerging in her mind, one that she didn't particularly want to lend too much credence to, no matter how real it was beginning to feel.

If Roger didn't know how long it had taken the women to die, was he really the one holding the knife? He would have had to be the one to tie them up, to put the bags over their heads, but was it all him, in the end?

Margot let herself imagine, briefly, Mateo being the one with the knife in his hands, but it just didn't *work*. He couldn't even do more than bruise his father's abdomen with a pen. No, Mateo had been involved but it was the man across from her with the literal blood on his hands.

"I didn't stick around to watch them die," Roger said finally.

"Didn't want to see what you'd done?" she asked. "You

killed them anyway, even after Hector did what you asked. Why?"

Roger continued to stare at her for a long time before he finally leaned back in his chair and crossed his arms over his chest. "I think I'd like to speak to my lawyer now."

FORTY-ONE

Mateo, at nine, was smarter than Roger. He'd said yes when asked if he wanted a lawyer present, and that lawyer had precisely zero interest in letting the boy implicate himself. They already had Roger's confession, and his confession pointed a big, meaty finger in the direction of the boy as an accomplice, but independent confirmation was going to be hard to come by.

The lawyer, a stern-faced woman of about fifty, managed to turn her lips into a cartoonishly straight line every time the detectives tried to ask Mateo a question.

"Mateo, do you understand why we've brought you in here today?" Wes asked.

"I don't think we can expect the boy to answer that question," the lawyer interjected. "There's no way he can possibly know what the nuances of your investigation might be."

Wes looked about ready to reach across the table and throttle her. They'd gotten lucky with their initial questioning earlier, as it was perfectly legal to question a minor who was a witness to a crime, even without a parent or guardian present. Margot had hoped they might get away with only having

Mateo's cousin in the room this time, someone who might not know when to stop the kid from talking.

Jerri Andover, on the other hand, was a brutally efficient defense lawyer, and one who evidently had plenty of experience working with children. She wasn't going to let a single whisper get past Mateo's lips that might give them a case against him.

"Roger has told us what you told him. About your parents and how they treated you?" Margot made it a suggestion, hoping to goad the boy into speaking.

Instead, he looked at them both blankly, as disconnected and uninterested as ever. It was like he wasn't even in the room with them. He leaned back in his chair, his feet not reaching the floor, and kicked his legs out one at a time, over and over.

"Did you ask Roger to kill your parents, Mateo?"

"He's not going to answer that."

Something flickered on Mateo's face though. A hint of recognition, finally, as if he hadn't been in his body this entire time and something had finally brought him back.

"I wouldn't do that. Roger is lying."

Jerri put her hand on his shoulder, her shiny red nails gleaming under the dull lights of the interrogation room. "Don't answer them unless I tell you to, OK?"

"But I didn't tell Roger to kill them." He pouted at her, and Margot watched in absolute astonishment as Jerri melted, yielding to the lie he was selling.

"I know, sweetheart, I know."

Jesus, thought Margot. If she hadn't so recently seen the way Ed's expressions changed like leaves scattering in a breeze, she might have bought what Mateo was selling, too. She certainly had leading up to this. Now, watching the boy play his lawyer like a marionette, Margot was glad they'd gotten to him early, before he'd been strong enough to commit crimes on his own.

She tried to catch Wes's eye, but he was too busy watching the scene across the table from them, a faintly queasy expression on his face.

So, he noticed it too.

"Your family had a lot of photo albums in the den, didn't they?" Margot asked.

This question, innocuous enough, and Jerri still under Mateo's spell of innocence, allowed to hang in the air, uninterrupted.

"Yes."

"Did you like to look at them?"

"Uh-huh."

"Were you looking at one the night your parents died?"

Mateo fell quiet, and this time Jerri did interject, saying, "Don't answer that."

He did, anyway. "I wanted them to see it. To see what they had done. They pretended we were so happy. We weren't."

"Mateo," Jerri scolded. "That's enough."

"So, you had the album out for them to see. Before they died." Margot wondered if this might be the closest thing they'd get to a confession with Jerri in the room.

"Don't answer that," she said.

Mateo smiled at them, softly, his innocent face so practiced and perfect. "I was in the basement."

"Of course you were," Margot replied. "Right where I found you."

"I think we're done here, Detectives," the lawyer said.

"Are you sorry they're gone?" Wes asked, as Jerri hustled the boy up from the chair. Outside, officers were waiting to take Mateo into processing. He could avoid questions all he wanted, but he wouldn't be going home that night, or any night soon.

Mateo looked back at them from the door.

"No."

.   .   .

In the lobby of the police station, Evangeline's cousin Yolanda Encarnacion was sitting in one of the hard plastic chairs, tapping her toes nervously. Margot approached her first, sensing the younger woman might feel more comfortable speaking to a female officer.

"Ms. Encarnacion? Yolanda?"

She looked up, brushing thick black hair away from her face and getting to her feet quickly. She was plump and short with a pretty face and had obviously spent a considerable amount of time crying. "You're the detectives? The ones from Mateo's soccer game?"

"I'm Detective Phalen, this is Detective Fox. You can call me Margot, if you'd like."

"Yoli," Yolanda replied, shaking Margot's extended hand. "Is Mateo OK?"

"He's being processed. You understand he won't get to come home with you, right? He's being held on suspicion of a connection to the murders of his parents and sister."

Yoli sat down again, her breath escaping in a whoosh. "I was sure I'd misunderstood. You arrested his coach, too, right? Ralph?"

"Roger."

"I never liked him. He was too focused on Mateo. Too touchy. He asked me so many questions when I brought Mateo to soccer. At first, I thought maybe he was worried about him, after what happened, but it seemed like too much. I wasn't even sure Mateo was ready to be doing things like soccer again, but he really wanted to go, almost begged me."

"Ms. Encarnacion, how would you characterize Mateo's behavior in the week he's been with you?" Wes asked.

Yoli shrugged, but she was twisting the hem of her shirt between her fists in an almost violent way. She looked past the two of them and up the stairs, as if waiting for Mateo to emerge any moment.

"I didn't know him before, not really. We weren't close, me and Eva. Not since we were kids. But... I'm all he had? That's what the estate lawyers said, that everything went to Mateo, of course, but since he had no closer relations, and they didn't have godparents for him, I was it. I was the closest thing. So, I don't know. How do you know what's normal for a kid you've never met? How... how do you know what's normal for a kid who has been through what he has? I just don't know."

"Has it seemed to you like he's been in mourning?"

"He's been really quiet."

"Has he cried? Had bad dreams? Does he talk about his family with you at all?" Margot asked.

Yoli shook her head. "He plays video games a lot. He's got one of those little hand-held consoles? Spends all day looking at that thing. When he asked to go back to soccer, I thought that might be a good sign, so I said yes. I mean, you want me to tell you if he's been weird, right? I don't know, Detectives. I don't have my own kids, and yeah, he's weird, but maybe that's just the way he is?"

She was still playing with the hem of her shirt, and Margot decided to try one last thing.

"Yoli, were you ever scared of him?"

The younger woman's head whipped around, and she focused on Margot squarely for the first time since they'd met. It took her a very, very long time to answer, and when she finally did, her chin dropped, and she stared at her trembling hands.

"Yes."

FORTY-TWO

Wes took the lead at the Potter house this time, letting Margot wait a few steps down when they arrived at the cheerful Victorian house for the second time. The street was quiet, charming. The ideal sort of place to raise kids in a city that was otherwise bustling and busy everywhere you went.

A few houses down a purple bike leaned against the front steps of a pink and cream-colored Victorian, as though its owner had no worries in the world about someone walking away with it.

It was the illusion of comfort that you could buy if your annual income was high enough. The Ramirez family probably thought they were safe, too, because they had money and their kids could play outside after dusk.

But what went on behind closed doors had robbed those children of any sense of security. She thought about Mateo, and about how far he had been pushed by those who were supposed to love him the most, to protect him.

And it made her wonder about Ed, and about all the other killers she had known in her time, and whether Mateo was a monster that had been created by his parents, or if that was who he was going to be no matter what.

She stared at the purple bike, and the life it represented, and she swallowed hard.

Illusions, unfortunately, were only useful until they shattered, and then you were left with nothing but shards, vapor, and a crushing sense of reality weighing you down.

Peter Potter answered the door, and he looked a good ten years older than he had the first time they'd visited. Gone was the man who had cheerfully tried to offer them drinks and couldn't seem to understand the reasons why homicide detectives might be standing at his front door.

He was wiser now, and Margot hated the change. He'd been so jubilant and bubbly in the moments before he'd learned what had become of Emily. She wished she'd been able to know who he was, in a time before tragedy.

"Mr. Potter," greeted Wes, toeing that perfect line between friendly and apologetic. That's why he was in charge here, he handled people better than Margot ever could. He could soothe with his tone, warm with his smiles. She only made things worse when nuance was called for.

"Detectives. It's a pleasure to see you again." He seemed to realize after saying it that it wasn't entirely the right word choice, but it was out now, and politeness required he leave it there, in the air between them. "Did you have news about Emily?"

Jean appeared in the doorway behind him, a pale ghost of the woman she'd been. She'd lost weight in the time since Emily's death, and her skin had taken on a sallow, gray quality. The bags under her eyes suggested she and sleep had parted ways some time ago, and had not yet reconciled.

Margot hoped their visit today might help, at least in that regard.

Wes nodded. "Yes, we have some important information to share, would you mind if we came inside briefly?"

Jean clung to Peter's shoulder, wordlessly watching them as if admittance into their home might bring only more bad news. In a way, she was right. This wouldn't be easy news to hear, and would probably hurt them, but at least they would know the truth.

That was more than a lot of families got.

Peter stepped out of the doorway and guided Margot and Wes into the familiar sitting room they'd been in before. Again, the detectives sat wedged together on a much too small love seat, while the Potters sat in adjacent armchairs.

Margot noticed a bottle of pills and a glass of water on a table in between the armchairs. She recognized her old friend Xanax even from twelve feet away.

"What's happened?" Jean asked, inching toward the edge of the chair, her hands clasped together so tightly in her lap that her knuckles were white. She had put herself together, wearing makeup and a mint-green cardigan layered over a floral button-down top. Her hair was perfectly coifed.

Peter, too, was wearing a sweater over a button-down and his khakis were freshly pressed. Margot had to admire their ability to put on a good face for friends and neighbors when it was obvious from even the most casual glance that they were falling apart.

Margot thought about the way her mother had unraveled after Ed's arrest. He had held one end of the sweater that was Kim, and as she moved across the country to get away from him, he'd simply kept pulling the thread. She'd never been the same.

Margot hoped that Jean and Peter would be able to find solace in each other, to get through this in one piece.

"We've made two arrests in the murders of Emily and the Ramirez family," Margot said, unable to keep herself out of the conversation. She desperately wanted to be able to give the Potters something, *anything* they could use to heal.

"Arrests?" Peter asked. "There was more than one person involved?"

Jean looked extra pale, bracing herself for a blow.

"Yes. We arrested Roger Davis as the primary assailant who we believe is responsible for the actual murders."

"Roger? *Roger?*" Peter was clearly stunned, but beneath that was a building fury that turned his white cheeks a ruddy crimson shade, the mottling extending up to his bald head. "Roger was Emily's soccer coach, what, five years ago?" He glanced to Jean, whose hands were now hanging loose, trembling violently. "Why on earth would Roger do this?"

Wes and Margot exchanged glances. "We have reason to believe that the Ramirez parents were Roger's intended victims, and that he was under the impression the girls would be *here* that night."

"Oh my God." Jean collapsed in on herself, bending double in the chair and dropping her head into her hands. Her sobs shook her entire body.

"Jesus." Peter looked past them, out the window into the unapologetically sunny day outside. "They were. They were supposed to be here that night, but at the last minute we asked if they might stay with the Ramirezes. We had a contractor coming early in the morning to look at the bathroom." He lost his focus, and simply stared blankly for a moment, before remembering why they were all sitting together. "Why would Roger want to kill Hector and Evangeline?"

Again, Margot hesitated, knowing what came next would be the hardest part. "The other arrest we made in the case was Mateo Ramirez."

This stunned the sobbing Jean into silence, and both she and Peter stared at Margot with disbelief.

"M-Mateo?" Jean stammered. "No, there must be a mistake."

Margot shook her head. "While he didn't confess, Roger did. He and Roger conspired together. He convinced Roger that his life was in danger, and that if his parents weren't killed, that he would die soon." Margot figured this was enough of the truth for them. Since Mateo was so young there wouldn't be a trial, he would go into detention until he turned eighteen. So there was no point in telling them that Roger's confession had gaps in it; he'd left out a lot of the more insidious details, and the unsettling reasons a thirty-five-year-old man might have been so easily manipulated by a nine-year-old. They didn't need to carry a burden that ugly.

"Mateo." Jean sounded dumbfounded, and Margot couldn't blame her. It was the least expected outcome for any of them. "I-I don't understand, they were such a nice family. Why would he think he was in danger?" Judging from the expression on her face, Margot imagined she was going through all her past interactions with Hector and Evangeline, trying to recall any reason she might have overlooked for mistrusting them.

"Mateo killed Emily?" Peter seemed to have lost the train, blindsided by the new information.

"No, we think Roger killed the girls because he was surprised to find them there and wasn't sure how to get out of the situation without killing them as well. They were never the intended targets." She wasn't sure if that made things better or worse. Emily was collateral damage in a disturbing family drama, and the Potters now needed to live with the knowledge that a contractor's schedule might have made the difference between life and death for their daughter.

None of this was their fault, but Margot knew logic had no place when it came to personal blame.

"We're terribly sorry for your loss, again," Wes said. "We thought you would want to know that the case is now closed.

Roger and Mateo have both acknowledged their participation, to some degree, and we're going to hand over the investigation materials to the DA to begin prosecution."

Peter nodded, though Margot wasn't entirely sure any of this had sunk in yet.

"We appreciate you coming in person," Jean mumbled. "Instead of us finding out on the news."

Margot and Wes got to their feet, but before they could show themselves to the door, Peter asked, "Will you see him again? Roger?"

With the investigation largely wrapped up, it wasn't likely they'd have much contact with either Roger or Mateo again at this point, but sensing a deep need in Peter's question, Margot said, "Yes."

"Can you tell him something for me?"

Margot anticipated an offer of forgiveness, or something to give Peter necessary closure. "Of course."

"Tell him I hope he burns in hell for what he did to Emily." Peter glanced over at Jean, who nodded, tears streaming down her cheeks. "You tell him that for me, OK?"

FORTY-THREE

Margot should have felt relieved. Usually, the solution to a case brought her some sense of closure, a door being closed, things put right in the world for at least one small moment in time. More often than not, solving a murder meant giving someone peace of mind, but she still wasn't sure that's what she had given Emily's parents, or Mateo's family.

This was one of the rare situations in her line of work where solving a case only managed to make her feel worse. Even now, almost a week later, she didn't feel good about the Ramirez case.

It had been a complicated case, and even now she wasn't sure how she felt about Mateo. She didn't know if he was a victim of circumstance, or something much, much worse, and she *hated* that even in a nine-year-old she couldn't tell the difference.

She also had a lingering, gnawing anxiety that hadn't faded about how a family had been able to abuse both of their children for *years* and no one had noticed or done anything to stop it until one stupid man was convinced that killing them was the only solution.

Why hadn't there been someone to stop it before it got that far?

Surely there were signs that had been missed.

But none of that was for Margot to solve. She had done the one job she'd been brought in to do, even if the results were not as satisfying as they usually were when she closed a case.

Yes, they knew who had murdered the Ramirez family, and her bosses would be thrilled by a closed case on the board, but they were condemning a young boy to a very uncertain future, and there wasn't anything rewarding about learning the truth of what had happened behind closed doors with the Ramirez family.

Sometimes you open a door, and you just find skeletons.

Closing one case meant it was time for her to acknowledge there were others out there that still craved conclusion. She didn't want to be involved, at least not with Ed, but she had promised Andrew she would hear him out, and she owed him that much. Margot, not wanting to deal with the brutal parking in the Opera Plaza area, opted to take an Uber to the FBI field office. She had already mentally planned the route to Philz, one block away, so she could get coffee after the ordeal, but decided to face Andrew and his team first and get it out of the way.

The Uber driver brought her right to the front door of the headquarters, a plain, ugly building that tried to make itself unique with four glass and metal art facades above the doors, but it just looked like someone had glued some old computer racks together and called it a day.

The place looked cold and uninviting, which was probably the point, at least subconsciously. It's not like the FBI wanted people coming in off the street for no reason. Still, Margot was meant to be there, and even she didn't want to go in.

She entered from Turk Street and made a beeline for the reception desk, where a middle-aged woman with a perfectly smooth bun and stylish black glasses was working at a computer.

"Good morning," she said. "Can I assist you?"

Margot wanted to say no and walk right back out, because there was already a sense of looming dread hanging over her like a pregnant storm cloud. Andrew had gone ages without talking to her, without needing her, and now he had called her asking her to come visit. She didn't like it and knew deep down she wasn't going to be happy about his reasons. Whatever he wanted to show her, whatever new evidence was uncovered, it was one more thing that kept her from leaving the past buried.

"I'm here to see Special Agent Andrew Rhodes. He's expecting me."

"Margot." Andrew's voice was soft, yet managed to fill the whole lobby. He crossed the room and gave her a friendly handshake, patting her shoulder. "Mary, can you get Margot a visitor badge, please? I'll be escorting her."

Mary, the receptionist, dutifully collected some information from Margot, checked her ID, and printed off a hard plastic badge that Margot clipped to her blazer. After being reminded to return the badge before leaving the building, Margot was allowed to enter a secured staff-only area with Andrew leading the way.

He obviously knew the staff, seeing as he was based out of the San Francisco field office, but it only managed to make Margot feel more like an outsider as he nodded to people and exchanged friendly good-mornings while they walked through the halls. After a quick elevator ride to the fifteenth floor, Andrew led her to an open glass door and ushered her inside.

The space surprised her. It wasn't the cold, dark-colored basement she had imagined his team being shut away in. If anything, the area felt more like a workspace for a new app development company or a Google office. It was largely open concept, with bright blue paint on the walls and a graphic outline of the Golden Gate Bridge on one wall. Big windows filled the area with natural light, and a team of about six agents was milling around speaking in low tones. On one wall there was even a little coffee station set up with a single-cup brewer and a variety of mugs that had clearly been brought from home.

World's Okayest Dad.

A Starbucks mug from St. Louis.

A Stanford University mug, maroon with the green tree logo on the front.

One even had a graphic from *Lilo & Stitch* on the side, cartoonishly depicting Lilo's drawing of Stitch's "badness" level.

If the mugs were any indication, at least the team working here had a personality.

At the back of the room was a raised table with several tall chairs around it, though only one agent was currently seated there. There were four desks in the center of the main room, and almost every wall had a whiteboard on wheels pushed against it. Dozens of photos adorned the boards, showing the faces of women Margot didn't recognize. The pictures were all old, yearbook photos, candids from the eighties and nineties based on haircuts and makeup trends.

The agents looked up as Margot entered the room and for a moment, a hush fell over the office.

Talk about a warm welcome.

Margot forced a smile but knew it looked like just that: a forced smile. Her teeth hurt from faking friendliness she didn't particularly feel.

"Team, this is Detective Margot Phalen of the SFPD. We're hoping she'll be able to assist us with the ongoing case as a consultant." He glanced over at her, raising an eyebrow as if to ask her permission to continue.

Margot grimaced before she could stop herself. She knew what he was asking, and also knew that the FBI case on Ed would reflect the name changes her family had made. As had been pointed out to her many times in the past, she had made a legal name change, but the truth was on record with the FBI. Everyone in this room probably already knew who she really was. She shrugged, which was all the invitation Andrew needed to continue.

"Margot, as most of you know, is Megan Finch, the eldest daughter of Ed Finch. Her willingness to go visit Ed earlier this month helped us identify Theresa Milotti's burial location and retrieve her body successfully, for which we are grateful to her."

No one in the room moved or spoke, no one looked particularly grateful. They were all grim-faced and attentive. Margot, however, turned her attention fully to Andrew. "So, we were able to confirm it was Theresa?" she asked, having just heard this news for the first time.

Andrew nodded. "Successful match of her dental records. We've already spoken to her father, and we'll be having her remains sent back to Illinois for burial once we've completed our investigation. It hasn't been easy to pin down a cause of death with the hyoid missing, and there's no indication of weapons or blunt trauma on the remaining bones, but we obviously want to be thorough. Ed's confession should be more than enough to secure prosecution though."

"And what, add another death sentence onto the existing one?" Margot scoffed.

She obviously knew prosecuting Ed for the murder was more to give the Milottis a sense of closure, and to make sure people knew who had killed their daughter, but Margot couldn't help but think of her recent visit to Emily's parents, and how little good knowing the truth really did them.

Andrew said nothing, probably knowing he didn't need to.

"Agent Rhodes?" asked a young woman. Her hair was twisted into a few dozen long braids and wrapped up on the top of her head in a thick bun. She looked to be in her late twenties, which made Margot feel especially old for some reason.

"Yes, Kam?" He paused then. "Agent Brady."

"I don't mean to be rude, but how exactly is she going to be able to help us with this?" Agent Brady looked to Margot apologetically. "Sorry."

Before Margot could respond, Andrew interjected. "Margot's connection to Ed gives us unexpected access to him, as we saw with the Milotti case. We never would have found that body, let alone closed that missing person's case, if not for Margot's involvement."

Bile started to rise in Margot's throat, burning, causing her eyes to water. She suddenly understood why she was here, and it had nothing to do with updates on Theresa's case, as Andrew had indicated over the phone. She felt like she'd been pushed on stage in the middle of a concert and told to perform, when she had no idea what song she was supposed to sing.

She froze, wishing she could run from the room.

He had tricked her, whether he realized it or not. She wanted to slap him, but knew it wasn't the best plan in a room filled with eager FBI agents who probably thought he hung the moon. Margot herself had thought that for a long time, but now she began to see that Andrew wasn't a hero, wasn't perfect, he was just a man with a job to do.

And Margot wasn't a surrogate daughter, wasn't someone he cared about or wanted to protect. She was a means to an end.

For the moment, her anger and sense of betrayal were keeping the panic at bay, and she clung to that, hoping it would last until she was home again, or at least out of this room. She couldn't have an attack here, they'd think she was an absolute lunatic.

Just like her dad.

That sobering thought let her swallow the lump in her throat, the sickly acidic taste of vomit leaving her wanting water, or a stiff drink.

She stared at Andrew and waited for him to admit why he'd

brought her here, using his agents as a shield to make his request when he didn't have the balls to ask her directly. He wanted her in a position where she didn't think she could say no.

"Given that Ed seems willing to share the details of his crimes with Margot, we're hoping she'll continue visiting him on a regular basis, as we have reason to believe Theresa is only the first of many victims we were previously unaware of. We also know based on our extensive understanding of serial killers that Ed started quite old, comparatively, so we may soon confirm a theory that he started killing before we originally believed he did." He glanced over at her then, a fake, friendly smile on his face, one that didn't fit the discussion of unsolved murders. Andrew's book had hypothesized that a string of Peeping Tom incidents around Petaluma in the late seventies had likely been Ed's early handiwork, but Margot knew Andrew believed there might have been more violent episodes before Laura.

Margot didn't speak for a long time. She stared at the faces on the boards around the room, little cards next to each one that listed the women's names, last known locations, and last known contact. Some of them had been missing almost as long as she'd been alive.

She looked at the eager, attentive faces of the agents on Andrew's team, waiting for her to speak.

If she said no, she was saying no not only to the people in the room, but also to every face on the boards around her.

Andrew had backed her into a corner and dared her to make herself the villain.

Fuck you, she thought in his general direction.

"How could I say no?" was what she said out loud.

FORTY-FOUR

When Margot was young she used to have nightmares about monsters.

She often woke up at night screaming, babbling about creatures under her bed, or eyes in her closet. She was a nervous child, and wore her emotions on her sleeve at all times. At night, that would manifest itself as monsters.

At the time she didn't really understand the wicked beings as real entities. They weren't *visible* to her, but slipped through the shadows and rustled in the billowing curtains of her window. They were footsteps in gravel and laughter in other rooms.

Whenever she woke up screaming it had been her mother who came to her side. Often, in the night, her father wasn't home, citing nights out with his friends or busy overtime hours at work. Little did she know at the time that those overtime hours never seemed to show up as more money in the family account for things like groceries or new shoes.

Margot hadn't understood what was at the root of her parents' arguments, she only understood that there was a deep-seated resentment between the two. They rarely showed warmth toward each other, something she took for granted as being normal. In retrospect, she wasn't sure her parents had even *liked* each other. But it was the same old story of couples in that era. High school sweethearts who did what they thought was right and got married after graduation.

Then kids, bills, and a growing distance.

Still, none of that had been on Margot's mind when she was small, and fearful over shapes she couldn't make sense of. So, Kim would come to her bed and sit with her, cradling Margot in her arms and singing her anything she could think of off the top of her head. She was a big fan of Fleetwood Mac and Huey Lewis, so often Margot would be lulled to sleep by "Rhiannon" or a lullaby version of "Hip to Be Square."

Kim was a pragmatic person who didn't particularly condone weakness in her children. She was the kind of mother who would brush off a scraped knee and say, "It's not broken, get back out there" or "A little blood never hurt anyone." But in Margot's tender moments of nocturnal fear, Kim softened. She'd never lie, though. It wasn't in her nature to say, "Everything will be OK."

She'd sing her daughter to sleep, brushing her red hair between her fingers. A color that matched Kim's own. She'd mutter, "Go to sleep, baby, sleep can change the way we see the world. When you wake up in the morning, all the shadows will be gone."

But the one thing Kim never said was, "There are no monsters in the house."

Which made Margot wonder if her mother had known, deep down, that there was one with them all along.

Rubbing her sweat-soaked hands on her jeans, Margot stared at the double doors she knew he'd be coming in from. Like last time there were only two guards in the room, and Ed's lawyer was in attendance, though he was sitting at a table a little ways off, pretending not to pay attention. His darting eyes gave him away.

The tension in the room was so thick it made her want to gag.

What was she doing here?

The door alarm buzzed, and the sound of the lock disengaging was as loud as a shotgun. In a precise reenactment of the last time she'd visited, two guards escorted a shackled Ed into the room, led him to her table, and once he was seated, they removed his chains.

The entire time they worked with locks and cuffs, Ed stared right at her, attentive, but his expression otherwise blank and unreadable. Margot mirrored it right back to him, hoping her disgust wasn't too apparent.

When the guards had taken a few steps back, father and daughter continued in silence, their eyes locked across the short distance of the table, neither willing to be the one who broke first. Margot didn't want him to think he had the power, and Ed *wanted* her to think he had the power, and for a solid, agonizing five minutes, they were at a stalemate.

At last, Ed cleared his throat and adjusted in his seat.

"You know, they let you buy snacks."

"Excuse me?" Of all the things she'd expected him to say, this hadn't been one of them. All her carefully thought-out quips and retorts evaporated on her tongue.

He pointed in the direction of the bank of vending machines on the wall. "They let visitors buy snacks. For inmates."

Margot sat back, pulling away from him, her face twisted in an unexpected grimace. "You want me to buy you... chips?"

"I mean, I won't be picky, but if you were taking requests, I wouldn't say no to some chocolate-covered raisins."

This floored her. She was so stupefied by it she actually

patted her pants, recalling that she'd been warned at the visitor center she could only bring in a certain amount of cash with her, and not understanding why she would need cash at all.

She glanced at one of the guards, who gave her an almost imperceptible nod, then crossed the room to the glowing array of machines, finding one with a familiar purple box inside, and selecting the appropriate number. The machine did not give her change.

Returning to the table she dropped the box in front of him. A nearby guard watched as Ed tore open the box and dumped the small brown chocolates onto the white tabletop, arranging them in a neat little pile.

Margot wasn't sure such rapt focus was necessary. Ed might be a killer, but he'd never managed to murder anyone with a small strip of cardboard.

"Happy now?" she asked.

"Ecstatic."

"I thought you were always more of a peanut guy."

Ed popped a raisin in his mouth and smiled. For the first time since she'd been here to see him, the smile actually looked genuine, not like something he was wearing for show.

"You remembered that?"

"Fifteen years under the same roof, Ed. I remember a lot of things."

"Your favorite ice cream used to be cotton candy," he said with a chuckle. "Things change, Buddy."

"They sure do."

"Tell me, did you find her? Right where I said you would?"

Margot couldn't tell if this was curiosity, or if he wanted to hear more about it to get the contact high of reliving his crime. Might have been a bit of both, so she reminded herself to keep the details as spare as possible. "We did."

"How was she?" He continued to eat his candy, savoring each bite on its own, closing his eyes with pleasure.

"She was just how you left her. But bonier."

Ed observed her through barely opened eyelids. "Bonier."

"Things change. They fall apart."

"Mmm."

"Can I ask you something?"

"You just did."

Rage bristled inside her, a red-hot sizzle of pure anger that made her cheeks flush. She was here to solve a murder and he wanted to play *games*? "Oh, fuck you, old man. Forget it." She moved to stand again, the nearby guards bristling at her sudden shift in tone, hands hovering near weapons.

"Megan, *sit down*."

His voice wasn't loud, but it was drained entirely of all the friendly, joking cadence it had carried when they first began to chat.

This time Margot did *not* sit.

"Would you have ever said anything about Theresa if I hadn't come? You said you only wanted to share it with me, you said I had to be here. But you could have gotten all the attention and press without me. I didn't need to be a part of this. So *why*?"

"Maybe I would have. I don't know. Would you sit down?" His gravelly tone was laced with anger, annoyance, but he was trying to school it into something resembling politeness. "Please?"

Margot, sick of the vibrating presence of the guards, sat once more, her knees bouncing restlessly under the table against her will.

"Can't it simply be that I wanted to see my daughter, but there was no other way to get her here?"

"You think playing with my guilt is fair?"

"What do you have to feel guilty about?" The question sounded so genuine, like he couldn't possibly imagine the burden he'd left behind to be carried by others.

"Someone has to."

Ed scoffed. "The dead are dead, Megan. They don't care what happens once they're gone. Don't make yourself a martyr for those who don't feel anything."

His cavalier tone made her feel sick. "You really don't get it, do you? It's not about them, it's about all the people they leave behind. Jesus, Ed. You really didn't hear a word when they read those victim impact statements at your sentencing, did you?"

"Why would I listen to strangers?" He shrugged.

"You don't feel anything, do you?"

His cheeks flushed slightly, as if embarrassed that he'd been caught letting his human mask slip askew.

"I care about you."

Somehow that was even worse. Margot felt a wave of nausea roll inside her. She looked him square in the eye. "I tell people my father is dead. When anyone asks about you, I say, 'He died when I was fifteen,' because as far as I'm concerned, you did. You played your little game, and I let you, but I'm here to tell you it ends now. Special Agent Rhodes asked me if I would keep talking to you. I think he hopes you're going to tell us more about your quiet years. But you know what those years were? That's when Justin was born. Or when I had the accident and you had to be home with me every night. Mom's miscarriage. The blips in their calendar are my *life*. And I don't feel like walking down memory lane with you."

Ed watched her carefully, his eyes darting over every inch of her face, and down to her twisted hands.

"Even if there are more?"

"Maybe it's time I take your advice, Ed. The dead are dead. You can't use them as pawns. When I leave here today, you're never going to see me again."

She got to her feet, stepping away from the table.

"Megan," he said sharply, panic on the edge of each syllable.

"What?"

"There are more, you know. More I could tell you about."

"Tell someone who cares."

She walked out, her head held high, never once looking back. When she got back to her car, she let it all out in one body-wrenching sob.

This time, though, she didn't throw up.

This time, *she* had walked away with all the power, even if it had destroyed something inside her to do it.

This time, it was going to happen on her terms, or it wasn't going to happen at all.

FORTY-FIVE

The house in Forest Hill wasn't haunted anymore.

Margot sat in her car across from the former crime scene, with all the yellow tape and police vehicles gone. A white van was parked in the driveway bearing the name of a company Margot knew specialized in crime scene and biohazard cleaning services.

There were a surprising number of such specialty cleaners in the San Francisco area, something that probably shouldn't have surprised her, given the number of homicides and suicides she saw in a year, but still seemed a little unusual when she thought about it.

The blistering heat wave that had chased her through the duration of the Ramirez investigation was gone, replaced with a chill in the air that said fall was coming. In the mornings, fog hung over the Bay as it was meant to. Things felt like they had gone back to normal in the city, now that the case was solved.

For Margot, though, she didn't know what normal felt like anymore.

It had been almost a week since her second visit with Ed, and he hadn't tried to make contact again. Andrew was disappointed, frustrated with her for not trying harder, but she couldn't play nice just for the sake of his investigation. She wanted to help, and she knew she could have been more of a team player in all this, but what was the sacrifice on her end? How much of herself did she need to give up for others?

She still wanted to parse through all Ed's old letters to the newspaper—something she was sure the FBI was doing as well —but life was relentless, and she hadn't found the time. Or perhaps more accurately she hadn't *made* the time.

When would her efforts be enough to make up for what Ed had done?

Never.

Never was the most honest answer she could think of.

She sipped her iced coffee, chewing nervously on the straw until the plastic was totally mangled and she was barely able to get any liquid up it anymore. The crime scene cleaners went from the house to their van a few times, carrying specialty cleaning equipment, and pails filled with sprays and jugs of liquid. They laughed at a private joke, while one helped the other move a carpet extraction unit through the front door.

That's how Margot knew there was nothing left lingering inside. The memory of Hector, Evangeline, Valentina, and Emily wasn't in the carpet or the walls. No spirits hung over the shoulders of the cleaners as they did their work.

Everything inside the house was gone. Yolanda had called her and Wes to confirm she and her husband were allowed to begin the process of getting the house ready to sell. Mateo would soon need the money to cover legal fees, while the state decided the best recourse for him. Because of his young age he wouldn't be subject to a standard trial and would likely be put into a special psychiatric facility until he was of legal age.

Who really knew what would happen to him?

Margot remembered clearly the dead-eyed way he'd looked

at them in that interrogation room, and wondered if it might not be for the best that he never see the light of day again.

He was still a child, yes, but Margot knew enough about psychopaths to know how early the signs began to manifest. Maybe Mateo could be helped, now that he'd receive special attention. There was, perhaps, still a chance for him to live a normal life. But he'd live that life knowing he was responsible for the deaths of four people, including his entire family.

If he was ever able to acknowledge that guilt, it would be enough to ruin even the strongest person.

She watched the house, not totally sure why she'd been drawn back to it. The case was over, there was no reason for her to be here anymore, and yet she'd been compelled, drawn like sea to shore, finding her way back here again.

It reminded her, she realized, of being parked in front of her old house in Petaluma. The way a house could continue to be a house, in spite of the secrets and horrors that went on behind closed doors.

This was just a place, now. Walls and rooms and square footage. Someday soon a new family would call it home, and while a realtor would be required to share its past, the house would go on being a house.

Her old home in Petaluma wasn't blackened by the presence of Ed Finch living there. Some other family had moved in, they'd painted, they'd made new memories.

Maybe if a house could go on and reshape itself, so could she.

Margot's phone began to buzz and she put her coffee back in the cup holder, checking the caller ID to see if it was Leon. Things on the Muir Woods case had gone ice cold, and even with Wes offering his help in the background, they didn't feel any closer to finding out who had killed Leanne and Rebecca. She felt like the answers were there, but they simply couldn't figure it out.

It wasn't Leon, though, it was Ford Rosenthal.

She considered not answering, but since it had been a week from the time of her last visit, she knew she couldn't put him off. Ed had been silent that whole time and reaching out now meant something.

Margot answered. As it turned out, exorcising the ghosts of the past was a lot easier for houses than it was for people.

Rosenthal cleared his throat, choosing his words carefully.

"He's ready to tell you about Seventy-Eight."

A LETTER FROM THE AUTHOR

I wanted to take a moment to thank you so very much for reading *The Killer's Daughter*. I hope you were invested in Margot's story. If you'd like to hear all about my new releases with Storm Publishing, you can sign up for my mailing list here:

www.stormpublishing.co/kate-wiley

I have a lot of exciting things coming up, so if you want to stay in the loop on new releases and bonus content, you can sign up for my newsletter:

eepurl.com/ASoIz

If you liked the book and could spare a few moments to leave a review that would be hugely appreciated. Even a short review can make all the difference in encouraging a reader to discover my books for the first time. Thank you so much!

This book was a huge labor of love (and a little bit of scaring myself by writing those Ed chapters). I have long been a lover of the thriller genre and Margot's story has been following me around for almost eight years. I'm so thrilled that after all that time it's finally in your hands.

Thanks again for being part of this amazing journey with me and I hope you'll stay in touch—This is just the beginning!

Kate Wiley

KEEP IN TOUCH WITH THE AUTHOR

www.katewiley.com

facebook.com/SierraDeanAuthor
tiktok.com/@sierradeanauthor

ACKNOWLEDGMENTS

First and foremost, I'd like to thank whoever monitors scary Google searches for not wondering too heavily about my research on decomposing bodies and lividity timelines. I have no doubt I'm on a bunch of weird lists, especially after writing this book.

Second, I want to thank Vicky Blunden, my editor at Storm Publishing. This book had a heck of a time finding a home, and in publishing that just means you're waiting for the right person to say yes, and Vicky said yes with so much enthusiasm I knew it had been worth the wait. She just *got* this book from day one, and her excitement to share it with the world really told me I'd found the right place.

Writing a book like this can put you in a dark place and I spent far too many hours listening to *Crime Junkie* and *Red-Handed*, podcasts that go to those dark places on the regular.

I want to thank my mother, who never ceases to be my biggest champion, and my friends who continue, as ever, to show enthusiasm for each new book.

Printed in Great Britain
by Amazon